Aired

by

J L Wilson

Remembered Classics Romance #10

Aired

Cover Art by *Kim Mendoza*

The Wild Rose Press, Inc.
PO Box 708
Adams Basin, NY 14410-0708
Visit us at www.thewildrosepress.com

Publishing History
First Edition, 2022
Trade Paperback ISBN 978-1-5092-4639-7
Digital ISBN 978-1-5092-4640-3

Remembered Classics Romance #10
Published in the United States of America

"How many guards are in the house tonight?"

A nightlight behind John's desk highlighted his movements. I could see him remove a gun and a shoulder harness from the drawer. "Paul, Frank, and Mark. Paul is outside. Frank and Mark are inside."

"How long before the police arrive?"

"Five minutes, maybe ten. Possibly longer given the weather."

I gestured to the automatic he held. "Do you have another? Mine's in my room."

John straightened. "You're remarkably calm about this."

"It's not my first rodeo."

"I expect you to explain that remark later." He reached into the desk and pulled out a 9mm in a belt clip and handed it to me. It was heavier than my S&W but familiar.

I checked the safety then attached the belt clip onto my jeans, holding the gun at my side. "Where do you need me?" I whispered.

John went to the door. "Stay with Adele. I think she's in her room."

"If we need to evacuate, I'll take her to the woods and the patio below. From there we can hide if we have to."

"You're not a regular nanny, are you?"

"I've done some security work."

Dedication

To librarians everywhere and the books I read, which
set me on the path I'm on today.

Author's Note

While obeah and other similar religions are followed in
the Caribbean, it is important to state clearly that the
religious practices described herein are solely the
product of the author's imagination and have no basis
in reality. All characters, locations, events, and cultural
descriptions are completely fictitious and have no
relationship to actual people or events.

Chapter 1

"Are you crazy? They need somebody who can handle teenagers and act as a hostess for business dinners." I regarded Burns Allen, one of my oldest and most exasperating friends, who held a clipboard in one well-manicured hand. "I can't do that."

"Of course you can." He bent over the clipboard, pen raised. "Charlotte E. Rochester," he said, filling in the top line. "Do you want me to use your cell phone or home phone?"

"Neither."

"Okay. Home phone. Age." He looked at me enquiringly. "Do you want to lie?"

"Why would I lie? I'm fifty-six and it's nobody's business." I pulled off my garden gloves and wiped sweat from my forehead, adding dirt to the smears already there. Burns interrupted my Monday morning tussle with the weeds in my front garden when he came by to implore me to help him. "Why are you so anxious to land this account?"

"It's a big client." He didn't raise his head, focusing on the application form. "Previous employment. Well, I can give them your resume, I suppose. I'll fill in the major ones. *Technical consultant*, Lerner Corporation." He grinned at me. When he saw my thunderous expression he ducked his head again. "I'm not lying. You're a technical consultant. *Visiting Professor*,

Central Iowa College." His pen hesitated on the page. "No need to go into details, I guess."

"How am I supposed to hostess a business dinner when I don't even own a black dress?" I worked for Burns now and again, usually as a tech guru for women who weren't comfortable letting a man into their homes. Allen's All-Around Aides was one of the premier employment agencies in Stratford, our bustling little suburb outside Des Moines, Iowa. I enjoyed the occasional jobs which could be wedged in between my consulting jobs at Lerner and my sporadic teaching at the college.

"You're a natural for this. Well, except for the part about hostessing. And kids." Burns leaned back cautiously in my wicker chair, probably not anxious to get dirt on his pristine white shirt. My front porch was, admittedly, a bit on the rustic side. It was badly in need of a coat of paint. My once-white furniture bore the brunt of the northerly winds that kicked in dirt from my garden and the farm fields a mile away. Burns' khaki pants were already smudged by a run-in with my lilac bush, which overhung the sidewalk leading to my house.

"So what part am I a natural for?" I chugged lemonade from my National Wildlife thermos, trying to wash away some of late August's cloying humidity.

"The gun part."

"Gun part?" I snatched the clipboard from his hand and read the job description aloud. "Mature woman needed for teenage girl as nanny and companion. Business social skills required, as well as teaching experience and knowledge of video game technology. Knowledge of firearms preferred." I looked up. "Okay. I can cover firearms, teaching, and technology. Why me?"

"This is a plum assignment. If my firm gets it, we'll have an in with the other rich clients in town." Burns regarded me with his big puppy-dog brown eyes, such a beautiful contrast with his stylishly trimmed blond hair. "Plum. Absolutely top notch."

"Wait a minute. Who's this for?"

Burns took a deep breath. "John Aire."

"What?" I shoved the clipboard back at him. "No way."

"Charlie, come on. Consider it." Burns regarded me imploringly. "Think of the kid. You could have such a good influence on her."

"The kid?" I pulled off the fabric headband which held my curly white hair away from my face. "You mean Adele? The daughter of two murdered parents and grandchild to a suspected murderer in America and a drug lord in Jamaica?"

Burns waved one manicured hand. "Gossip."

"Truth."

"Okay, yes. Her parents were murdered. By persons unknown. The Jamaican grandparents haven't been heard from in years. And John Aire was not charged in the disappearance of his wife."

"The charges weren't brought because there wasn't enough evidence," I said. "That doesn't mean he's not culpable."

"You would know that, of course, because of your police background and your work at Lerner's."

"My late husband's police background," I snapped. "And yes, I do happen to know about that kind of thing."

"And you know about firearms, which makes you perfect for this job." He smiled triumphantly.

"The girl needs a bodyguard, not a nanny. Her

3

grandfather—Aire—is one of the richest men in the state. Hell, he's the richest in the Midwest. And her other grandparents are involved in God knows what kind of illegal activities, if they're still alive."

"She has several bodyguards. He wants a companion for her. A mature companion."

I snorted. "Well, I'm not sure I'm qualified there. I may be in my fifties, but some people might question my maturity level."

"Why?" Burns blinked innocently at me. "Because you have a yard full of unusual metal sculptures you've welded yourself? Because you teach Tai Bo Kwan Do or whatever it's called? Because you fought City Hall and won?"

"It's not welding, it's soldering. Otherwise, I'd say yes to all of the above." I smiled, unable to stay peeved with Burns for long. He was such an amiable goof and had the charm of a good salesman, which is what he really was.

I regarded my yard, the reason for my fight with City Hall. My little acreage was recently designated a Monarch Habitat. Thus I was exempt from the stupid rules about mowed lawns and manicured hedges. Most of my neighbors were laid back about my overgrown oasis, but one neighbor in particular was a thorn in my side and tried to have me arrested. "Seriously, Burns, I don't think I'm the right woman for the job."

"Well, I considered Liza Reade," Burns admitted.

I flopped back in my chair and shot him an incredulous look. "Rigid Reade?" My few interactions with the woman in question revealed a puritanical young woman with scathing opinions about today's immoral society.

"Or Georgie, her sister," he added.

"Good Lord, Georgie's a harlot and Liza's a saint. Surely you have someone on the payroll who is half-way between the two of them?"

"I do and it's you. You're between cats, right? So you can be away from home?"

"Yes," I said reluctantly. I provided foster care for elderly and ill cats. I found homes for them or, more often, they remained with me until they died. I was currently B.C.

"There's another big point in your favor."

I wiggled my feet in my well-worn red Crocs. "Jamaica."

Burns nodded. "The kid is Creole. Her father was John Aire's son and her mother was Jamaican."

Old memories bubbled up in my mind. During my sophomore year in college, I was an exchange student in Jamaica. I met Art Nichols, a young policeman in Kingston. We had a steamy love affair that broke off when I returned home. But he followed me back to the University of Iowa and within months we were married. Nick died seven years later of typhus, contracted when he returned to Jamaica on family business.

"It's been thirty years. The last time I was there was for Nick's funeral. I haven't been back since."

"You might be able to make a connection with the kid." Burns touched my hand. "I didn't mean to rake up old memories."

"*Feel no way.* Don't worry," I translated when I saw Burns' blank expression. "I still know some of the old patois."

"I imagine the kid is out of her element here. Or maybe not. She and her parents were in witness protection for more than eight years. Who knows? Maybe they were in a town like this."

I smiled. "In case you haven't noticed, we don't have a very large Jamaican population in the Midwest. I doubt they were housed near here."

"Good point. It's because of Aire's son, the kid's father, that the Jamaican drug cartel was almost eliminated."

"It'll never be eliminated. It can only be subdued for a time. That gang has its fingers into everything on the island. No wonder Aire needs a bodyguard for her."

"I told you," Burns said with exaggerated patience. "He doesn't need a bodyguard. He needs a companion. It's not dangerous, if that's what you're worried about."

"I'm not worried." I was more intrigued than worried. This would definitely be a once-in-a-lifetime job, that's for sure.

"Think about it, okay? I'll submit your paperwork then you'll have to go for an interview. Just consider it, please?"

I sighed. "Go ahead and submit it. But don't you dare exaggerate my talents."

"Thanks for helping with this, Charlie. Like I said, if I score this contract, I'll have an in with the other Richie Riches in town."

"In that case you'd better start recruiting more nannies and companions. The folks on your staff aren't quite the type."

Burns jumped to his feet. "I'm already on it. I'll let you know when the interview is scheduled."

"If it's scheduled."

He smiled, his perfect teeth so white in his tanned face. "No, when. I'm sure you're a shoo-in. I'll be in touch." Burns hurried down my sidewalk, giving the lilac bush a wide detour before hopping into his SUV.

I waved to him when he drove past the house then considered my front yard. It was noon and getting too hot to do much more work. I walked around the side of my small Craftsman house to the two-car garage. Half of it housed my car. The other half was my work area where I kept my tools and supplies. The two sides were separated by heavy fabric to keep the dust on the working side away from my car.

I entered the house through the mudroom/laundry room where I kicked off my shoes. I peeled off my clothes, dumping them into the basket on top of the washing machine. The mudroom connected to my bedroom straight ahead or to the kitchen on my right. I considered a snack but opted for a shower instead.

Half an hour later I was freshly scrubbed and dressed. I looked around for Shirley, the diabetic and elderly orange tabby who was with me. Then I remembered. She died a week before. I sighed, wondering what perverse part of my personality allowed me to form attachments to animals who could not be saved.

I made a sandwich and settled at my computer in my small office before placing a few calls to friends in the police department, confirming much of what Burns said. An Internet search unearthed a plethora of information about John Aire, millionaire recluse and founder of Air Play, a consortium of theme parks based on different media motifs. The one in California was all about the movies. The one in Boston was based on U.S. history. The one in Kansas City was culinary-based, focusing on barbeque. And the one in Nashville was centered around the music industry. Willing patrons spent large amounts of money participating in virtual reality games and adventures at the different parks.

I munched my sandwich and chips while I read. Aire was now in his late fifties. When he was in his early twenties, he married Alberta "Bertti" Mason, a Creole Jamaican super-model. Before marrying Aire, she was the arm candy of a man who supposedly was a mucky-muck in the drug trade. Aire and Mason met in Jamaica, where he was vacationing. It was a whirlwind romance between two young lovers. They married and immediately had a child, Edward, who was born when Bertti was only twenty and Aire was barely twenty-two.

The relationship fell apart immediately, with Bertti returning to Jamaica and resuming her partying lifestyle. The child, Eddie, was put into boarding schools. Aire threw himself into his work, creating playgrounds for the wealthy. Oddly enough, he and his wife didn't divorce, they simply led separate lives. Gossip had it that her Roman Catholic family threatened her with expulsion if she considered divorce.

I took a break from my research and went to putter in my She Shed. This was a tiny structure I built the year before among the three oak trees shading the back yard. It was my craft shop, office, and inspiration space, ten-by-ten feet of recycled furniture and odds and ends. I cranked up my stereo, put on my Bluetooth headphones, and spent the afternoon reading, writing a few pages on my never-ending novel, and sketching ideas for my next metal sculpture. I ended up dozing for an hour or so, my feet propped up on the couch while the ceiling fan moved lazily overhead.

I stirred myself at cocktail hour and went inside to

mix a drink. I was considering the inside of my fridge when my home phone rang. I glanced at the display. *Private number.* I let it bounce to my answering machine. "Hey, it's Charlie," my voice said. "Leave a message. I'll call you back, sooner or later."

"Miss Rochester, this is John Aire. I'd like to speak with you as soon as possible." A male voice, scratchy sounding but polite, echoed in my office.

I stared in surprise at the answering machine before fumbling the phone out of the base. "Yo, hey. I'm here," I said breathlessly.

"Ah, good. I was hoping we could talk this evening. I understand you're interested in a job I have advertised."

"Actually, Burns Allen is interested in the job. He feels I'm the right woman for it. You need to discuss an interview with him, not me." I wouldn't participate in an end-run around Burns.

"I see. Can you hold?" Without waiting for a yea or nay, the line blipped at me. Damn Musak began to play.

"Asshole," I muttered. I set the phone to speaker and put it on the counter so I could resume staring at my fridge. Leftover chicken from the takeout place or leftover Chinese from the takeout place. I opted for Chinese, dumping it into a dish to pop into the microwave.

"Miss Rochester, I spoke to Mr. Allen. If you're amenable, I can interview you tonight."

I snatched up the phone, glancing down at my comfortable, faded capri jeans and loose, off-the-shoulder purple knit top. "I suppose that's okay. How about seven o'clock?"

"How about now?"

"What?"

"I'm not far from your home."

"Oh. I thought you meant at Burns' office."

"I don't see any reason for formality. You can call Mr. Allen to verify my credentials if you'd like."

Verify his credentials? I grinned. I think Aire had a big enough bank account, which was all the credential Burns cared about. "Sure, that's fine. Give me a minute to change my clothes."

There was a slight pause. "I don't mean to be rude, but I'm between appointments at the moment. Believe me when I say your choice of clothing is irrelevant to my hiring decision. I would appreciate it if you could make time for me now."

I gave up arguing. This was a man who was accustomed to getting his own way, no matter how polite he made it sound. I may as well get the damn interview done with so I could get on with my life. "Sure, that's fine. I live at—"

"I have your address. Thank you." He hung up.

I took a long swallow of bourbon then went to the front door mat to grab a pair of sandals. I straightened when I saw a large black car pull to the curb in front of my house. The biggest man I've ever seen in my life stepped from the car. He was linebacker big, with no neck and a buzz cut, wearing a suit coat that could have sheltered a family of four.

He opened the back door and a man in a business suit stepped out. I recognized him from the Wikipedia picture on my computer screen. John Aire, big as life, in my driveway. Compared to the bodyguard, he appeared short, but he was probably six feet tall with a lean build. He wasn't a handsome man, but he had an unusual face, one that showed his years and his experience. Cropped, thinning gray hair, a long, lined face, and a gray goatee framing his downturned mouth. The richest man in town, in my driveway.

I glanced at myself in the mirror near the door. Flyaway, curly chin-length white hair, no makeup except for mascara and a sunburned nose. I tugged my blouse so it hung more evenly and opened the front door. "When you said you were nearby, you weren't kidding." I stuck out my hand.

Aire shook my hand briskly. "Thank you for seeing me on such short notice." He turned to eye my garden. "Your yard is quite abundant."

I smiled. "That's one way to phrase it. Please, come in." I moved to one side. Aire stepped past me into the house.

The bodyguard—I suppose that's what he was— towered over me. "Do you mind if I check your house?"

"Sure, that's..." My voice trailed away when he pushed past me, walking to the kitchen and into the side hall to check the two bedrooms. He returned in less than a minute, nodded to Aire then went outside, closing the door behind him. "Well, that was interesting," I murmured.

Aire looked around my living/dining/kitchen space before his gaze settled on me. "I thought you'd be taller."

I regarded him with amused understanding. "I get that a lot. I sound taller on the phone." A lifetime of being the shortest person in the room inured me to surprise such as his.

"The way Mr. Allen talked, you're a giant."

"Burns is prone to hyperbole." I gestured toward the armchair. "Have a seat. I warn you, I have cats so there's cat hair everywhere." I eyed his crisp dark business suit.

It appeared professionally fitted and expensive.

He glanced around. "Cats?"

"I did have cats. I will have cats." I waved him toward the chair. "It's a long story."

He sat without a backward glance, leaning back and unhooking his suit jacket in one smooth gesture. The man obviously kept an account with a professional dry cleaner. "Why do you want to work for me, Miss Rochester?" he asked in his raspy voice.

I took the matching armchair. "I don't particularly care about working for you, Mr. Aire. But Burns would like me to work for you because he feels it will be good for his company. And Burns is a friend of mine. If I can accommodate him and earn money at the same time, that's fine." I frowned at my fluorescent pink toe polish. I needed a touch-up.

Aire glanced at my feet then my hands. "I don't bother with manicures," I said. "I do too much gardening for that."

"But you bother with pedicures," he murmured.

"A girl has to have some color in her life," I countered. "Can you tell me about the job and what your expectations are?" I figured it was best to get the details out of the way so I could deal with any misconceptions up front.

"As you probably know, my granddaughter, Adele Verrens, lives with me." He pronounced her name "Ah-dell," not "A-dell" as I expected. "Adele was in protective custody for two years following the death of her parents when she was ten years old."

What a cool, detached way to talk about his only son's murder. "I seem to remember reading about it."

"I was assigned custody of the child when she was

twelve, almost thirteen. That was four months ago. I'm in need of a person to act as a companion for the girl." He regarded me steadily, his pale blue eyes neither warm nor cold. Disinterested, dissecting, and direct. The words bounced through my mind when I met his gaze.

"In what capacity?" I hurried on before he could speak. "I mean, do you want me to teach her? Socialize with her? Act as a parent would?"

He frowned, the deep lines around his eyes creasing further. "I'm not sure. I think you can better evaluate that once you've met her. She is intelligent but not a very social child. I've tried two other nannies. They didn't last long."

"Really." I waited for him to elaborate but he didn't. "Did she dislike them?"

He rested his elbows on the chair arms and steepled his fingers in front of his chest. "She can be difficult sometimes. From what I can gather, she simply doesn't interact with them. She refused to follow their instruction."

From what I can gather. Assigned custody. What odd phrasing. "Does she attend school?"

He shook his head. "I don't think it would be safe for her."

"Does she have friends her age? Does she socialize with other children?"

He shook his head again. "I don't think so."

"So she's still in protective custody. Just a different kind of custody." I laced my fingers together in my lap. I had to still my need to get up and pace, a habit of mine when I was working on a difficult subject and needed action to help me think. "As I'm sure Burns told you, I don't have much experience with teenagers. Most of my

JL Wilson

teaching work is done at the college. I work in the Information Technology department on an as-needed basis."

"He did mention that."

I considered him and the job. The kid sounded like she was in desperate need of a friend, but was I the friend she needed? Well, no harm, no foul, I guess. I could always try it and leave if I didn't suit. "I'm willing to meet with her and see if we hit it off."

He kept his gaze fixed on me, his blue eyes so pale they seemed devoid of color. It gave him an odd, blind look. "You're aware I was investigated about the disappearance of my wife when I had her declared legally dead?"

"Yes. No charges were brought due to lack of evidence. Her body wasn't found nor was there any evidence of foul play. Your wife simply disappeared."

His lips compressed into a tight line. "The media is still anxious to prove me guilty. You may be questioned by the press. If you speak to them, you'll be dismissed. Do you understand?"

"I don't gossip."

"This isn't idle gossip. Anything you say could affect my business relationships. Are we clear?"

I bit my lip to restrain the words I longed to hurl. "Perfectly." I met his cold blue eyes with my own icy blue stare.

"I expect you to live at my home so you can stay with Adele around the clock. Will that represent any problem for you?"

"No, it won't." I had assumed that. It was good to get confirmation.

"I expect Adele to meet a few of my business and

14

social acquaintances. I would appreciate it if you would be with her. I'm not sure she's aware of the necessary social conventions such events entail."

"She and I will be in the same boat because I'm not sure I am, either. I can certainly try not to embarrass you or your friends, though. And I can try to help her navigate those kinds of gatherings."

He frowned. "I suppose that will have to do."

I inclined my head. "I suppose it will."

He was silent for a moment. I waited for the next barrage of questions. I was getting the hang of his interrogation technique. "You're a widow."

"Yes."

"Your husband was Jamaican."

"Nick had dual citizenship. His mother was American and his father was Hakka."

"Chinese Jamaican," he said, interrupting me when I began to explain. "Yes, I'm familiar with the term. That means you understand the customs of the island."

"Some of them. I didn't live there long."

"Do you know what obeah is?"

"Of course. It's a form of religion practiced in the islands. It's more of an individual religion rather than an organized religion per se. There are countless variants practiced throughout the Caribbean."

He stared at me, his face unreadable, for a long few seconds. I could imagine the wheels turning in his head. "One of the requirements for this job is a knowledge of firearms."

"I know. I have a gun permit. I've passed the licensing exams and tests. I've owned a gun for a long time."

"Do you carry a weapon?"

"Very seldom."

"Why?"

I had a ready answer because I often needed to defend my decision to my few gun-rights friends. "Most of the time I feel quite safe and am willing to let the police defend me."

"What about those times when you don't feel safe? Those places where you might not feel safe?" His gaze and his steepled fingers didn't waver. I thought I saw a hint of emotion in his eyes.

"At those times I do carry a gun and I am prepared to use it." Of course, nobody could honestly say that. I knew I was ready to use it, but would I? It depended on the situation. I suspected I would if my life or a child's life was threatened.

Actually, to be completely honest, I didn't just suspect. I knew I would.

"If I asked you to carry a gun while being with Adele, would you?"

"No." I answered without hesitation.

"Why?"

"From what you've said, you're concerned about her safety. Therefore, I shouldn't have a reason to carry a gun. If I do join your household and feel I should carry a gun I would discuss it with you before doing so."

He stood before I finished speaking. "I'd like you to start work tonight."

"Tonight? I can't. I need to—" I looked around my living/dining/kitchen space. "I have things to do."

"I can wait."

"What's the rush?"

"Why delay?"

"I need to make arrangements." I stopped when I

saw the way he looked. Or rather *didn't* look at me. No humor, no understanding, no empathy. "You won't take no for an answer, will you?"

He smiled briefly.

I stood. "I'll need to pack a bag."

"I'll wait outside. I have calls to make." He headed for the front door. The bodyguard must have been listening. As soon as Aire touched the handle, he opened it and moved to one side so Aire could exit.

I scowled at the door when it closed behind them. Next I called Burns while I considered my wardrobe. "I know, I know," Burns said before I could even speak. "He's like a force of nature. He wanted to talk to you and I couldn't say no."

"I'm starting tonight," I snapped. "I'm warning you, Burns. If you misrepresented me in any way, shape or form, I'm blaming you totally."

"It's good. All good. Call me if you need anything. I have a client on the other line, I have to go. You'll be fine, just fine." He was babbling, which wasn't unusual for Burns. "Don't keep him waiting, Charlie. Call me tomorrow. Tell me how it's going."

"Okay, but you owe me, Burns."

"I know, I know. Double bonus for you on this one. 'Bye."

I nuked my Chinese food and alternately ate, packed, and sipped bourbon. I tossed in an assortment of clothing, mostly jeans and tops. At the last minute, I threw in two swimsuits. I'd seen pictures of Aire's estate and I knew he had a nice pool. Besides, I'd only be a few dozen miles away from my house. I could always come back and get more stuff if I needed it. After an internal debate, I also put in my S&W 9mm with a spare magazine and the belt clip holster. I might not need it, but it paid to be prepared.

Packing my tech gear took longer because I had to dig around for power cords and couldn't find any carrying cases. They were probably buried somewhere in the attic along with my other luggage. In the end I jammed a laptop, my tablet, and cords into my bookstore tote bag emblazoned with the movie poster from *Jane Eyre* with Welles and Fontaine. I decided that Byronic setting might be suitable to my current situation. At the last minute, I also jammed in my wine-in-a-box. I enjoyed a little toddy before bedtime. God knows what it might take to get a glass of wine at Aire's place.

I set a couple of lights on timers and exited the car side of my two-car garage. The bodyguard was standing outside the black sedan like a rock keeping the car in place. "I'll follow you." I manhandled my suitcase, tote bag, and purse into the back of my small Fiat 500.

Aire exited the sedan, phone in his hand. "You can ride with me."

"I'm taking my car. I'll follow you. Just don't drive fast."

"I'll call you back." Aire touched the Bluetooth receiver in his ear. "You don't need a car. If you need a driver, I'll have someone take you where you want to go."

"I'll take my car." I went to the driver's door of my pale green mini-car. "Please stop arguing before I change my mind about taking this job." I turned to look at him.

I caught a glimpse of surprise, maybe bemusement, before the cool, disinterested mask settled back into place. "As you wish." He got into the sedan. The bodyguard slammed the door behind him and raced around to the driver's side.

I followed the sedan out of my neighborhood to the Interstate a mile away. The car drove at a sedate pace. It was easy to keep up, so much so I was tempted to pass them and show them what a zippy little car could do.

I restrained myself, though. After all, Aire was my employer. Maybe I should at least pretend to be sedate in turn. The sedan drove five miles south on the freeway then took the Woodland exit. I followed it into a suburb of three-acre lots full of McMansions. We left it behind and drove into the countryside, dotted here and there with large homes on ten or more acres, set back far from the road.

The sedan finally turned into a driveway, barely seen through the surrounding woods. It was wider than a normal drive, with room for two cars. The denseness of the foliage made the sun disappear so it felt like deep nighttime.

The road twisted and turned, finally emerging from the trees to a bluff overlooking the river below. The house was a sprawling expanse of glass and stone anchored by garages on the right. Brick paving was in front, enough to easily park five or six cars. Sunlight glinted off the exposed windows, making it wink in the late day light. It was only two stories tall but it seemed massive.

"Holy crap," I breathed.

The sedan disappeared into the depths of one of the garages. I drove forward and found a motor court behind the house. I parked my car so it faced out, lest I need a quick getaway. I slipped out of the car and saw Aire waiting for me in the open door to the garage.

"Let the adventure begin," I murmured.

Chapter 2

I tugged my bags from the back hatch. The bodyguard hurried to me and scooped up the roller bag. I held on to the tote bag when he reached for it. "Sorry," I said. "Nobody touches my tech but me."

He frowned. "I won't break it."

The guy looked so miffed I handed it to him, reluctantly. "Be careful. Oh, wait." I reached into the car, unhooking my iPod from its accessory slot in the console. I locked the doors and followed him across the open brick drive to Aire, who watched us from the depths of the garage.

"This is Paul." He nodded to the bodyguard, who preceded us into the house. "You can leave your car keys here." He pointed to a panel on the wall where other keys hung. "If we need to move it we can." He didn't wait to see if I agreed or not. "The other guards will be introduced to you when they come on duty. I've made sure they have your photograph so they're aware you're here. If you need to leave the grounds, ask one of the guards to enter the security code for you."

I reluctantly hung my car keys on a hook. "Security code?" I glimpsed two other cars next to the black sedan. One was a small red sports car. The other was a Humvee. Another car was in the far slot, hidden in the shadows. It was a dark color, long and sleek.

We passed through the garage into a hallway.

"Laundry is here." Aire gestured to the left. "My office is here." He continued walking while he rattled off rooms. "Dining room is here. Kitchen there and beyond it is the game room. The sunroom is off the living room. My suite is at the far end of the house. Here are stairs to the upper floor."

I would need breadcrumbs to find my way around. "What did you mean about security codes? What if I want to take a run? Go for a swim?"

He stopped in the entrance to the biggest living room I'd ever seen with a balcony above us on three sides. The room faced south. Long fingers of setting sun shone in, lamps lighting the dark corners.

"We set an alarm system once everyone is in for the night. You're free to come and go throughout the day if you don't leave the grounds." Aire looked at Paul, who stood near the stairs, my bag in his hand. "Miss Rochester will sleep in the green room." The big man went up the steps, my bags in tow.

A man stood on the other side of the living room in an alcove with a desk and books, turning when he heard our voices. He was younger than Aire, maybe in his thirties. He had dark red hair, a square, boxy sort of body and a plain, non-descript face. Like Aire, he wore a suit but his wasn't as fitted or as expensive-looking. "The papers we were waiting for came in from France," he said, stepping away from the desk.

"This is Miss Rochester, Grant. She'll be working with Adele." Aire took the folder the man handed him. "Miss Rochester, this is Grant Pool. He's my aide."

I shook the man's hand, noticing with a small smile the way he swept his gaze over my casual clothing. "It's a pleasure to meet you, Miss Rochester."

"Perhaps you can meet Adele tonight," Aire said to me. "It's not too late."

"She said she was going to sleep early," Pool murmured. "She ate dinner and went to her room."

"Is she unwell?" Aire asked.

"I don't think so. She was tired." Pool smiled at me. "I'm sure she'll be anxious to meet you tomorrow."

"I'm sure she will," I agreed, keeping a straight face. I glanced at my watch. It was only eight o'clock. If Adele was like the few other teenagers I knew, she was gearing up for a long night. She'd be on the Internet and the phone, chatting with friends and hanging out on social media sites. That reminded me. I turned to Aire. "I'll need the Wi-Fi password for the house and any other technology information you feel I'll need."

"Grant will provide you with those details. Now if you'll excuse me, I have work to finish." Without waiting for my reply, Aire went back the way we came and disappeared into a room on the right, across from the kitchen.

"Breakfast is usually at seven o'clock." Pool gestured me into the living room. He paused while I looked around the room, which was easily the size of the entire living space at my house. "The cook comes on duty at six. Lunch is usually at noon and dinner is at six-thirty or seven. Neither Mr. Aire nor I take meals here. We're often at the office by seven in the morning and are frequently in meetings until late in the evening. I know he was anxious to finalize the details for Adele today, which explains his early return home."

Early return home? Eight at night? I went to the opposite side of the room where large windows led to a massive porch full of skylights. Beyond it was the swimming pool and beyond it the land dropped off in the bluff on the river. "Does Adele swim?"

"I don't believe so."

I turned, taking in the expensive paintings, groupings of furniture, and the wall full of bookcases filled with precisely aligned spines or expensive knick-knacks. "What kinds of games are in the game room?"

Pool went to the far corner and I followed. We passed into the kitchen, a pristine white space with two islands and a stove that appeared big enough to cook a whole pig. Pool opened a door and we entered a room about as big as a two-car garage. A ping pong table and pool table took up part of the space. In one corner was a large TV with a bank of chairs in front of it. A door was between the TV and the treadmill, and a set of stairs near it led upward. Behind a screened-off portion of the room were weights, three weight benches, a treadmill, and an elliptical machine. "The guards frequently use this room during their down time. You're welcome to use it when you aren't with Adele."

"Where's the door go?" I asked. "And the stairs?"

"The door goes to the back yard. The stairs lead to a room upstairs where the guards relax between shifts."

"Does a guard remain here at night?" I gestured around me. "In the house, I mean."

"There are two guards on duty at all times, plus one is always with Mr. Aire when he leaves the house. The guards have overlapping hours and the schedule is random." Pool led the way back through the kitchen, speaking over his shoulder. "I'm sure the guards will introduce themselves when you see them. We have a regular rotating group of ten men."

"No women?"

Pool stopped in the middle of the living room, if such a large space could be called that. "No, we don't have any women on assignment. Is that a problem for you?" His tone was blandly polite. I thought I heard an undercurrent of challenge.

"Just curious. I wondered if Adele would be more comfortable with a woman guard."

"Adele seldom leaves the house. I don't know if she even notices the guards."

I was getting the impression no one in this house even noticed Adele. I headed back to the kitchen.

"Can I get you something?" Pool asked, hurrying after me.

"I want a glass for my toothbrush and one for my nightstand, so I don't end up stumbling around searching for water in the middle of the night." I approached a bank of dark cherry wood kitchen cabinets, opening one at random.

"We have bottled water here." He opened what I thought was a pantry cabinet but which turned out to be a double-wide fridge. "Feel free to help yourself."

I opened another cabinet and spied an array of glasses. "Bottled water is a waste of plastic. Tap water is fine." I took two heavy cut-glass tumblers and joined him at the fridge. It was so neatly organized I wondered if anyone ever foraged in there for a midnight snack.

As though reading my mind, Pool opened a door next to the fridge. "We have an assortment of bread, crackers, and other items here, if you're hungry between meals." He smiled briefly, but it didn't affect his pale brown eyes. "And of course, you're welcome to anything in the refrigerator. Mrs. Fairfax runs a tight ship. She doesn't like her kitchen in disarray."

"Mrs. Fairfax?" I considered making a grab for a package of Oreo cookies, but Pool closed the door before I could make up my mind.

"Our cook. If you have any particular dietary restrictions, please let me know so I can keep her informed." He waited expectantly.

"No moldy cheese. Other than that, I'm fine." I went back to the living room, looking up at the balcony. A door in the corner was closing. I glimpsed a dark-haired figure disappearing behind it.

"I'll show you to your room now, unless you have other questions." Pool led the way past a wall of paintings, going back to the hall where I entered.

"Do the guards sleep here? Do you?" I followed him up the stairs.

"The guards come on duty in shifts, so they don't sleep here except in unusual circumstances. I often sleep in the lower bedroom under yours." He paused at the top of the stairs. "That's the library and TV room."

I peeked into the big room ahead of me. "What a marvelous place." I surveyed the long room with chairs, bookcases on walls, and tall windows opposite the door.

"Yes, quite nice. Beyond the TV room is another bathroom and the room the guards use when they aren't on duty." Pool ignored my rapture about the library. We walked along the balcony overlooking the living room below, coming to a door in the northeast corner of the house. "This is your room. You have a private bath, of course." He swung the door open and I went in. "The bedroom next to yours is empty. It's a guest room, as is this one."

A lamp was lit near the double bed with a pale green flowered coverlet on my right. Straight ahead was a window with a chintz chair near it and a bench under it. Across from the bed was a dresser with a small television on top. The walls were painted a pale mint green and the dark wooden floors glowed around a thick green area rug.

"Your bathroom is here." He opened a door inside the room. I glanced in to see a shower and sink, with another door presumably leading to a private toilet area.

"Very nice. I'm sure this will be acceptable." I put my two glasses on the dresser. Pool's eyes widened at this desecration of furniture. "Don't worry. I'll be careful."

"I'm sure you will. If you need anything, dial zero on the house phone." He gestured to the phone in a charger on the nightstand. "Either I or one of the guards will answer. If you need an outside line, dial nine first."

"Good to know." I went to my roller bag, which lay on a suitcase stand near the window, my tech bag on the floor nearby.

"I hope you'll be patient with Adele," he said.

I turned. "Of course I will be."

"I mean, well, she's a difficult child sometimes." He smiled weakly, pretending to be compassionate. He actually looking sly and cunning.

"She's at a difficult age. And she's had a difficult life, far more so than most teenagers."

"I suppose you're right." What he really meant was *That's bullshit*. "Mr. Aire mentioned you lived in Jamaica."

"Very briefly and a long time ago." I unzipped my bag. "You were going to give me the Wi-Fi password."

Pool reached into his inner suit pocket and extracted an index card, crossing the room to hand it to me. "This should be everything you need. We change the passwords every Tuesday, Thursday, and Saturday. The new password is posted on the chalkboard in the kitchen near the game room."

I glanced at the information. "You have two networks?"

"Mr. Aire and I use one for work and there's one for the home, which you can use."

"Which does Adele use?"

"The home network, of course."

I checked the card, which only noted one password. "Do you change the password for your business network every day?"

"No, we change it randomly."

That meant they probably seldom changed it. "Thank you. I'll try to log in tonight to verify it's working okay."

"Mr. Aire mentioned you have a technology background."

I opened my suitcase. "Yes, I do. Now if you don't mind, I'd like to unpack and relax."

He backed up immediately. "Of course. I'm sorry to detain you."

"No problem." I went to the door and held it while he left. "I'll see you in the morning."

"Oh, I doubt that. We usually are out early."

"So am I. Good night." I closed the door firmly in his face. For some reason, Pool bugged me. It wasn't just his unctuous mannerisms and implicit criticism of a girl I hadn't yet met. He gave me the creeps. The less time I spent with him, the better.

I unpacked and inspected the bathroom, which was twice the size of mine at home and far more luxurious. It was only eight-thirty so I left to explore. When I went to the library, I saw John Aire below me in the living room, standing at the windows overlooking the sun porch. The room was in darkness except for one lamp on his left. He had shed his suit coat and wore a white dress shirt rolled up at the sleeves, his arms clasped behind him.

He turned, hearing me on the balcony. I edged back into the shadows and thus missed the door to the library, ending up instead at the TV room. A big black man in a dark business suit approached me from the hallway ahead. "It's okay," I said softly. "I work here."

He smiled, white teeth appearing in his dark face. "Yeah, so I heard. You're the new governess or whatever it's called. My name's Charlie. I'm on duty until seven in the morning."

I stuck out my hand. "I'm Charlie, too. Good to meet you."

He shook my hand. "I thought you'd be bigger. He made you sound pretty big."

"Who did?"

"Mr. Aire. I guess your employment agency talked you up."

"Yeah, Burns does that sometimes. I hope I can live up to the expectation."

He passed me, going to the staircase. "Good luck, Charlie. You'll need it." He disappeared before I could question his cryptic remark.

I surveyed the TV room. It held a dozen theater-style chairs facing a TV taking up most of one wall. I examined the controls on the table in the middle of the room and decided I could figure it out. I left the room and ducked into the library, taking a minute or two to examine the bookcases. An eclectic collection of volumes filled the shelves. They appeared to be sorted by genre with a preponderance of titles in non-fiction. Of all the rooms I'd seen in the house, this was the only one that appeared used.

I went back to my room, eyeing the length of the balcony to Adele's door. I considered introducing myself, but a noise below made me stop. John Aire stood at the edge of the living room outside a door directly under Adele's door. He watched me, his face highlighted by the lamp in the corner. "Good night, Miss Rochester," he said, his voice drifting up to me. "I hope you'll be comfortable."

"I'm sure I will be. Good night." I ducked into my room and closed the door, my heart pounding erratically. Aire had a habit of appearing, well, out of thin air. It was unnerving. I poured myself a glass of wine from my stash then got out my tech gear and plugged in my phone and tablet.

The blinking icon on my phone told me a message was waiting. "Hi, Charlotte. It's Richard St. John. I wanted to check with you on our time tomorrow night. The lecture begins at seven. I suppose we should arrive at least half an hour early to get good seats."

I rolled my eyes. Richard was a man I met in my Tai Chi class. We occasionally attended public lectures at the college. I doubted whether a lecture on "The Meaning of Joy Through Exercise" would be heavily attended, so it didn't warrant going early. But that was Richard. Better to be safe than possibly have a bad seat.

I glanced at the clock and decided it was too late to call him back and cancel. That would involve a long discussion which would lead to his doubts about the advisability of me staying in a strange person's house.

Richard was cautious that way. I'd call him in the morning.

I settled on the bed with my laptop on my knees. I logged in to the network to run a couple of programs of mine that monitored network traffic. As I expected, there was one other user currently logged in to the home network, probably Adele. She wasn't using an excessive amount of data, but her usage was active. That meant she was on the Internet. I could view usage on the other network and one person was logged in there. That was either Aire or Pool, who was presumably in the room directly below mine.

I checked my email and sent a quick note to Burns assuring him I was in place and doing okay. I set the laptop aside and changed into my nightgown. I enjoyed fresh air while I slept, but given how tight security was in the house, I was reluctant to open the windows. However, the air-conditioned room was nice and cool and outside was muggy and hot. Given the possibility I might have a hot flash made me decide not to risk it. Instead, I opted to take an OTC sleep aid and flick through channels on the small TV until it kicked in.

I dozed off and woke when a noise outside my door made me jerk upright in bed. It sounded like someone crying or maybe coughing. I checked the TV, thinking a movie was on. The station was showing an infomercial for some kind of rotisserie cooker. I pushed my covers aside and jumped out of bed. My dark purple nightgown was relatively modest, reaching to mid-thigh. However, it was thin and depending on how I moved, it could accent every bulge and lump I had. I grabbed a throw from the window bench and draped it around me.

I cautiously opened my door and peeked out. The

hallway opened onto the balcony. It was empty or so it seemed. A faint glow of light showed over the railing but otherwise everything was dark. I inched through my door, glancing to my left where another bedroom door was closed.

The sound came again, this time from ahead of me, at the end of the run of balcony where it stopped at Adele's room. It was more like a man's laugh followed by a woman's exclamation of surprise or maybe dismay. I thought of the child, essentially alone in the house with a bunch of men. My hesitation vanished. I strode along a tastefully decorated hall, several hidden sconces highlighting paintings or an object d'art piece on an end table.

I was nearly to the double doors set at an angle to the balcony when movement below me made me stop. John Aire once again looked up at me. He was barefoot and wore washed-out jeans and a navy T-shirt. "What is it? Is something wrong?"

I leaned over the balcony. "I heard voices. What time is it?"

"It's midnight. Perhaps Adele is watching television or a movie." He sounded surprised, not worried.

"Doesn't she have a curfew?" When he didn't answer, I prompted, "A set time to turn off electronics and go to bed?"

"I know what a curfew is, Miss Rochester. No, she doesn't have one. Adele is an intelligent girl. I trust she knows the importance of a regular schedule."

I tugged the throw tighter around me, attempting to cover more skin. The hallway was chilly and my body was reacting with goose and other unseemly bumps. "She's a teenager. She may be intelligent, but at her age, her hormones are probably far stronger than her reasoning." I went to her door but hesitated before knocking. If she was watching a movie, I didn't want to appear like a nervous Nelly. But if there was a problem, I had to know about it.

"I applaud your concern but everything is fine. Good night, Miss Rochester." Aire said it firmly and with finality, leaving no room for arguing.

I turned to go back the way I came. When I did, I tripped on the throw. It ended up on the floor and I ended up mostly exposed to my employer. I didn't bother apologizing. I snatched up the offending blanket and scurried back to my room.

I stopped outside my door, straining to hear any other noises. I heard soft footsteps below me, but I didn't hear the voices or laughter or whatever it was. I finally went into the room and settled back into a deep sleep.

My eyes snapped open at five-thirty, as always. It didn't matter how late I fell asleep. I always woke at five-thirty and I always woke instantly, with none of the groggy transition other people talked about.

I went to the tall front windows. They faced north. The small porthole-type windows high above the bed were east facing. Faint light told me dawn was starting. Even from the confines of an air-conditioned house the outdoors looked moist and warm.

I checked the weather app on my phone. Seventy degrees at five a.m. with eighty-percent humidity. I rolled my eyes. The dog days of summer, indeed. We were a week away from Labor Day but it felt like July. I dressed in my modest blue one-piece swimsuit covered by gym shorts and my *I took the road less traveled, now where the hell am I?* T-shirt. Grabbing my flip-flops, I left the room and headed for the ground floor.

Charlie, the large black guard, met me at the bottom of the stairs. Today he wore a dark blue polo shirt and jeans, presumably his overnight uniform. "You're up early. Couldn't sleep?"

"Early to bed, early to rise. I'd like to get in some exercise and a swim before the house is stirring. Is it okay?"

"Sure, not a problem. Come on." He led the way through the living room to the sunroom, opening the door for me. He gestured to a set of double doors to the left, below Adele's doors above. "Mr. Aire's suite is there. He has a private patio that opens into the backyard. I don't know if he's awake yet, so keep the noise to a minimum and you'll be fine."

"It's some Tai Chi, then a swim," I assured him. "Virtually noiseless. If it's okay, I'll use the weight room later, maybe get in a run on a treadmill or lifting. I try to do some kind of workout every day."

"Mr. Aire usually exercises first thing in the morning. If you don't overlap with him, that's fine. He likes the weight room to himself."

The king, high in his castle. "Thanks. I'll make sure we don't coincide." I exited the sunroom onto a beautifully paved brick patio, an inset design of lighter colored bricks making me pause to examine it. The artwork was apparently a seal or crest, but it was hard to get a sense of it from this angle. I studied the house, noticing for the first time an exterior balcony overlooking the pool and patio. It would have the best view of the patio design. At one corner, near Aire's suite, was a spiral staircase leading upward to the balcony. It was like something in a Romeo and Juliet sketch.

I walked onto the lawn, carrying my shoes. The earth was cool between my toes, the grass luxurious and damp. It was a foggy morning, the air so thick with humidity it was transformed into mist. A pale glow to my left was the sun creeping over the horizon.

The lawn was a strip of greenness about thirty feet wide separating the house from the pool, which was in turn surrounded by ten feet of concrete. Trees denoted the edge of the bluff. The pool appeared to slide off the edge like one of those infinity pools from a TV design show. It was not quite Olympic sized but still decent for lap swimming or splashing.

I left my shoes near the concrete verge of the pool and faced the sun, the house on my left side and the pool on my right. I spent a few moments in silent contemplation, inhaling the tangy smells of flowers from the beds around the house. I felt the moist air of a breeze and heard the beginnings of birds in the trees beyond the pool. I slipped into my Tai Chi practice, moving carefully through the postures, repeating them to myself as I did.

Commence. Part the Wild Horse Mane. Brush Knee. Play the Lute. Reverse here, now facing the motor court and my small car, dew glistening on the roof. *Repulse Monkey. Grasp Sparrow Tail.* Turn to the left, now facing the bluff and the wheeling birds flying over the river below. *Single Whip. Wave Hands Like Clouds.*

Turn again, the house once more on my left. My mind flowed with the movements, clearing and calming. I focused on a shrub in the distance, a bright pink hydrangea so overburdened with blooms it appeared to be collapsing. *Single Whip 2. High Pat on Horse. Right*

Heel Kick.

I put my energy into the kick while I swiveled, staring at my car and Charlie, who watched me from the motor court. Sweat ran down my face and dropped onto my pale blue T-shirt. *Strike Ears with Fist. Turn and Left Heel Kick.* This was the tricky part, requiring balance and concentration. *Left Lower Body, Stand on One Leg.* Switch. *Right Lower Body, Stand on One Leg. Shuttle Back and Forth.*

Sweat made my shirt cling to me like a second skin. I barely noticed except to blink it from my eyes. *Needle at Bottom of Sea. Fan Through Back.* Deep breath. *Turn, Deflect, Parry, Punch.* Release breath. *Appear Closed. Cross Hands. Close.*

I remained standing for another long moment, reveling in the exhausted feeling of an exercise well done. Then I shook off the sweat and strode to the pool, peeling off my shirt and shorts before diving in.

The water was shocking and marvelous, warmed by the sun but refreshingly cool. It instantly erased the sweat better than any towel or shower could do. I surfaced halfway along the length and began a lazy freestyle stroke, flipping at the end and coming back with a backstroke. I did one more length with sidestroke then rolled onto my back to float, arms extended while my body bobbed with the faint ebb and flow of water.

The sun was up now, burning off the mist in the air. I stared at the sky and the last remnants of stars, the almost-full moon still fat and heavy at the horizon. *Not a bad gig. Of course, I haven't met the kid yet, so maybe she'll be a monster. Odd. No one has discussed a curriculum or anything.*

What did they expect from me? Companion? What

an old-fashioned term. Wasn't the narrator of *Rebecca* a companion at the start of the book? I dipped my head back, water tugging on my curls, tickling me. I knew little about kids, so this might be a short-lived job.

I sensed more than saw movement to the right, near the house. I dibbled my feet so I had a better view of the lawn, expecting to see Charlie or one of the other guards. What I saw was John Aire, running from the house, barefoot. He wore the same faded jeans and T-shirt from the night before. He tossed a coffee mug to the side where it bounced in the lawn, liquid spilling out.

I jackknifed upright and treaded water. "What's wrong?" I called. "Is Adele okay?" I peered up at the house and spied someone on the overhead balcony. The minute I saw the figure, though, it vanished back into the house.

I turned back to Aire. He was stopped now, staring at me with an odd expression. "What is it?" I swam to the shallow end of the pool where I could stand, propping my arms on the concrete surround.

"I thought…" He approached the edge. "You were floating."

I pushed my fingers through my hair. "Sorry. I didn't mean to disturb you. The guards said it was okay. I guess I wasn't as quiet as I meant to be. I apologize."

"No, it's not that." He looked away from me to the trees, as though searching for an answer there. "I thought you—you were floating and—"

Holy crap. "You thought I was drowning? Oh my God, no, I'm fine. I'm an excellent swimmer. No, I'm sorry. I'm fine." I was stammering but I didn't know what else to say. Crap, was I a goof? The man thought he needed to jump in and save me. Here I was, bragging about my swimming ability.

"You were just, well, I've never seen anyone lie on the water like that." He backed away from the edge. "I'm sorry. I didn't mean to interrupt your swim."

"Women are more buoyant than men. It's easy to float." I clambered out of the pool on the side ladder.

He stepped from me, stumbling on the uneven concrete. I realized I didn't have a towel. I headed for my dropped shorts and shirt. "As I said, sorry if I disturbed you."

"Towels are there." He gestured to the low wicker table between two chaise lounges.

"Oh, great. Thanks. I guess I forgot to bring one." I took one of the thick, luxurious towels from the shelf under the table. "I've never—" I was talking to no one. John Aire was striding back across his lawn, making a beeline for his dropped mug. I blotted myself somewhat dry and put on my shirt, wrapping the towel around my bottom half in a sarong. I picked up my shorts and sandals and headed for the house.

Charlie the guard emerged from the sunroom. He and Aire spoke then Charlie joined me midway across the lawn. "Did I piss him off?" I asked.

Charlie looked at Aire, who entered the house through a set of French doors on the brick patio. "I don't think so." He fell into step with me. "You know, he can't swim."

"What? It looked like he might jump in the pool for a minute there."

"Yeah. I thought so, too. Weird. Oh, oh." His eyes narrowed and his mouth thinned into a tight line. "Trouble ahead."

I followed his gaze. A girl stood on the patio outside

the sunroom, leaning against an open door. She had straight and thick long black hair and warm, chocolate brown skin. She wore what passed for age-appropriate clothing these days: white shorts showcasing her long brown legs and a see-through slip-off-the-shoulder red blouse over a sports bra. She was a child masquerading as a woman.

"That's her, right? Adele?"

"Yeah. She's a kid in too much of a hurry to grow up. See you later." He made an abrupt left turn and headed for the motor court.

The girl watched him go before turning her gaze to me. Her chin jutted out and she straightened. I recognized her defiant posture. I'd seen it often enough on undergrads when they wanted to spin a story about lost homework or a missed exam.

I smiled. "Let's get this show on the road." I walked forward to meet the kid.

Chapter 3

Adele straightened when I approached. "Who are you?" she asked in a surly, dismissive voice.

"My name is Charlie Rochester." I stuck out my hand. "Who are you?"

Instead of shaking my hand, she twisted a long black strand of her hair around a finger, eyeing me suspiciously. "You know who I am. I'm John's granddaughter. How come you were doing all that standing and moving stuff earlier on the lawn?"

I lowered my hand. "It's called Tai Chi Chuan. It's a form of meditation."

"I thought meditation was about sitting in one place and staring at the wall and making your mind empty."

"Not really. Meditation is about understanding your mind and how it works. Tai Chi helps me understand it."

"It looked stupid. Starting and stopping and the weird postures." She pushed her hair over her shoulders and crossed her arms on her chest.

"I suppose it does appear odd to an observer." I refused to defend my choice of exercise to this rude child.

"You're the new governess, aren't you?" she challenged.

"Yes, I am." I dabbed at my face with my T-shirt, more to hide my annoyed expression than to dry my skin.

"I don't want a governess."

"That's irrelevant. Your grandfather gets to decide what you do and don't have."

Adele rolled her eyes, such a typical reaction of teenage angst I was hard pressed not to laugh. "He doesn't give a shit about me." She eyed me sideways, as though gauging my reaction to her mild profanity.

I considered my several options regarding how to handle this. I decided on the blunt approach. "That, too, is irrelevant. You're his legal ward. He can do whatever the hell he wants with you. What he did was hire me."

"I can get you fired," she shot back.

"Go ahead." I took a step forward and stared into her face. She was a tall girl, but still a child, so she didn't have much of a height advantage on me. "I'm doing this gig as a favor for a friend. If you get me fired, I'll go back to my life and you can go back to yours. But I'm pretty sure if you get me fired, your grandfather might decide it's not worth his time to have you here with a nanny at your beck and call. You might be shipped off to a private school where you don't have any freedom at all. So think about that."

I could see she longed to fling back a retort, but she didn't. To her credit, she did consider it. Her eyes, pale gold-brown, narrowed when she regarded me. For an instant, she reminded me of her grandfather, so coolly arrogant and self-confident. "So what are you supposed to do with me?"

"That's for us to figure out." I stepped back. "Let's start over, shall we?" I held out my hand. "Hi. My name's Charlie Rochester. Who are you?"

This time she took my hand and gave it a limp shake. "I'm Adele Verrens."

"The first thing I'll teach you is how to give a proper

handshake." I released her hand and went inside the open door. "Your handshake tells the other person about you. Come on."

"Where are you going?" She followed me, probably from curiosity more than anything.

"I'll get changed then we'll have breakfast and decide where we go from here."

"I don't usually eat breakfast." She slowed when we crossed the sunroom and entered the voluminous living room.

"Humor me. Have a slice of toast or something. Meet me downstairs in twenty minutes. Do we eat in the kitchen or the dining room?"

She pointed ahead and to the left. "Dining room. Mrs. Fairfax usually sets up a buffet."

"That's a waste of food if you don't eat much," I said.

"That's my concern, not yours, Miss Rochester," a male voice said behind me.

I turned. John Aire stood in a doorway on my right, the one leading to his suite. He wore brown trousers, a starched beige shirt and a brown tie, looking every inch the businessman he was.

"Actually, it's everyone's concern." His condescending tone grated on my already flighty nerves. "Food waste is foolish if not immoral when so many people are hungry in the world. There's no excuse for it."

I didn't wait for his reply but brushed past Adele. With a startled squeak, she hurried after me. "You told off my grandfather," she whispered excitedly.

"Stick with me, kid," I muttered. "I'm sure I'll do it again sometime. I'll see you in twenty minutes." I headed for the staircase and took the steps two at a time, not pausing to see if she followed my instructions.

I showered and dressed in a pair of lightweight khaki pants and a dark brown linen blouse. It was casual yet somewhat business-y, or so I told myself. I slipped on a pair of sandals and tucked my phone into my pants pocket. That reminded me to call Richard to cancel the night's lecture. I dampened my curly hair's enthusiasm with styling gel then left.

To my surprise, John Aire was seated at the far end of the dining room facing the doorway across the expanse of the table. And what a table it was. Ten people could easily fit around the long rectangular length of mahogany. Three low vases of fresh flowers were stationed in the middle on a runner of embroidered silk. The table itself was laid with glittering china and crystal stemware, items I associated with dinner not breakfast. In fact, the table held as much dinnerware as I owned. All of this was matched, unlike my own mish-mash of cutlery and glasses.

I paused inside the doorway to get the lay of the land. Three chafing dishes were set on a sideboard to my right. Small burners glowed under the gleaming pans. I smelled bacon, bread, and something sweet, possibly warm honey. Adele sat in the middle of the table, separated from Aire by one place setting.

"Good morning, Miss Rochester." Aire glanced up from the newspaper folded next to his plate. His pale blue eyes swept over my business casual ensemble and he frowned.

"Hello again." I went to an empty seat across from Adele, who stared at her phone, positioned next to her plate. "Good morning, Adele. What do you have planned for today?"

Adele and her grandfather both looked at me as though I spoke in tongues. "What?" Adele asked.

"What do you have planned?" I repeated. "I find it's useful to have an idea of what I want to accomplish in the day. It helps me map out what I'll do." I moved aside when a small gray-haired woman bustled into the room behind me, moving with a slight limp. She wore a plain blue chef's coat with navy blue pants and bright pink Croc clogs.

"Is everything to your satisfaction, Mr. Aire?" she asked, lifting the lid on one of the dishes on the sideboard.

"Yes, Mrs. Fairfax. Fine." Aire didn't even look up from his paper.

I followed her. "I'm Charlie Rochester. I'm working with Adele. If you're the cook, I need to thank you. The aroma of your food positively pulled me into this room." I took a plate from the stack on the sideboard and peered into the pan whose lid she held.

The little woman seemed to puff up. "That's good of you to say, miss. Let me serve you. These eggs are local, you know."

"I get mine from Bass Farms on Highway 30," I said while she put a healthy dollop of fluffy scrambled eggs on my plate.

"I get our vegetables there. I get our eggs from a friend of mine who has a small farm east of here."

"Local food is the best," I agreed, peering at the next pan. "Oh, my. You can't find sausage like this in the grocery store."

She positively swelled with pride. "Indeed. It starts with the right meat, of course."

"This did not come from a feedlot pig." I lifted one

plump sausage in the tongs and brandished it before putting it on my plate. "My compliments, Mrs. Fairfax. I will need to be careful I don't overindulge while I'm here." I plucked a piece of toast from the warming basket. "Is this homemade jam?"

"Strawberry. From my garden."

I sighed. "My mother used to make strawberry jam. Sometimes she would warm it in a pan until it was more pourable and serve it on French toast for special dinner meals." I spooned a large glob of jam and put it on the thick piece of bread. "Breakfast was never my favorite meal, but I can see you may change my mind."

"Can I get you anything else? There's coffee here. If you'd like something else to drink, you let me know."

"I do like a glass of milk with my meals if that's not too much trouble. Not now, but perhaps for lunch?"

"Absolutely. I'll make sure it's here."

I smiled at her. "Then everything will be perfect. Thank you."

Mrs. Fairfax beamed at me then left, her pink Crocs a blur of motion. I went to the table and put down my plate. John Aire watched me, his blue eyes cool and evaluating. "It appears you're good with people."

"I suppose that's because I'm a people, too." I filled a china cup with coffee and took a seat across from Adele. "I've found letting someone know you appreciate what they do can be pleasant for them and for yourself."

He propped his elbows on the table and laced his fingers together, staring at me above his hands. "I pay her a very good salary for what she does."

"And I'm sure she's happy to receive it." I sampled the eggs. They were heavenly, light and fluffy with just the right amount of seasoning. "But it's still nice to be told you're doing a good job and your hard work is seen and valued. She's an excellent cook. The fact she's seeking local food sources is outstanding. She not only cares about how food tastes, but she cares about the quality as well."

"Why does it matter if it's local?" Adele asked.

I took a bite of sausage. The casing cracked when I cut into it and the meat inside was juicy and flavorful. It was probably handmade and local, too. "There are several reasons to use local food that I feel are important." I savored my bite of sausage before continuing. "First of all if it's local and in season, you know it's fresh and it hasn't been transported a long distance. The cost of fuel adds to the cost of the food and can keep prices high. Secondly, if it is transported a long distance, the food was specifically bred to endure the trip. That means it's been altered from the way it would grow naturally. Think about winter tomatoes. So different than summer tomatoes. Lastly, if it's local, you can examine the growing conditions, which I feel is essential for the items in the food chain."

"Food chain?" Adele darted a glance at her grandfather, who continued to gaze at me, a speculative expression in his eyes.

"Meat is at the end of our food chain." I paused to consider the notion. "Although I suppose the earth is truly the end of the food chain because after we die, we go back to dirt if we're allowed to decay naturally. But for now, let's say our meat is. It's important to know what goes into the meat. Was it grass fed on land not chock full of chemicals? Was it allowed to take exercise and live a somewhat normal life? Was it caged and not allowed to move? That causes an enormous amount of stress on an animal. Stress is translated into the food we eventually eat." I held up the last of the sausage, speared on my fork. "This was a pig once. Was it full of chemicals and forced to live in an unhealthy environment? Was it allowed to have access to fresh air and sunlight? Was it slaughtered humanely?"

Adele wrinkled her nose. "That's gross to think about. Besides, the government makes sure everything is safe so why should we care?"

"Oh, to be so trusting again." I leveled the fork at her. "It's important to develop critical thinking skills. Never assume a ruling body is doing what is best for you. That body is supposed to do what is right for the *majority*, which sometimes does not translate into what is best for the individual. And in addition, lobbyists and other powerful parties can influence decisions. What if the government decided it was essential its citizens have access to organic foods and foods treated with chemicals were illegal? What would happen to our mega-food companies? How would they adjust?" I stared at her across the table then popped the piece of sausage in my mouth. "That's your first assignment for today," I said after swallowing.

"What?" She sounded outraged, as though a homework assignment was an insult.

"I'll give you a couple of clues. Find which companies spend the most money on lobbying Congress regarding food laws. Maybe research those companies and see how many people they employ. After that, I suggest you study the towns where the companies have factories. If the company was forced to change the way it does business, how would that affect the workers? Don't forget to consider shipping costs, which will change radically, and other factors. For example, those strawberries." I pointed to my half-eaten toast. "Those are local. Where do you think your strawberries come from in January? They're grown in California. Winter fruit is a large part of the California economy. Can a company safely ship organic produce across the country in wintertime? And in what quantities?" I glanced at her grandfather. "What time is it?"

He checked his large watch. "Seven thirty."

I regarded Adele, who stared at me in wide-eyed wonder. "You and I will chat about your findings at ten o'clock. You don't need to write it out in detail, but I would like you to prepare a summary of your research. Have you been home schooled in the past? Do you have a set school schedule? I don't want to interfere with that."

"I, no, I do online classes. I can do them at my own rate."

"Have you established your own schedule?" I took a bite of toast. Good Lord, the jam was like ambrosia, so fruity and fresh.

"No, I just…I mean, whenever I—"

"We'll set up a schedule later." I interrupted her stammering. "That way it will be easier for me to assess your progress. If you're done eating, I suggest you get started. The research is only part of it. You need to think through your conclusions and organize it in such a way it makes sense."

I thought she might rebel. She wanted to, I know, but her grandfather was there, watching everything. Adele picked up her phone and stood. "I've never done anything like this before. We don't have assignments like this in the school I use."

"Then it will be a new learning experience." I smiled at her. "Perhaps when you finish, we can discuss where you'd like to go for our field trip this afternoon."

"Field trip?" Aire's chilly voice echoed in the room.

"I think a visit to the local museum might be fun. The St. John's Bible is on display. It's a chance of a lifetime to see such a work of art."

Adele wrinkled her nose again. "A Bible?"

"Not only a Bible. It's a hand-illuminated Bible, every page individual and unique. I suggest you do research about it, too, before we go. We'll go after lunch."

"I don't think that's advisable, Miss Rochester." Aire stood and picked up his newspaper.

"You're excused, Adele," I said to the girl, who stood near her chair, her eyes wide with surprise. "If you need any help with your assignment, I'll be in the upstairs library later." I waited until she reluctantly left the room before I faced her grandfather over the expanse of table separating us.

It was time to get the rules established. "I will not participate in home arrest for your granddaughter. A visit to a local museum and other outside activities are things I feel are important. I understand your concern for her safety. I'll discuss any outings with the guards you have on duty. If they express concerns for my plans, I'll consider a change. Otherwise, Adele and I will have an outing every day." I took one last bite of eggs and stood. "If that's not acceptable, you'll need to make other arrangements for her schooling and her care."

He stared at me, his face as still as stone. Then he nodded, once. "That's acceptable."

I blew out a long breath. "Good." I headed for the

door, glancing reprovingly at the food in the chafing dishes. "I think I'll speak to Mrs. Fairfax about the leftovers. I'm sure there's a place where it can be donated."

"Miss Rochester?"

I stopped in the doorway and turned to face him.

"You said your mother made French toast for special dinners. That's usually a breakfast item."

I met his gaze across the mahogany table. "As you already know, my family was quite poor. Oftentimes the only thing we had to eat was the bread my mother made, the fruit she and my father grew, and the eggs we gathered from the chickens we raised. We had meat on occasion when we slaughtered an animal. My parents did the best they could with what they had to work with."

His lips softened in a faint smile. "Thank you, Miss Rochester." It was a clear dismissal.

I left before I got even more pissed off than I was. What an arrogant, condescending jerk. He undoubtedly had a dossier on me an inch thick. Well, I hope he enjoyed reading about my less-than-wealthy upbringing and my struggles to put myself through college via an assortment of odd jobs.

I barely avoided Grant Pool, who was striding out of the living room, his eyes intent on the tablet in his hand. "Oh, Miss Rochester. Have you seen Mr. Aire?"

I gestured behind me. "Finishing breakfast."

"Really? He seldom eats here."

"He did today." I headed for the sunroom but stopped. I told Aire I would check with the guards before our outing, so I suppose I needed to do that. I hurried up the stairs and onto the balcony. Instead of going to my room I went left at the top, past the library and the TV room.

The hallway ended with another short hall on my left and a room on my right. The open doorway on my right revealed another laundry room, companion to the one on the main floor. I went to the door on my left and knocked. It opened and a young man in exercise clothes with short hair and a grim face stared at me.

"You're the governess," he said flatly.

"Yes, indeed." I stuck out my hand. "Charlie Rochester. And you are?"

He ignored my hand. "Baxter. What do you want?"

I lowered my hand while I peeked past him. From what I could see, the room held two couches, several armchairs, and a wall covered with bookcases, a television in the middle of them. Three men were seated on the couches, one of them eyeing the door where I stood. In the middle of the room was a large table.

A table covered with guns. Good Lord, I spied enough firepower to handle a gang war.

Baxter moved and my view was cut off. "What do I want?" I babbled. "An outing. That is, I mean, Adele and I will be having an outing this afternoon. Mr. Aire suggested—well, he insisted—or rather, I volunteered— to discuss my plans with you and your fellow security people to determine if it meets with your approval. Of course, I don't need your approval. Adele and I will be going out. But I did want to keep you in the loop, so to speak." I shrugged, using the action to let me lean to the left and hazard a glimpse into the room again.

"She never goes out." Baxter crossed his arms on his impressive chest, obvious in the tight black T-shirt he wore. His thick thighs strained his gray sweatpants. Even his bare feet seemed muscled and taut.

"She will be going out now and henceforth. We will go to the Art Museum this afternoon. After lunch. If the weather cooperates, I believe tomorrow we'll go to the Iowa Arboretum."

His eyes narrowed. "The what?"

Another man joined his fellow at the doorway. This one was older and slender, reminding me of a grandfatherly James Garner with dark eyes and an engaging smile. "Mr. Pool mentioned you were considering a field trip. It might not be such a good idea on such short notice."

"I believe six hours will be sufficient for you to review my plans." I smiled when both men straightened to tower over me, as though it would add weight to their words. I was accustomed to such tactics from the taller set. It didn't bother me in the least. "The Art Museum is located at the corner of Grant and Ninety-Fourth Street. We'll see the St. John Bible exhibit, which I believe is on the first floor. Shall we say two o'clock? It's rather an extensive exhibit so we'll need two hours, I think."

The second man's genial look began to appear strained. "Perhaps tomorrow."

"Today, gentlemen."

"Mr. Pool thought you should wait until we can verify the location."

"I was hired by Mr. Aire. He agreed this outing would be acceptable." Well, he agreed if the guards agreed, but why muddle the waters with a little detail? "I do not take my orders from Mr. Pool." I frowned. "I don't take orders from Mr. Aire, either. That's a figure of speech. Are we agreed, gentlemen?"

The first man, Baxter, glared at me. "No, we aren't."

"Then Adele and I shall leave without you. If you

try to prevent us in any way, I will call the police."

"That isn't necessary, Miss Rochester."

I turned. John Aire stood in the hallway behind me.

"I was explaining to your security detail about Adele and I."

"I heard." Aire looked past me to the two men blocking the doorway. "It might be good for my granddaughter to see more of town. I think Miss Rochester's idea of a field trip is a step in the right direction."

Odd phrasing. I didn't know we were stepping in any direction. Regardless, I was grateful for his support. I was going to say as much when I noticed the expression on the faces of the two guards and John Aire. The three of them shared a secret. It wasn't only one of those male, *I know more than the little lady* kind of looks. This was something else.

The moment passed. The older guard said, "If you think it's a good idea, we'll make sure the area is sufficiently safe for your granddaughter."

"And for Miss Rochester," Aire added softly.

"Of course," the older man said. The two men went back into the room, the door closing behind them.

I walked to Aire, stopping directly in front of him. "Mr. Aire, I think it's important for you to tell me what's going on. You are being overprotective of your granddaughter. I'd like to know why."

"I don't think it's overprotective."

"Nonsense."

"Do you always disagree with whatever a man tells you?"

I drew breath to disagree then realized what he did. I decided to twist the words to suit myself. "I think it's important for me to set an example for Adele. She needs to know that just because she's a girl she doesn't have to always do what the men around her tell her to do. She needs to know she can and should stand up for herself."

"She's a child."

"Children learn from the grown-ups around them." I brushed past him. It wasn't until I got to the hallway leading to the library that it struck me how he deftly avoided answering my question. That prevented me from asking anything about the armory I saw in the guard lounge or whatever it was. Well, I'd get to the truth sooner or later. I wasn't concerned about that. I was good at ferreting out information.

I hurried downstairs and into the sunroom. The day was already warm and muggy with a moist breeze stirring the trees in the distance. I settled into a wicker chair and stared at the pool, trying to calm my overheated brain. I dislike confrontation of any kind, but John Aire seemed to bring out the combatant in me. When my blood pressure was somewhat settled, I called Burns, hoping to catch him at home before he left for his office.

"How's it going?" he asked eagerly.

"I haven't been fired yet, so I suppose it's going fine. The poor kid isn't allowed to take a step anyplace without a bunch of guards around her. And I think the guards are armed. Very armed."

"She is related to a billionaire," he pointed out. "And her other grandparents were in the drug trade."

"I know, I know." His rational explanation was irritating. "But it seems like too much protection to me."

"Do you feel unsafe? Do you want out?"

It was tempting. Granted, I only caught a glimpse of the room. Perhaps I was wrong. After all, I saw three men. If each of them carried at least one firearm and had a backup, and they were on the table, then I suppose it added up to that many guns. "No, I guess not. I met the kid. She seems nice enough. I don't think she's had much discipline. I'll have to play it by ear how to handle her."

"What's the house like? I saw pictures of it in the newspaper. It looks like a real mansion."

"Oh, it's great if you like Ostentatious Extravagance." I crossed my legs, one sandal dangling off my foot. "Aire has a library that's to die for. I'm not sure if it's ever been used or not, but I plan to take advantage of it." I sensed movement on my right, at the far end of the property. Then I heard a garage door opening. The dark sedan backed into the motor court before disappearing around the side of the house. The king was apparently leaving the castle. "I'll check in with you tomorrow if I'm still here."

"I talked to Aire. I bet you'll still be there."

"What?"

"Talk to you later. 'Bye," and he hung up.

"You rat." What did Burns know he wasn't telling? I made a mental note to call him back later in the day and pump him for information. I checked the time on the phone. It was eight, so next I called Richard. He exercised every morning at precisely seven o'clock and always ate breakfast at eight.

"Oh, I'm so glad you called back," he said when he answered. "I was wondering what time you want to meet tonight at the lecture hall."

"That's why I'm calling. I'm on a temporary job assignment and I can't meet tonight. I'm sorry."

"A temporary job assignment? What kind of job prevents you from going out at night?"

I could imagine Richard, his large blue eyes indignant on my behalf. He was tall and slender, with classically handsome features. They were so smooth and unlined I often wondered if he had a portrait aging for him in the attic. His thinning blond hair would be tidily parted on the right and he'd be wearing his exercise "togs" as he called them: long yoga pants and a pristine white T-shirt. "It's a long story," I said. "But I'm on duty around the clock so I won't be able to meet you tonight."

"Are you staying on-site? Charlotte, we've discussed this before. You know I don't think it's prudent to stay in a stranger's house."

I repressed a sigh. This was the third time I took a job "on-site." The others had been to assist elderly ladies while they sorted through possessions prior to moving into assisted-living accommodations. Richard acted as if I might be murdered in my bed at any time by an eighty-something year old woman and her cane. "It's fine, Richard. Nothing to worry about."

"Well, I suppose you know best, but I still think it might not be safe. I admit I'm disappointed. I always enjoy our conversations after these lecture outings. If we can't do that, perhaps we can get together and see the exhibit at the museum before it leaves. I know you wanted to do that sometime."

"I'm doing it today, actually." I caught sight of something in the woods on the bluff. A flare of light snagged my attention, something shiny and bright. "I'm going there this afternoon."

"That's perfect, then. I'll meet you there. What time? Would two o'clock suit? I have a meeting at three-thirty. I think it will give us ample time to view the exhibit."

"No, I can't, Richard, I'll be with someone."

"I'll see you there. Perhaps if we have time we can also take in the exhibit of Japanese landscape art. 'Bye."

"Richard, I can't." Damn. He hung up. Oh, well. I would have to make sure we went to the museum earlier or later in the afternoon. I didn't want to bother with Richard when I was trying to establish a rapport with Adele.

I slipped my phone back in my pocket and went outside, pausing on the brick patio to see if the shiny object was still there. I didn't immediately see anything. Then I caught sight of something moving in the shadows of the shrubs under the trees. The glossy leaves of the rhododendrons were shifting. There wasn't enough breeze to warrant that kind of motion.

I went to the left around the swimming pool, approaching the spot from the bluff. On my left was a hillside with trees below me. I took a step down on the concrete walkway separating the edge of the pool from the edge of the drop-off. A high metal fence on my left kept me securely on the walkway. I hurried past the pool above me, conscious of a steep fall on my side.

When I got past the pool, the walkway diverged. I could descend a set of steps to a large patio where chairs sat. They overlooked the river far below with a view of the distant city. Or I could go back up to the lawn where the trees formed a border. I chose that route and emerged near the motor court, not far from the shrubs where I thought I saw something.

The dense grass muffled any movement I made. I suppose I somewhat blended in with the foliage with my khaki pants and blouse. When I neared the densest part of the landscape, I now saw a man crouching there, his back to me with something large and dark in his hands. A gun? Binoculars? I couldn't tell and I didn't wait to see.

"Hey, what are you doing here?" I called, striding toward him.

He scrambled to his feet, grabbing hold of a low tree limb to help himself upright. I was almost to him when he let the tree limb go and it slammed into my head.

I was knocked off my feet, pain exploding on the left side of my face. I clamped my hand on my eye and wheeled around, stumbling away. Then my feet went out from under me and I was falling head over heels.

Chapter 4

"Are you okay?" a voice asked.

I blinked and opened my eyes. My left eye hurt to open so I clapped my left hand on it. When I did that, I discovered my hand hurt, too. "What's going on?"

"You fell. How many fingers?" Two meaty fingers hovered in the air above my face.

"Two and who are you?"

"Do you feel sick? Nauseated?"

"No, but I'm starting to feel annoyed. Who are you, where am I, and what happened?" I tried to sit up. When I put my left hand on the ground, pain shot into my palm.

"Take it easy." Strong hands clasped me under my armpits and I was lifted to my feet.

I swayed and someone steadied me. The world around me swam into focus. I was on the pavement below the swimming pool, the iron railing behind me. A man in a dark blue polo shirt and jeans stood in front of me. "Who are you?"

"I'm Frank. I'm on duty on the grounds. You fell down the hill."

"How many of you are there?"

"Are you seeing double?"

"No, I meant how many guards are on duty?" I cautiously removed my hand from my eye and blinked. My vision was blurry but okay. "Did you catch him?"

"Catch who?"

"The guy in the woods."

"I didn't see anybody. I saw you, falling down the hillside."

"Because a guy hit me," I said with what I thought was admirable patience. "Did you get him?"

"Hold on." Frank put his finger to his ear. I saw a little gadget there, something Bluetooth. "Governess says she saw an intruder in the woods. Verify."

"My name is Charlie Rochester, not Governess," I snapped. "You can call me Charlie or Miss Rochester." I checked my hands. They were scraped and bloodied. "I saw him in the woods. I went to investigate. He was holding a tree limb and it hit me. I stumbled back and I fell." I scrambled up the incline to return to where I was a moment earlier. "Right there." I pointed.

"If you see anything, get one of us. That's our job." He approached the woods.

"If it's your job, why weren't you out here patrolling?"

"We were and we didn't see anything."

"Well, I did." I decided he had matters in hand so I went across the lawn toward the house. My hands and face hurt like hell. All I wanted was an ice pack and ibuprofen.

He hesitated. "We're checking on it."

"Good. You do that," I said over my shoulder. I headed for the sunroom.

Before I got there a door opened to the left of it, near the garage. The older guard from earlier stepped out. "Miss Rochester? Come in. I'll take care of that cut."

"What cut?"

He tapped his arm and I looked down at mine. Blood dripped off the end of my hand from a puncture in my left forearm, probably from a tree branch. "Damn." I joined him at the doorway. It was the entrance to the game room, next to the kitchen. He gestured to the stairs. I preceded him upwards, emerging into the guard room I saw earlier.

Two men were there, sitting on the couches and talking in low voices. When I came in they stood. "Sit there," the older guard said, going to a First Aid medicine chest on the wall near the stairs.

I sank into the armchair next to a couch, nodding at the men staring at me. "Hey. I'm Charlotte Rochester. How's it going?"

"What happened to you?" one of the men asked.

"A run-in with a guy and a tree."

"Go and help Frank," the older guard said. "He's checking it."

The men left the room by the stairs while the man who escorted me came to stand next to me, a small First Aid kit in his hands. "My name is Mark Temple." He opened the kit, setting it on an end table.

"What's going on, Mark?" I eyed the table in the middle of room where I'd seen the weapons. Now magazines were there. "There's an awful lot of guards here to watch a teenager."

"We don't ask questions. We're paid to keep an eye on her and that's what we do."

"Yeah, right." He approached, a sterile pad in hand. "Are you a medic?"

"Not really. Tilt your head back."

I did as he asked. He fussed around my face and my arm then slid a bandage onto the cut, stepping away to look at me. "You'll have a black eye. Hold on." He went into an adjoining bathroom and emerged with a wet washcloth. "Here. Keep this on your eye."

I pressed the cold cloth against my face. It felt marvelous.

"Why didn't you call for help?" Mark asked, putting the various tubes and packages back into the small case.

"I didn't think I needed it." I stood up, wincing when a bruise I didn't know was there made itself known. I handed him the cold cloth but he waved it away. "Thanks."

"Miss Rochester?"

I paused at the door leading to the outside hall, which led in turn to the interior balcony. "What?"

"Don't hesitate to call us in the future."

I met his speculative gaze with one of my own. "I'll tell you what. I'll start trusting you when you start telling me the truth. Okay?" I didn't wait for his reply but left the room, heading for my bedroom.

When I got there, I examined myself in the bathroom mirror. Good Lord, I looked like death warmed over. A dark bruise was forming along the left side of my face, my left eye was puffed and bruised, and my hands were scuffed like I'd wrestled with sandpaper. "All this before nine in the morning," I muttered. "Who knows what the rest of the day will bring?"

I gingerly washed my face and went to the library, where I sank into one of the overstuffed armchairs and propped my feet up on a hassock. I was only there a few minutes when Mrs. Fairfax burst into the room, a tray in her hands. Her round face was red and she puffed with exertion, a testament to her hurry up the steps.

"Oh, you poor thing. Here now, you have a sip of this." She set the tray on the hassock and put a frosty glass of iced tea on the side table to my right. "And keep this on your eye." A small plastic bag with crushed ice was plucked from the tray and wrapped in what appeared to be a cotton dishtowel. "Ten minutes on and ten minutes off. There's a little fridge in the TV room next door. I've set the icemaker so it gives the smallest size cube. If you need more ice, you get it there. Don't you be going up and down those steps."

"Thank you, Mrs. Fairfax. I appreciate it." I rested the cloth against my face, grateful for the coolness.

"We have people in this house who can handle trouble, Miss Rochester. Make sure you call on them in the future." The little woman smiled brightly at me. "We'd hate to lose you so soon after we got you, wouldn't we?" On that cheerful note, she hustled out of the room.

I rested back in the chair, swallowed by its plump deepness. I checked my phone, thankfully not damaged in my mishap. My vision was blurry and I didn't feel like answering any email or checking any social media. I let it drop to my knee, leaning back into the comfort of the overstuffed chair.

"Does this mean we're not going out today?"

I managed to lift my head to see Adele in the doorway, a tablet in one hand. "Of course we're going out. Why wouldn't we?" I checked my phone, surprised to see it was ten o'clock. Did I doze off? "Why wouldn't we?"

"You're hurt."

"I'm not incapacitated. Come in."

Adele entered the room like a wary animal, unsure if an enemy lurked therein. She sank into a matching chair on my right and put her tablet on the table between us. "I heard you fell down the hillside."

No reason to scare the kid, I decided. "I'm klutzy that way, I guess. At least I didn't break anything." I swiveled my head to regard her. "Did you think about what we discussed earlier? About food sources?"

"I wrote some stuff." She reached for the tablet.

I knew I wasn't up to the task of reviewing anything in a size smaller than a newspaper headline. "Print what you have and I'll check it later. Maybe for now we can talk a bit."

"About what?" She sat back in her chair, her golden eyes wary.

"Tell me about yourself. What do you like to do? Who are you?"

She shrugged, her small breasts in the sports bra barely jiggling with the motion. "You probably know about me."

"I don't hang out on social media sites and I don't read gossip rags. You tell me. Where were you born? Where did you live?"

She hiked up her long legs, crossing them gracefully and sitting in a yogi position. My bruised body ached to see it. "I was born in Jamaica. My father was John's son. My mother was Antoinette Verrens. Her father is Antoine Verrens. He's a drug dealer."

Interesting way to phrase it. Not "my grandfather" but "my mother's father." As though she could distance herself from the family. "I know about him. I lived in Jamaica for a time. Everybody there knows about the Verrens family."

Adele stared beyond me, to the wall of books. "He killed my parents." She said it flatly, with no emotion except her avoidance in meeting my eyes.

"Why did he kill them?" I asked softly.

"My father and mother testified against him in a trial. But it didn't work. He never went to prison. I don't know why he killed them. But I know he did it." Her left hand, resting on the arm of the chair, tightened into the fabric. "I was at school. I came home and our house was on fire. My parents were inside."

Silence stretched between us. I didn't know what I could say to something like that. I finally broke it by saying, "My parents died when I was young, too. I was fourteen. They were in a farming accident. My father was sick before he died. I think he was too weak to handle the equipment and that's why it happened. My mother tried to save him but she died, too."

We were silent again for a time, then Adele tilted her head to one side, her eyes still fixed on the bookcase. "I don't remember Jamaica much. We were moved when I was four. The police put us into a house in Santa Fe. We were supposed to be safe there." She smiled at a private memory. "Mama always said *Everyting cook and curry.*" Her eyes met mine.

"That means everything's fine. My husband was Jamaican."

"Where is he? Doesn't it bother him you're staying here?"

"He died. A long time ago."

"Oh."

I looked at the tablet. It was an Android model, thin and lightweight. Very new and expensive. "What apps do you use?" I picked it up and viewed the icons on the screen. "I use that one. It's kind of fun. And Angry Birds. That's fun."

"They're okay. I like that one." She pointed to an icon with a woman's face on it, someone like a flamenco dancer with black hair and a sultry expression. "It's called Guardians of the Gems."

I tapped it. The screen opened showing what looked like a treasure map with different locales on the map depicted: a pirate ship, a train station, a workshop among others, maybe a dozen or so. "How does it work?"

Adele took the tablet from me and tapped one of the locations. It opened to show a drawing of a pirate ship, surprisingly lifelike and real, at least as real as any imaginary pirate ship could be. "You have to find these hidden things." She pointed to the list at the bottom of the screen. Vase, clock, cutlass. At least a dozen objects were noted.

"You have to find them and tap them." She focused on the pirate ship on her screen, tapping objects so quickly I barely recognized them. When she tapped and cleared an object, more names showed up in the list at the bottom until finally when she tapped, no more names appeared.

Within a minute she finished a list of perhaps twenty items. The screen cleared and small objects appeared on top of the location's icon: a sword, a jewelry box, a piece of ribbon, and a claw of some kind. "That's it?" I asked. "You don't get any prizes?"

"Those are the prizes. You add them to other prizes to get chests of stuff. There're campaigns and adventures and contests. See, I won an Infinity Chest." She tapped a treasure chest icon at the bottom. It opened. "That means I get free energy for four hours. That's big. I've gotten good at it. I know where they hide things."

They being pimply-faced young programmers in China or Russia, I suppose. "Do you have to pay to play?"

"No. Well, you can. You can buy extra tools and stuff to help you find things."

"Do you buy tools? How do you buy them?"

"It's done through the app store. Like with any app. You register your credit card there. If you want to buy something, you tap on the icon. It goes to the app store and charges the card."

Good heavens, she made it sound like such an everyday occurrence. Of course, for children her age, it was. "You don't have a credit card, do you?"

"I have an account." She hurried on when I started to ask for more details. "You get prizes for getting to different levels. Every time you solve a puzzle you get items that go into prize bags. You can combine the prize bags into even bigger bags. There are forums where you can talk to other players and share things. Like if I need a tool and somebody needs a crown, I can trade with them." She focused intently on the screen. "I've met a few neat people there."

"You've met them?"

"Well, you know. Online. I haven't really met them. We have secret names we use." She glanced up. "My name's Princess Ava."

What an apt name. "That sounds like fun." She was so excited, tapping around and showing me what the icons meant. Poor kid, I thought. I'll bet I'm the first person she's talked to in a long time. Or maybe the first person who sat with her for any length of time.

"See, if you win these hammers you can defeat a gargoyle. If you defeat the gargoyle, you win a blow torch. With that you can go to the armory and buy..." She showed me screen after screen of wonders, each more complicated than the last.

I figured I'd try again for a straight answer. "So do you pay to play this game?"

"You can pay if you don't earn enough coins to play." Her tone of voice clearly said *That's all and back off.*

I longed to push her for more information. I knew if I did, she might shut down completely. "Well, you're so good at it, I'm sure you earn enough coins. How do you keep track of it all? How do you know what defeats a gargoyle or how many coins buy what?"

Her suspicious scowl was replaced by a wary smile. "I have a chart."

"Can I see it?"

Adele bit her lip, obviously evaluating me. "I suppose," she finally said grudgingly. "It's in my room. Come on." She unwound her legs and headed for the door.

I followed, stopping to leave the damp dishcloth in my bathroom before traversing the length of the interior balcony to the double doors at the end, open now. I entered a spacious suite with an enormous bed set into a bay with two floor to ceiling windows on either side. A long white vanity table was against the wall on my right. A white desk was on my left with a computer monitor mounted on the wall above it. Next to the desk, covering most of the wall space, were over-sized sheets of graph paper with writing, sketches, arrows and drawings.

I approached the wall where Adele stood, eyeing her handiwork. "Is this it? Your chart?"

"That's the world, there." Adele pointed to a sheet of paper that was a copy of the landing screen for the game. "And that's the different villains you have to defeat and what kind of weapons you need to beat them."

She rattled on, pointing to trunks and chests and armories, complete with small hand-drawn pictures of the objects inside with lines and arrows connecting them all.

"You did this?" It was amazing, with a level of detail that showed she truly cared about the subject matter. It was Important Stuff to her.

Adele drew away and frowned. "I suppose you think it's a waste of time."

"Not at all. Why, did somebody tell you that?" When she didn't answer, I said, "I did something like this once about Middle Earth and the hobbits. I drew a map of their journeys."

"It was a movie, wasn't it?"

I smiled. "First it was a book. Actually, it was several books." I looked around the room. "This is a beautiful room." The wallpaper was a pale satiny blue with flowers scattered on the surface at random intervals, big bursts of peonies and roses giving the room a cheerful, vibrant feeling. The bedspread was in a matching fabric and the armchair in the corner was covered in the satiny blue material. Several paintings on the wall looked like Wyeths. I suspected they weren't copies. I went to the nightstand and checked the stack of books there, making a mental note about the titles.

"Yeah, it's okay. I didn't decorate it." The sulky teenager was back. Our brief moment of sharing was past.

I decided to let her choose our roles, so I acted like the grown-up she expected. "Did you have a chance to research the Bible we'll see today?"

"No. I'm not sure I want to see it." Adele went to the vanity table and lifted her hairbrush, running it through her long hair.

"Is there somewhere you'd rather go?"

"I don't know if I need to go out at all. I need to play Gems today."

"You need to play it? Why?"

"There's a contest going on. It runs until tonight. I'm in third place, so I need to keep playing it today to try to take the lead."

I considered several different replies and settled on, "You need to eat and you need to breathe. You don't need to play a game." I went to the double doors. "We're having an excursion. And I think we'll begin with the Bible exhibition. Maybe when you research it you'll have more interest." I glanced at the clock on her bedside table. "I'll meet you for lunch at noon and we'll talk about it then."

"I don't want any lunch." She was moving toward her tablet while she talked.

I picked it up from the desk. "I'll review your notes about food distribution we discussed earlier. Is there a password?"

"No, but you can't take that. It's mine."

"I'll give it back to you at lunch. You can keep me company while I eat whatever Mrs. Fairfax has taken the time to prepare." I left before she could argue.

Outside her door was another door, leading to the exterior. On impulse, I went outside. Muggy air surrounded me on the balcony, which provided an excellent view of the lawn, the swimming pool and the motor court at the far end of the property.

A door at the other end opened and Mark, the guard, stepped out. "I thought you'd be resting." He joined me in the middle where I leaned on the ornate cast iron railing.

"I'm on duty. Just like you."

He looked beyond me, to the door leading to the inside of the house. "Are you still set on taking a field trip?"

"I am. She's like a prisoner here. She needs to get out."

"That's for her grandfather to say, not you."

"He agreed."

Mark smiled briefly. "From what I heard, you didn't give him much choice. I get the feeling you do it often."

I straightened. "Sometimes that's the best way to get things done." I went back into the house and made a detour to get more ice before going to my room. I changed my now wrinkled and stained slacks and blouse for black jeans and a lightweight sweater set of black and white dots. I made a mental note to ask Mrs. Fairfax about using the laundry facilities.

I got my tablet and downloaded the Guardians of the Gems app. There were no obvious rules. Images of people appeared on the screen from time to time, directing me to do things like search a location for a certain item, or assemble a box of items from things I won by searching. I played for an hour and ran out of 'energy' so I bought more. It was as easy as Adele said.

Next I checked Adele's tablet, noting the usage statistics for the different apps. She spent most of her time on the Gems game and on the Internet, presumably to use the forum she mentioned. As I suspected, she stayed logged in to her apps, so I could access her accounts. I jotted notes about usage information and usernames, then shut the tablet off. I needed to talk to her grandfather about what I suspected was too much gaming on Adele's part.

The kid did appear for lunch, but she ate little of the excellent chef salad Mrs. Fairfax prepared. "Mr. Aire said he'd be home for dinner tonight at six thirty," the cook said when I stood to leave. "He asked you to approve the evening's menu."

I looked at Adele, who appeared as surprised as I was. "What would you suggest?" I asked Mrs. Fairfax.

"I have two nice T-bone steaks. I could get another one and make twice baked potatoes to go with it and perhaps a nice salad. But are you sure you're up to dining tonight? Would you like dinner in your room?"

"Of course not. I'll be fine. It's only a bruise." I touched my face gingerly. It was puffy but it didn't hurt as much. "Don't get an extra steak on my behalf. I'm sure Adele and I can split one. I normally don't eat much meat. That sounds like a nice summer meal."

"Good, I'll plan on that then." Mrs. Fairfax left the dining room, gesturing to the young man who came in. He appeared too muscular to be a bus boy, but I suppose he was because he began gathering the dishes onto a tray.

Adele and I left the room. I spied Mark coming toward us across the living room. "Ready to go?"

"What's the rush? I thought we were leaving at two."

"The last time I checked, we don't have a schedule." I turned to Adele. "I suggest you change into something more appropriate for the viewing of a Bible. A pair of slacks and a nice blouse should be okay. We'll wait for you here." I went into the living room.

Mark followed me, watching Adele while she stomped along the balcony to her suite. "I'm starting to see how you get things done."

"Speaking of getting things done, did you find any sign of the person I saw in the woods?"

He didn't answer immediately. "We're not sure who was there. We did find broken branches and footprints. How did you see them? We have security cameras panning the whole area and they didn't pick up anything."

Security cameras? Good Lord, the place was a fortress. "I saw light glint on something."

"Something?"

"Light on metal. I thought it might be a gun."

He didn't blink an eye. "And you went to investigate? That's brave."

"Some people would say it's stupid."

He smiled briefly. "You're not stupid. Maybe impulsive, but not stupid." He glanced at his watch. "I'll get the car."

I considered trying to contact Richard again, but it would probably be futile. Knowing him, he was en route to the museum, anticipating non-existent traffic snarls and imaginary parking problems. I would have to get rid of him as soon as possible. This was my chance to spend time with Adele outside the home. I wanted to take advantage of every moment.

She joined me ten minutes later, dressed in black yoga pants and a tunic top with bright flowers imprinted on it. The outfit was an improvement and I said as much. "Thank you for changing clothes," I commented while we went to the garage.

"I didn't have much choice," she grumbled.

"Of course you did. And I appreciate that you took my advice." I approached the large black sedan where Mark stood.

He gestured me to the back seat. "You and Miss Verrens ride in the back," he said. The muscular young busboy hurried from the house, pulling on a sports coat over his dark polo shirt.

I ducked into the spacious rear seat, Adele sliding in after me. She immediately pulled out her phone, huddling against the door so I couldn't see what she was doing. I saw Mark watching me in the rearview mirror. I rolled my eyes and rested against my side of the car, taking my phone from my pocket and mimicking her.

I had an email from Burns, asking for an update. I decided to let him sweat a bit. I checked the weather forecast and saw a break in the heat was predicted for tomorrow night. It couldn't come soon enough for me. Heat, humidity, and my curly hair were not good companions.

I ordered a couple of the books I saw on Adele's nightstand, having them delivered to my Kindle app. By then we were pulling up to the museum. Mark drove to the front and we got out, accompanied by the young man who informed me his name was Jason. He followed Adele and I into the main entrance, where we waited for Mark to join us.

It wasn't crowded, although there were small groups of people moving through the hallways. I headed for the exhibition hall, Mark ahead of me. Adele and Jason trailed behind.

"He seems young for this," I said to Mark.

"He's older than he looks." Mark gestured to Jason. The two men split up, pacing around the big exhibition space.

I joined Adele, who stared at one of the framed pages from the handwritten Bible on display on the wall.

"Impressive, isn't it?" I read the information plate next to the display. "It took four weeks to letter this page." I peered closely at the fine script and the intricate illustration. "The page size alone is amazing. Fifteen by twenty-four. Where did they find the vellum to do this? I doubt if there is a readily available supply."

"Vellum?"

"The paper it's printed on. Vellum is animal skins that were cured in a particular way to act as paper."

Adele wrinkled her nose. "Animal skins. Euw."

"That's all people had for a long, long time. Paper is a relatively new invention." I read the information panel for the next page under glass for display. "What an effort."

"Why do it?" Adele asked. "Aren't there enough Bibles in the world?"

I considered how to answer her while we moved to the next case. "You play your game, right?" She nodded warily. "It feels good to get good at it, right?" She nodded again. "It's a process, to get good at something. There aren't shortcuts."

"Yeah. A friend and I were talking about it. He said something like that. He said you can't buy your way through the levels. You have to learn your way."

Friend? He? Buy your way? Red flags sprang up in my mind. *So many questions. Proceed with caution.* "He's right. Does he play the game?"

"Yeah, that's how we met. Well, we didn't meet-meet. We met in the online forum for the game." Adele peered closely at the page in the display case.

Tread carefully. "That's great. It's great to have somebody who knows the game so you can talk about it." I moved to the next case. "Did you ever buy anything in the game? I have a friend who plays online poker. He has to keep himself on a strict budget." I smiled in what I hoped was a grownup-to-grownup way. "It's so easy to buy stuff online, isn't it?"

She scowled. "John makes sure I can't spend much."

Points to your grandfather. "Well, it's more satisfying. I guess it's like your friend said. It's good to learn knowledge, not just buy it." I pointed to the illustration on the page. "Calligraphy is a unique art form. It requires intense concentration and discipline as well as talent. I guess if a person has to focus so deeply on Holy Scripture, it might bring the artist closer to the Word."

"The word?"

"The Word of God. You need to understand the Bible in context. For many people, it is the Word of God, a set of rules by which to live. They take it very seriously. Creating a book like this is an act of devotion."

"I suppose." She moved to the next panel, this one a stunning illustration of Jacob's Ladder. "I don't know if I believe in God."

"I find it hard to not believe in God," I said. "Every time I see a butterfly or a dog or a child, I think something created it, something designed it." I studied the information panel, which detailed the weeks of work that went into the page. "I don't believe in religion, but I think there has to be a God."

"My grandmother believes in the devil. My Jamaican grandmother." She said it overly casually, which told me how serious it was to her.

"If you believe in the devil, I think you have to believe in a god of some kind. The world is balanced. If there's evil, there must be good."

Adele shot me a disbelieving look. "Who said the world is fair and balanced?"

"Touché," I admitted. "Perhaps I am naïve. Or maybe optimistic." I stared at the enormous sheet of paper under the glass. It was full of text from margin to margin with small, perfect handwriting in a unique script. "When I see things like this, it restores my faith in the world. It's heartening to believe someone would take the time to give such attention to this."

"Yeah. I guess it is like learning the game," Adele said grudgingly. "The more I worked at it, the more I understood. It took me days to get past level 70. Jamie said I was moving fast, but it didn't take him that long."

"Jamie?"

"That's his name. My friend in the online forums. He's a junior at Washington High school." She glanced at me. "I asked John if I could go to school."

"What did he say?"

"He just said no. He said I needed to have home schooling. I think it's because—" She stopped, tugging on her purse strap, running it through her fingers.

"Think what?"

"Charlotte!"

I turned. Richard was heading toward me like a ship about to crash against the rocks. In this case, the rocks were Mark and Jason, who moved to intercept him.

"It's okay. I know him." I met Richard in the middle of the room. "I'm busy now, Richard. I'm with someone and we're busy."

"My God, what happened to you?" His voice rose. People began to shoot us covert glances.

"What do you—oh, my eye." I touched my face and winced. I'd forgotten my black eye and bruised face. The minute he mentioned it, I began to get a headache. Or maybe it was Richard. "I fell. It's nothing."

"Nothing?" His handsome face was full of disapproval. "It's terrible. You must see a doctor." He peered around as though a medical professional might be lurking in the corner, waiting to help.

"I'm fine." I kept my voice low and firm. "As I told you on the phone, I'm here with a friend."

"It's not safe to be in a stranger's home. Look at your eye. That's ghastly. You might have been blinded." He put his hands on my shoulders.

I winced. "That hurts, Richard. I fell, remember? I'm bruised." I felt movement on my left, but my vision was blurry so I couldn't tell what it was. When I finally managed to focus, I saw John Aire watching me.

Chapter 5

"What are you doing here?" I blurted.

"I wanted to join you. Do you mind?" He faced Richard when he spoke then he turned to me. "Are you all right? Would you like to see a doctor for your eye?"

"I'm fine. It's only bruising." I touched my face and resisted wincing. "I suppose Mark called you about it."

"Who are you?" Richard demanded. "Who is Mark?"

"He's my employer." I decided I'd better not mention Mark the bodyguard. Richard would go ballistic if he knew there were guards in the house. "Now if you don't mind, Richard, I'm here with a friend."

"You should take better care of your employees." Richard's gaze swept over Aire in his bespoke suit. He frowned, recognizing the quality and probably wondering who this arrogant businessman was. "What sort of job have you employed Charlotte for? What kind of an employer are you?"

"I'm a very good employer." Aire's voice was so frosty I shivered. "I would be happy to make sure Miss Rochester receives any medical attention required."

"I don't require any medical attention." I pulled Richard to one side. "This is none of your business. I did not invite you here. I would appreciate it if you would leave us alone."

Richard ignored my protests. "I have only your best

interests at heart, Charlotte. It appears you're unable to care for yourself."

I gave up. I didn't feel like dealing with Aire or Richard or any more disapproval. I headed for the bathroom. "I'll be back. Give me a minute."

"But we need to discuss this."

"I'm done discussing with you, Richard." I pushed past him and made for the exit sign.

Mark eyed me when I passed him. "What's going on?"

"Bathroom break." I made a beeline for the Ladies Room and ducked inside, thankful to get away from the raging testosterone in the outer room. I went into a stall and sat, trembling from anger and embarrassment. How dare Richard show up and act like that? I never gave him any reason to think he was more than a friend. Here he was, acting like an aggrieved husband.

Someone rattled the door. "Occupied," I called out, flushing the toilet for emphasis.

"Miss Rochester, can you tell me about your relationship with John Aire?" a voice asked outside my stall.

"What?" I emerged to find a tall brunette woman blocking my exit.

"We have photos of you and John Aire together at his house. Obviously, you're good friends." She stared at me, so close I could see the tiny lines around her mouth that her lipstick didn't quite cover. "Do you care to make a comment about your relationship? How does the CEO of Ingram feel about it? Have you talked to Miss White?"

I pushed past her. "I have no idea what you're talking about." I made for the sink but the woman interposed herself between me and the basin.

"Don't you want to make a statement to the press about your involvement with Mr. Aire? After all, he's one of the richest men in the city. How do you feel about the accusations surrounding his late wife? And what about your injury? Did it happen at his house? How did it happen?"

"It's none of your damn business what I do or what John Aire does." I gave up on sanitation and made for the exit.

"So you won't mind if we publish?" She thrust something at me.

I took it automatically. It was a photograph of me in the pool, smiling up at John Aire, who knelt next to the edge, his eyes fixed on me. "You're mistaken," I said, handing it back to her. At the last minute, I changed my mind and snatched it from her. "I have no comment."

"But you and Mr. Aire are obviously—"

I left the bathroom, pushing open the door so hard it slammed into the wall. Mark stood a few feet away. He was at my side in a second. "Problem?"

I looked behind me, expecting to see the pushy bitch. No one was there. "No, it's fine." I handed him the photo. "This explains who was in the shrubbery this morning."

Mark examined it. "Damn. I told them to stay the hell away. Those assholes. They could blow the whole thing." He jammed it into his coat pocket. "Sorry. This kind of shit happens sometimes."

"Really? It doesn't happen to me." I stalked away from him and headed for John Aire. Mark put a hand on my shoulder and pulled me to a halt.

"We'll talk about it later. Don't make a public scene now. It'll add fuel to the fire."

I spied Adele. She appeared worried and embarrassed. Mark was right. No reason to get the kid embroiled in more unpleasantness on our first outing. I took in a deep breath. "Okay. We'll talk about it later." I glared up at him. "We will."

"You're doing it again."

"Doing what?"

"Issuing orders."

I smiled at him and batted my eyelashes. "Does that make it better?"

He laughed. "Yes. Now let me handle it. You get rid of your boyfriend."

"He is *not* my boyfriend." I strode to Richard, who was trying to talk to Adele, pointing to something in the display case. She was doing a good job of ignoring him.

I stopped in front of him, put my hands on my hips, and said, "Richard, I'm busy at the moment. Perhaps we can talk next week. I'll call you." I looped my arm through Adele's. "Let's go see the Beatitudes. I've heard they're marvelous." I looked at John Aire, his icy blue eyes evaluating Richard as if measuring him for a coffin. "Care to join us?"

"Who was that?" Adele asked while I pulled her to the next room.

I glanced at Richard, who was trying to follow us. Jason somehow kept getting in his way. Mark said something to Richard and Richard paled, his eyes opening so wide it was comical. He scurried from the room. "He's someone I occasionally go to lectures with."

"How could you hear anything anyone said?" Aire muttered. He was keeping pace with us on my right, not quite with us but not separated, either. "He's probably too busy making comments for you to hear what anyone else says."

I wanted to snap a reply but honesty forced me to agree with him. "He can be a bit pretentious. And something of a know-it-all. Of course, I'm that way, too, sometimes, so perhaps we're a good fit."

"Trust me, Miss Rochester. You are not a good fit for him." Aire moved ahead of us into the next exhibition room.

Adele and I exchanged a surprised look and hurried after him.

We spent two more hours at the museum, examining the pages on display. I could have spent another day there, but I knew Adele was humoring me after an hour-and-a-half, so I hurried through the rest of the exhibit.

Our exit took us past the gift shop. I caught a glimpse of prints from the exhibit and I was drawn inside. "Aren't those beautiful?" Several different pages were on display, some complete illustrations and some with the text and the marginal illustrations.

"Which is your favorite?" Aire asked Adele. They stood together in front of me, not quite touching. It was the first sign I'd seen of them acting as though they knew each other.

Adele was focused on the illustration of Creation, the seven vibrant panels depicting the seven days of the world. "That one, I think," she said. "It says so much."

"What about you, Miss Rochester?"

There were a dozen different prints on display. I took my time, examining each one. "Proverbs, I think. But the one I really liked isn't here."

"You can order a print from any page in the book," a man behind me said. "They do custom print jobs."

I remembered one of the displays. "I liked the Song

of Solomon one. It was a two-page illustration, I think."
I checked the price on the Creation print. "Wow."
Definitely not in my price range. I went to a stack of
commemorative books. They were oversized and heavy.
I checked the price. Sixty dollars. Well, my budget could
afford that. It sure couldn't afford a thousand-dollar
print. "I think I'll get one of these."

"I think we need two." Aire picked up two of the
large volumes. "One for you and one for Adele."

I reached for my purse. "I can pay for mine."

"My treat," he said with a faint smile. "A souvenir
of such an interesting afternoon."

I was pleased, as much for Adele's delighted smile
as for such a generous gesture. He paid for the books then
left us at the museum entrance, saying he needed to go
back to his office. Adele and I oohed and ahhed over our
books in the back seat of the car on the drive home.

"Could you show me how to play the Gems game
tonight?" I asked Adele when we were in the house. "I
tried it but I'm stuck on a couple of things."

"Sure, when?" She was poised at the foot of the
stairs, her book clasped against her chest.

"How about after supper? Maybe if I study your
chart, it'll make more sense."

"Okay." She dashed up the steps. "I think I'll
research more about this Bible. I want to know how they
make those animal skins they used."

"I think there's Hebrew in here, too." I raised the
book. "Maybe check that, too."

She was gone in a flash, running to her suite. I
followed more slowly to my bedroom. I flopped on the
bed, using my laptop to check on the network usage. I
couldn't sign on, which reminded me that I needed the

new password. With a sigh, I got up and went to the stairs.

Charlie the guard was talking to Mark the guard below me. "...reporters almost blew the whole operation. We had a deal with them," Mark said.

I moved back into the shadows, straining to hear.

"We did have a deal. This was a new reporter. She heard some talk in the newsroom and decided to do some digging on her own. She found a photographer willing to take a chance."

"Is it handled?"

"It better be. I've never seen Aire so pissed off. I thought he'd go to their offices and tear off their heads. It wasn't only about the kid, either. He was mad about the governess. I think he feels responsible for her."

Their voices faded when they moved out of sight. "...our contact and...to keep them..."

I waited a few seconds before going to the kitchen. To my surprise, Mrs. Fairfax was there with the two men talking near the stove. I smiled while I entered the room, pointing to the chalkboard outside the game room door. "Password. I don't want to use my data minutes if I don't have to."

"How is your eye?" Mrs. Fairfax asked. "Can I get you more ice?"

"That would be great. I'm feeling puffy." I jotted the password on a notepad hanging near the chalkboard and took the small plastic bag of crushed ice from the cook. "Are you off duty soon?" I asked Mark.

"In an hour or two." He turned to Mrs. Fairfax. "Thanks for your assistance."

"I'm glad to help." The cook went to the fridge and opened it, leaning into its depths.

"I'll see you later." I sauntered away. I loitered outside the room but when I heard footsteps approaching I hurried upstairs. I wrapped the ice in the towel I used earlier then logged on to the network. There were two users on the home account, me and Adele. I wondered which network the guards used if they used one at all.

I rested back on the bed, the bag of ice wrapped once again in a towel. What an eventful first day. I needed to get more info about the person Adele contacted on the forum. I also needed more information about whatever arrangement Aire made with the media.

Well, that could wait for a few hours. I sighed with relief when the cool ice covered my face. Now I could rest.

At six o'clock I set aside the bag and went to the bathroom to inspect the results of an hour of icing. To my surprise, all that remained was a narrow welt of darkening skin along the left side of my face and an eye turning purple. Not bad at all. I peeled off the bandage on my arm and saw the cut was closed sufficiently, although it was bruised around the area. I put on a fresh bandage I found in the medicine chest before going downstairs.

John Aire was in the living room talking to Grant Pool. Both men turned when I appeared. "Why didn't you tell me about the photographer?" Pool strode toward me. "You should discuss those kinds of things with me, not the guards."

I stepped back. "You weren't there."

Mrs. Fairfax rounded the corner from the kitchen. "Ah, there you are, Mr. Aire. Which wine do you want with the steaks tonight?" She looked at me, her glance flickering disapprovingly to Pool first. "How are you feeling, Miss Rochester? I hope you were able to rest."

"I did, thank you." I sidled past Pool and his malevolent glare.

"We'll have the Rulo Syrah '07. You can open the wine to let it air and put the steaks on the grill any time, Mrs. Fairfax. We're ready to eat." Aire looked at the stairs, where Adele was descending. "Perfect timing."

"I thought we'd work on the contracts for the French park tonight," Pool said.

Aire gestured me ahead of him. "I think I'm done working for the evening, Grant. We'll touch base on those contracts tomorrow. I'm sure you wouldn't mind a night away from the office. Good night." It was a clear dismissal.

I hazarded a sidelong glance at Pool while I followed Aire. Pool's amazed expression changed to one of outrage when I scooted past, joining Adele in the doorway to the dining room. Salads were already at three of the place settings, one at the head of the table and one on either side in the middle.

I went to the seat on the right side of the table and Adele went opposite me. Aire moved to the head of the table but stopped. "Why don't you sit there, Miss Rochester?" he said, waving to the seat. "It might be nice to have a change." He went to the place setting across from Adele. "A change of scene, so to speak."

Adele's eyes darted to me. I saw her panic at the idea of being seated so near to her grandfather. I smiled reassuringly. "Fine. Tell me about your research today, Adele. What did you discover about the Bible we saw?"

"It takes a long time to make paper from animal skins," she said with a small laugh while she sat. "It's a complicated process."

"Why use animal skins? Vellum?" Aire shook out his napkin.

"It lasts longer and it holds ink better." Adele launched into a surprisingly comprehensive explanation of the vellum-making process, with Aire asking her questions along the way. That carried us through the salad course and well into the main meal. I kept out of the discussion, letting Adele and her grandfather carry the conversation.

It was interesting to watch them interact. Here were two people who knew little about each other, thrown together because of circumstance and obligation, not necessarily love. While they talked, I saw dawning appreciation on the part of Aire for this lively and intelligent girl. There was so little common ground between them. Perhaps I was seeing the beginning of a kind of détente.

When we were finishing the meal, Aire turned to me. "Could you please join me in my office after dinner? I'd like to discuss a few matters with you."

Oh, shit. Here comes the riot act because I was talking to Richard. "Adele was going to show me some of the things she's working on. I'll join you when we're done."

"That's okay," Adele said quickly. "We can do it later."

Aire stood. "I'll be in my office." He dropped his napkin next to his plate and left.

"Is he mad?" I asked Adele in a low voice while we trailed after him.

"He's surprised," Mrs. Fairfax said, passing us on the way into the room. "It's not often someone tells him to wait."

When Adele and I got to her room I went to the chart on her wall. "I don't understand how to get from this part to this one," I said, pointing to the map of the game.

"There's a secret door here." She tapped one of the locations. "You have to defeat the troll monster to…" and she was off and running, bringing up the game on her tablet which was paired to the large monitor on the wall. I was shown all manner of shortcuts, tips and tricks.

"How did you learn this?" I asked forty-five minutes later.

"Jamie showed me. He's the kid I told you about. And I like to play. I wish I knew how they did it. You know, how programs are written." She lounged on her bed and tapped her tablet, bringing up a YouTube channel of videos.

Jamie. The guy. "What's he like?"

"He's nice. We talk about all kinds of stuff. He sent me a link to some mashups." She started tapping on the tablet.

"The *Uptown Funk* one?"

"No, *Shut Up and Dance With Me.*" She brought up the video on the screen. "I like this one better."

I sat on the bed next to her, my feet bouncing in time to the music. "This one is good," I said, swaying with the song.

"I see you're studying."

Adele and I turned at the same time. Aire stood in the doorway to her bedroom, watching us. "We're having a moment," I said, turning back to the screen. "A cultural exchange."

"That's culture?" He frowned at the screen.

I took the tablet and paused the video. "It's a mashup."

"A what?"

"A mashup. You take a popular song from today and you find dance scenes from movies that match the rhythm." I played the video and watched him watch it. He inched into the bedroom as though drawn by a line, his gaze fixed on the computer screen. The light in the room was on his left side, leaving more of his face in shadow. I saw his smile when the different movie scenes flickered on and off the screen in time to the music. He wasn't a handsome man, not like Richard was handsome. Aire was more like Kevin Costner or Sam Shepherd, a kind of Everyman Handsome.

"I recognize that," he said, pointing. "That's *West Side Story*. It might be the only movie I do recognize." He smiled at a couple of the dances, shaking his head. "Who does this stuff?"

"Somebody with time on their hands."

"I liked *West Side Story*. It always reminded me of the warehouse district. I spent time there when I was a kid. It was fun to see the trucks coming in and unloading. I always wondered where they came from and where they were going." He tore his eyes away from the screen. "Can we chat now?"

"Sure. I think Adele and I are done for today." I followed Aire to the doorway. "Think about where you'd like to go tomorrow," I said to Adele. "I was thinking the arboretum, but maybe we can save it for a cooler day."

Adele rolled onto her tummy and regarded us, legs kicking in the air. "I'll lie awake thinking about it."

I laughed. "Yeah, right. And only one hour of games tonight."

She frowned. "But the contest is going on."

"One hour." I couldn't enforce it, of course, but I

was curious about her reaction.

"Okay." She sprang off the bed and went to her computer. We were already forgotten.

I joined Aire, who stood outside the door. "You seem to have developed a rapport with her," he said while we walked along the balcony to the stairs.

"She's an intelligent, inquisitive child. It's easy to find subjects to discuss with her. In fact, there are so many, it's hard to focus on one or two." I went carefully down the steps, using my right hand on the railing. My left hand was still too tender to use much.

I followed him through a short entryway into his office, a room about the same size as my bedroom with large windows facing the front and bookcases on two walls. A floor lamp cast a soft light throughout the room.

Aire gestured to one of three leather armchairs grouped around a small table. "Can I get you a glass of brandy? Wine?"

"A glass of wine would be nice." The walls held several large photographic prints of ocean and island scenes. The colors were vibrant and evocative. I could almost smell the vegetation on the shore and feel the breeze on my face.

Aire went to a wet bar in the corner of the room. He poured two glasses of wine then handed me a beautiful cut crystal glass with pale amber liquid in it. "How is your eye feeling? Are you recovering?"

"I'm fine. I won't be lying on my left side tonight when I sleep."

"Good." He sat in the chair next to me, separated by a small end table between us. "I wanted to apologize for the morning incident near the pool and the one at the museum. As I warned you, I'm often an object of media attention."

"I'm afraid I didn't handle that reporter very well. Plus I'd also like to apologize for Richard and his interruption. He can be overbearing at times."

Aire waved my apology away. "It's inconsequential. But I am surprised you're affiliated with a man who would want to control you."

I grinned. "We aren't affiliated. I usually ignore him and he eventually shuts up."

"Good policy." He sipped his wine. "Call me John."

"What?"

"John. My name. I see no need for formality."

I shook my head. "Sorry, but no. You're my employer."

He regarded me with a faint smile. "I think we're mature enough to not worry about any implications of an improper employer-employee relationship."

"I don't know whether to be offended or relieved." I sipped the wine. It was like velvet on my palate, faintly chilled with a bit of a flowery taste. I extended my right hand. "Hi, John. My name's Charlie."

"If you don't mind, I prefer Charlotte. It's such a pretty name." He took my hand and squeezed it gently. "Hello, Charlotte." His eyes met mine and he smiled, then released my hand and raised his wine glass.

I took another sip, giving me a chance to gather my scattered wits. "As I said, I was so surprised when I saw the photograph I didn't know what to do. The woman also asked me about someone named Ingram."

John's eyes widened. "Cat White? She's with Ingram Industries."

"Yes, I think that's the name." I sipped the wine. "The reporter asked me how the woman felt about my relationship with you. I had no idea what she was talking about. I suspect I sounded like an idiot when I answered."

"What did you say?"

"I said it was none of her damn business what you did." I blushed when he looked at me, one eyebrow raised. "Well, it isn't anybody's business."

One corner of his mouth quirked upward. "That's not what the media thinks."

"Jerks," I muttered.

"Succinct and true."

We were silent for a moment then I decided to broach a tricky subject. "Adele said she has a credit account she can use to buy apps and games and such things."

"Yes, she does. I have it tied to a credit card with a one-hundred-dollar a week maximum."

I choked on my swallow of wine. "One hundred dollars a week?"

"Isn't that adequate? Does she need more?"

"Good heavens, no. Most children her age don't have such a generous spending account."

He twirled the wine in his glass, the light catching on the liquid. "You think I'm spoiling her? Is she acting like an over-privileged brat?"

"No, not really. In fact, considering what she's gone through she's very, well, normal. Or as normal as a teenager can be."

"Then there isn't a problem, is there, Charlotte?"

I thought about Adele's talk of her online friend. Something told me her grandfather might not see it as an innocent friendship. I knew the Internet could be a treacherous place for a trusting girl, but I didn't think it was dangerous. I hesitated to alert him.

John tilted his head to regard me, his blue eyes intent. "I realize Adele has had an unusual life but I think she's a sensible girl. I trust with your guidance, she'll be fine." He was silent for a moment. "You lived in Jamaica. You know the obeah traditions."

"Like I said before. Obeah is a general term for a wide variety of religious practices. I'm familiar with some facets of it, but no one can really know it unless they know the particular sect involved. The practitioners have a great deal of influence on much of the island's population. It's like…" I considered an analogy. "It's like old school priests. Their word is law to some people."

John stared at the enlarged photo on the wall, at the white sand beach and clear, cobalt blue water. "Adele's grandmother, her mother's mother, is obeah."

"I didn't know that. Does Adele know?"

"She knows little about her Jamaican family. Adele's mother repudiated her island roots. Antoinette was horrified by her parents and their lifestyle."

"But Adele is safe now. Her grandparents are in hiding and it's over. She's safe."

He nodded.

"So why is she so heavily guarded?"

He stared at the picture. He reminded me of Adele, trying to decide if he could trust me or not. In the end, he didn't. "Just a precaution."

I stood, putting my glass on the table. "Good. I'm glad to know there's nothing to worry about. If you'll excuse me, I'm tired. I think I'll go to bed. Good night."

"Thank you for being here," he said when I reached the doorway.

"I enjoy the challenge."

"Are you talking about Adele or something else?" He leaned forward in his chair, his wine glass tilted in his hand.

I couldn't think of any polite answer so I left, darting up the stairs to my room. I poured myself a glass of my cheap wine and sat on the bench at the window, trembling while I drank it. I had no illusions about my attractiveness to a man like John Aire. He had been married to one of the most beautiful women in the world. No, he was a man who was accustomed to getting his own way and that included intimidating me in any way he could.

I shoved those speculations to one side. I would have to meet any challenge he threw at me head-on and deal with it as it came. I was here to do a job and nothing more.

****

Tuesday was a repeat of Monday without the excitement. I did my Tai Chi and swam. This time John Aire openly watched from the patio outside his suite, sipping his coffee. Adele did the same from her suite's balcony. I successfully ignored them both and enjoyed my exercise despite their attention.

John joined Adele and me for breakfast, where we decided it was too hot for an outdoor excursion in the afternoon. Adele and I settled on a visit to a library. Well, I decided on a visit to the city's main library. "It will be a good experience for you to do research there," I said while we were finishing breakfast.

"I can do my research online," Adele said half-heartedly, shooting glances at her grandfather while she spoke.

"You may be surprised what you can find in the stacks at a library." I smiled at John, who watched us with his usual inscrutable expression. "I'll check with the guards on duty, of course, and make sure it's okay with them."

"Of course." I saw a flicker of amusement in his eyes. "Speaking of outings, that reminds me. I have a dinner engagement on Thursday. I'd like Adele and you to join me."

"What kind of engagement?" I asked.

"It's a dinner party given by the CEO of a company with whom I do business. I'm considering adding areas to our theme parks for younger people. The company may invest in the project. I want to get Adele's opinion. There will be several other young people there as well, students in the Advanced Business program from one of the local high schools."

Just ask her for her opinion, I thought, but didn't say. "I suppose that's okay."

"Nothing formal. Black tie." John stood and picked up his newspaper. "There will be about fifty people there. Now if you'll excuse me, I'll be in my office."

"What does 'nothing formal' and 'black tie' mean?" I asked Mrs. Fairfax when she and Jason came in to clear the dishes.

"Black dress, not an evening gown." She scooped up the jam pot and toast plate.

"Thank God. All my gowns are at the cleaner's." Jason smirked and left, balancing an over-loaded try in his arms. "I may need to go shopping," I told Adele when we went into the hall outside the dining room.

"Ooh, let's do that instead of the library. I love shopping. It's my thing."

"Your superpower?" I asked with a laugh.

"What do you mean?"

"Everybody has a superpower. You know, a thing they're good at. Some guys can belch the "Star-Spangled Banner." Some women can walk in three-inch heels."

Adele tilted her head to one side, her long hair in its braid sliding on her T-shirt. "What's yours?"

I frowned. "Gee. I don't know."

"I do." John peeked from the doorway of his office. "You're confident."

I laughed. "Sometimes misplaced."

"I don't know about that."

"Often wrong but never in doubt. I think Max Perkins said that. He was a big-shot editor who worked with Scott Fitzgerald."

"Actually, Ivy Baker Priest said that. She was an early pioneer of women's rights." John smiled at me.

"Are you sure? I was sure it was Max Perkins."

"Look it up." He disappeared into the office.

"I'll do that." I followed Adele up the steps to the second floor. A woman was coming out of my room, her arms full of bed linens. "We have maid service?" I asked Adele.

"Twice a week. They come with the guards." Adele said it so factually I knew she didn't even find it odd. To her, having maids come with bodyguards was a normal part of life.

I smiled at the woman and ducked into my room, picking up my tablet and cell phone before rejoining Adele in the hall. "Let's review your schoolwork," I suggested. "I want to see this website you're using for homework."

"Can't we play Gems?" Adele pouted.

"First schoolwork, then games." I followed her to her room, glancing back once to see the maid going in the opposite direction, toward the guard room and the laundry. Several items in my room were in different locations than they were when I went to breakfast. I wondered if she found anything of interest.

Adele and I spent the morning reviewing her schoolwork, which was indeed on a website. It was a private "academy" and the curriculum she showed me seemed legit. She was studying history, French, algebra, and sociology. "Who set up your schooling for you?" I asked.

"John did, I guess. It was waiting for me when I got here. I went to a private school in Santa Fe when we lived there. It had high security. My grades and everything transferred over."

That explained why she was so at home with guards around the place. I wanted to ask John about how he found the school, but he wasn't at lunch. Mrs. Fairfax informed us he left on business. We should go without him on our outing. I approved her suggestion of roasted chicken for dinner, thankful I didn't have to come up with a menu on my own. My culinary skills were meager at best.

At one o'clock, Frank the dour guard escorted us to the car where Charlie the black guard was waiting to drive us. Like before, Adele settled in with her cell phone and I did the same, catching up on a couple of the books I downloaded.

The library was old-fashioned on the outside, an original four-story limestone Carnegie Library with massive stone steps leading to the glass-door entrance. It was in a grassy square in the middle of downtown. The library was smack in the center, like a big block of books.

To my delight, they kept one of the old card catalog cases. I showed Adele how to find information the old-fashioned way. She regarded me with wide-eyed amazement. "That's, like, a lot of work," she said when we moved to the computers.

"It was time consuming," I admitted. "I spent many hours in the library."

We found our subjects for the day—pirates and organic farming—and headed for the stairs, Charlie and Frank trailing behind us. When we got to the second floor I paused to help an elderly black lady coping with a large pile of books escaping from her arms. Adele went ahead of me into the stacks. Charlie followed her and Frank stayed with me, watching and not helping while I got the old woman's books organized and in a bag for her.

A few seconds later, Charlie came back. "Where is she?" He looked around. "Adele. Where is she?"

I shrugged. "I haven't seen her."

"She's gone."

Chapter 6

"She can't be far away," I said. "Maybe she went to the bathroom. Or maybe she went to a different part of the library."

"I was behind her." Charlie turned in a circle. "She vanished."

"Okay, then, let's split up and find her." I knew the library well, having spent many afternoons there studying when I was in school. "I'll take the middle section, you go right, Charlie, and you go left," I said to Frank. "The front part is mainly magazines so she's probably not there, but I'll look just in case." I checked the time on my phone. "Meet back here in ten minutes."

Charlie hurried to the west side of the building. Frank stomped away, muttering under his breath. I'm sure he would give Mark or whoever was in charge a full report when we got home.

I made a beeline for the rows of books stretching into the distance. Most of the light came from the overhead lamps. The long windows ahead of me at the end of the stacks also provided a faint glow. When I was taking classes at the nearby college my apartment building was noisy and low-rent, so I spent my study time here. I used to sit at the desks against the outside wall where natural light came in. I moved among the books, checking through gaps in the shelves to see if I could spot Adele in the middle of a row.

I got to the back of the library. Sunlight streamed in, making the musty air warm despite the air conditioning humming overhead. I decided to head to the far end of the stacks and zigzag my way through. I was on the third zag when I spied Adele at the back of the library, talking to a young black man. The guy had curly dark hair, the shadow of a beard, and a slender but muscular shape. He and she were in deep conversation, Adele listening intently to what he said.

I hurried toward them. He must have caught sight of me because he said something to Adele and wheeled around. He moved away from her so fast I barely caught a glimpse of his black T-shirt and blue jeans.

"Who was that?" I asked when I reached her.

"Somebody who wanted directions to the Capitol building for sightseeing. I told him he needed to talk to the librarian. I hardly ever leave the house. I haven't been to the statehouse. Maybe we could go there sometime." She took six books from the table nearby, a couple of them large and bulky. "I found good ones about real pirates and a couple about farming."

"Great. Come on." I steered her back to the main staircase. "Let's check in with Frank and Charlie and have them call off the search."

"Search? Geez, can't I walk around a library without a babysitter?" She stomped ahead of me, barely glancing at Charlie while he hurried after her.

"Where was she?" Frank asked, joining me at the top of the steps.

"In the back. Talking to a kid."

"What kid?"

"I don't know who he was. Some guy who wanted directions."

Frank pulled me to a stop. "Where is he? Do you see him?" He stared down into the main lobby.

I spied Adele, Charlie hurrying after her. She was heading for the checkout kiosks. "I don't see him. He's probably gone. He was going sightseeing or something."

"I don't like it," Frank muttered. "What are the odds we come here and a guy stops and talks to her?"

I went down the steps. "She's an attractive, outgoing kid. Why wouldn't somebody ask her for directions?"

"Yeah, right." He hurried away, catching up to Charlie at the front door.

Both men were over-reacting. So Adele talked to a stranger. So what? She wouldn't get cooties or anything. I filed away their strange behavior into a little spot in my brain where I was noting such oddities.

Adele kept her attention on her books on the drive home, sharing them with me to show me a few of the gorier pictures in the pirate books. When we got to the house I noticed black clouds piling up on the western horizon. Any thought I entertained of going for a run vanished. "I think I'll work out," I told her when we entered the house. "Do a few weights. Want to join me?"

"No, I'm going to read." She went up the steps. I followed and at the top, she paused. "Can I ask you something?" she said in a low voice.

"Sure." I waited expectantly.

"No, like, in private."

"Oh. Yeah, come on." I went to my room and ushered her inside. "What's up?"

Adele closed the door, her eyes flickering to my suitcase, my laptop, the dresser. To anywhere but me. "I had a question about periods. I wondered, well, you're a woman and I can't ask anybody else."

"Sure." I tried to sound casual and matter-of-fact. I was wrapping up my life in menstruation, in the beginning phases of menopause, but I still had the occasional bouts. "What do you want to know?"

"I just started having periods. I know about, you know, about sex and stuff. They taught that in school. So I know about, you know, how pregnancy happens and all that, with the penis and, you know." Her face was darkening as she struggled with her embarrassment. "But is it normal to have such bad cramps? And sometimes I seem to bleed so bad. It's kind of scary."

I put my hand on her shoulder and gave her a companionable squeeze. "Perfectly normal. Cramps are because your uterus is contracting and expelling the lining. I drink warm ginger tea. That helps me. Chamomile tea is good, too. And drink water."

"Really? Tea?"

"Yeah. You can take ibuprofen, too. That helps and so does heating pads. That's one reason I exercise. It helps me. And most women have a day or two where it's heavy. I've used a tampon plus a pad sometimes when it's bad."

"Oh, good." Her relief was so obvious she sagged.

"The time to worry is if you see big clots in the blood," I said as factually as I could. "That could be a sign of something wrong. And if you're using tampons, make sure to change them often, like every two or three hours. Never leave them in longer. Don't leave them in overnight."

"Yeah, I read it on the box. Some women got blood poisoning or something."

"Well, it's gospel truth so you follow directions." I smiled at her. "Any other questions?"

"Yeah, but I'll wait, I guess." She clutched the books tighter. "I have lots of questions. Maybe later. I mean, no offense, but I don't know you well, so maybe later."

I could only imagine. Poor kid, stuck here in a house with only men. "Any time. Now you go study and I'll go work out. I'm getting fat, sitting around the house."

Adele laughed, her spirits obviously lifted by our talk. "You're not fat. I heard John call you a sparrow. He said you looked as small and tough as a sparrow." She left the room, pulling out her cell phone and staring at the screen before she'd gone three steps.

A sparrow? Why not a wren? I suppose sparrow made more sense. I wasn't one of those petite little birds, but more the kind who could muscle my way at the feeder. I sighed. He was right. I changed into gym shorts and a T-shirt, grabbing my swimsuit from the bathroom. I headed back downstairs, making for the game room. When I did, I saw John Aire walking across the lawn, coming from the direction of the woods.

I ducked into the game room and inspected the equipment, especially the machine in the corner that reminded me of the all-in-one fitness apparatuses at my gym. I used it for leg curls, pull-ups, and sit-ups. Next I hopped on the elliptical machine for fifteen minutes. By that time I was sweat-soaked and ready for a swim. I went into the attached bathroom to change clothes.

While I was there, someone came into the game room. I heard male voices. I hurriedly dragged on my suit and pulled my T-shirt over my head, folding the rest of my clothes into a tight bundle. I stepped from the room. Charlie and John were at the weight rack, each man dressed in workout shorts and T-shirts. "I got the equipment warmed up for you," I said, taking a towel from the cubbyholes near the door.

They were so surprised to see me I thought they might drop a dumbbell. "When did you come in?" Charlie asked.

"I've been in here. Why? Were you talking about me? Is that why my ears were ringing?" I said it teasingly, but they both got chagrined looks, which told me I was probably right.

"What happened at the library today?" John began alternating bicep curls with two barbells, his tanned arms flexing with the effort.

"Nothing happened. Your guys are way too paranoid."

"Adele was missing," John snapped, his neck taut with strain. Compared to Charlie, he seemed slight. Yet his thighs and arms were solidly muscled and he didn't appear to have any businessman's flab around his middle.

"Adele was out of sight," I corrected. "It wasn't like she was a mile or two away."

"I don't think you understand. Adele's safety is important to me."

I stalked across the room and stood a foot away from him, glaring up into his face. "Mr. Aire, I don't think you understand that her safety is important to me, too. I will not do anything to put her in harm's way. If you don't think my opinion has merit, you can fire me."

He stared at me, the weights hanging at his sides. "Are you threatening me?"

"Not at all. I'm simply giving you a chance to get rid of me." I stared into his blue eyes, daring him to do it.

He smiled. "John, remember? You were going to call me John."

I took a step back. "I'm going for a swim. John." I tugged on the towel around my neck. Better that than strangle him. The man had a habit of irritating me then defusing my irritation with his rare smiles. It was disorienting.

I got in four lazy laps but soon the sky turned ominous, with fat clouds forming on the horizon. I finished just as Charlie called out of the game room door. "Do you want to move your car inside? The weather forecast said there might be hail."

I pulled on my T-shirt, scooped up my clothes, and jogged to him. "Is there room for it somewhere?"

"Sure. I'll pull the Jag forward. Your car can fit behind it." He grinned. "You have the abbreviated version of car. I'll meet you there."

"Hey, don't knock it 'til you try it." I ran around the outside of the house to the open garage door. By the time I got there, Charlie was getting into the car at the far end of the garage.

I went inside to get my keys from the rack. "Pull it into the far bay." John emerged from the house when I reached for my keys. He was still in his gym clothes. He looked about as wet as me, although his was from sweat.

"Thanks." I dropped my clothes on the steps and went back outside where dark clouds were boiling up on the horizon. The air smelled metallic, tangy and thick. It was cool now, no longer muggy. Big changes were in the offing.

I went to my car. That's when I realized John was keeping pace with me. "What are you doing?"

"Showing you where to park." He reached for the

passenger handle. "That is, if I fit in your car."

"You'd be surprised." I hopped in and turned the key in the ignition. My stereo blared to life. "Oops." I touched the volume button, tuning Pink Floyd to background music.

John slipped into the car. "I'm surprised. This isn't too bad. I actually have headroom and legroom."

"Told you so." I moved my car forward. "Are you sure there's enough space in the garage?"

"It'll be tight but it's okay."

I peered into the garage, brightly lit by overhead lights. Charlie stood at the rear of a dark burgundy Jaguar sedan, watching while my small green car inched into the space. He waved me forward and I let the car idle ahead.

"That's good," he called out.

I shut off the engine when he came to my door, bending over to check the interior. "This is one of the smallest cars I've ever seen."

"It's small but mighty. Thanks for giving me shelter from the storm." I got out, squeezing past Charlie to see how close I was to the pricy sedan. "Holy crap." Three inches separated my front bumper from the Jag's rear bumper. I went to John, who stood in the open garage door. "That's pretty trusting. Letting me park so close to an expensive car like that."

He shrugged. "It's a car. Looks like we're in for a storm."

"Well, at least I won't have to go home and water my garden." I drew in a deep breath of rain-soaked air.

"You have an unusual garden," John said, his voice carefully neutral.

"It's a monarch sanctuary," I said proudly. "A butterfly haven. It was designated a sanctuary by the

Monarch Society."

"Really? So it's a design? I mean, it appeared rather random."

"Well, it began with a design and sort of evolved from there. Now I'm enhancing what Mother Nature would do."

"Why?"

"Why what?"

"Why do it? Why fight for your yard the way you did? Why fight for monarch butterflies? Why rescue cats who have short life expectancies?" He stared at the rain. "Why take this job?"

"Because I can. Because somebody has to."

"But why you?"

"Because I can."

"Perhaps your childhood has something to do with that."

I froze. "What do you know about growing up poor?"

"True. My parents weren't farmers who struggled to make a living. They didn't die when I was young and leave me an orphan. I didn't have to work three jobs to get through school."

"Your research was thorough."

"I wanted to know who would be spending time in my home," he said quietly. "You worked hard to get where you are today."

"I did what I needed to do. I didn't need help."

"Didn't need it? Or didn't want to ask for it?" He nodded to Charlie, who stood near the entrance to the house. Charlie closed the outer door. I followed John through the garage to the house, pausing to pick up my clothes while I went. John went into his office and I continued upstairs, my thoughts in a whirl.

How much research did he do about me? It appeared he'd been thorough, but I didn't buy his glib response about getting know who would spend time in his home. Both he and the guards were far more protective of Adele than I expected. Charlie was panicked when she went out of sight for a few minutes. What were they anticipating? What didn't I know about this situation?

I called Burns but got no answer. I sent him a quick email, letting him know things were fine and asking— okay, demanding— he spill the beans about anything he knew.

I showered and dressed in jeans and a loose blue elbow-sleeved top. I took a chance and opened a bedroom window, drinking in the smell of rain-soaked lawn. My room was at the front of the house and the long driveway leading to it. The storm darkened the sky so much the driveway lights came on, triggered by the lack of sunlight. The drive was like a long tunnel with small flares of gold punctuating its darkness. While I watched, the lights flickered on and off because of moving tree limbs. It reminded me of fireflies and their pulsing beacons.

Grant Pool joined us at night for dinner, sitting next to me at the table with Adele across from us and John in his usual spot at the head. Both men wore jeans and shirts, John in black jeans and a dark gray shirt with darker gray lines in it. The colors highlighted the gray in his hair and beard. Pool wore blue jeans and a navy shirt. Both items of clothing appeared ill-fitting. Or maybe he wasn't comfortable in more casual clothing.

Perhaps it was my imagination, but conversation seemed more stilted, with Adele barely volunteering anything even after being prompted by her grandfather. She kept shooting glances at Pool and she was noticeably distracted.

She left the table immediately after eating and Pool left shortly thereafter. That bothered me for some reason. I fidgeted for a minute before saying, "Excuse me. I need to check something in my room." I stood and started to leave the room.

"Is there a problem?" John asked.

"It might be the weather. I have a headache."

"If you'd like to skip our talk after dinner, that's fine," he said immediately.

"I didn't know we were having a talk."

"I'm sorry I wasn't clear. I need to talk to you every night about Adele and her schooling and her progress." He twisted his glass of wine, the red wine coating the side of the delicate cut-crystal stemware.

"Oh. Sure. Let me check in with Adele and I'll join you." I hurried out of the dining room before he could reply. I headed for the staircase but stopped when I spied Adele and Grant Pool on the upper balcony, halfway to her room. They were partially hidden in the shadows. Adele was shorter than him and her head was bowed. She kept her head down while he spoke to her, his eyes fixed on her bended head.

I am a firm believer in gut instinct. The way he looked at her raised all kinds of red flags in my brain. I hurried up the steps. They must have glimpsed me because by the time I reached the top, she was on the way to her room and Pool was walking toward me.

"What's going on?" I asked in a low voice as soon as he was near.

"What do you mean?" He tried to get past me but I

moved to block him.

"What were you and Adele talking about?"

"That's none of your concern." He pushed past me, but instead of going away, he paused to grab my left arm, pulling me toward him. "*Puss no business in dawg fight*," he whispered.

Cat has no business in a dog fight. My mind automatically translated the old Jamaican proverb. "Adele is my business."

"She's allowed to have privacy. You can't boss her around every minute of the day." His grip tightened painfully on my arm.

I put my hand on his, twisting one of his fingers. It was a tactic I'd learned in self-defense class and one that always surprised opponents. He released me immediately but I didn't release him. I transferred my grip to his wrist and kicked at the back of his knee nearest me. It threw him off-balance and let me twist his arm behind his back while I pushed him into the balcony railing. "Don't pick on people," I whispered. "*Not everyting with sugar be sweet.* You might be surprised who fights back."

"Is there a problem, Charlie?"

Mark strode toward us from the hallway leading to the guards' break room. I stepped away from Pool, who turned, his hands gripping the railing behind him. "Not at all," I said. "Just a slight disagreement. Excuse me. I need to chat with Mr. Aire now." I headed for the steps but not before I saw Pool's startled and frightened expression. I smiled at him. "He likes me to give him a full report about Adele every day."

I went downstairs but only made it halfway before Mark caught up to me. "What was that about?" he asked, keeping pace with me on the broad staircase.

"What do you know about Pool?" I asked in a low voice.

"What about him?"

"He gives me the creeps."

"So you beat him up?"

"I didn't beat him up. He tripped and I helped him."

Mark stopped at the bottom of the steps. "What's going on? What's got you worked up?"

I pushed past him. "You haven't seen me worked up. Yet." I hurried ahead and ducked into John's office.

A lamp cast a circle of light on John's hands where they rested on his keyboard. A low-wattage lamp in a corner provided the only other light, with most of the room in darkness from the storm outside. John's shirt sleeves were rolled up, exposing his tanned forearms. "I thought you might be spending time with Adele after dinner. More cultural exchanges." He smiled briefly.

"Maybe later. I'm sure there are more mashups I haven't seen." I went to the window. The rain was loud on the shrubs outside the window and on the brick driveway in front. "I love rainstorms. Unless they're downpours. Our house used to get water in the basement during heavy rain. I hated that. We always had to mop up."

"It's odd how certain memories are so strong."

I looked over my shoulder. He was staring at the photographs on the far wall. "Did you spend much time on the island?" I asked.

John was silent and I wondered if he heard me. Then he stood and shook his head. "Long enough to remember the harbor. Sometimes I think I can hear the gulls and smell an odor. It's hard to describe." He joined me at the window.

"Rot and oil and ocean?"

"Exactly. I think it was the same in every harbor on the island." He went to the bar in the corner. "I'd like you to try this port wine I have. I think it's special."

"Then it will be wasted on me." I went to the seats we used the night before and sat.

"I would appreciate the opinion of someone who doesn't know the quality of the product." He handed me a small glass full of ruby red liquid. "Sip it. Let it sit on your tongue."

I waited until he seated himself then I did as he said, allowing a tiny sip of the liquid to enter my mouth. It was a complex flavor, at first dry but thick, with a faint taste of flowers or honey at the end. I frowned, not sure what words I wanted. "I think it's more effort to enjoy than I'm accustomed to."

"Things we truly enjoy do take time to savor, don't they?" He sipped the wine, his eyes fixed on me. "It is delicate," he agreed.

"It's nice, but I'm more of a slurper, not a sipper."

John grinned, the first expression of pure enjoyment I'd seen him display. "That's an interesting way to categorize yourself."

"It sort of hits the nail on the head."

We drank in companionable silence, the only sound the rain outside and the thunder, which was getting progressively louder. It was accompanied by lightning, which cast the shadows of the room into startling relief.

"Can you tell me about Grant Pool?" I asked casually. "How long have you known him?"

"He's been my assistant for five years. Why do you ask?"

I sipped more port, deciding how to proceed. I didn't like Pool, but I didn't have any concrete evidence of wrongdoing on his part. I decided to be somewhat honest. "I don't particularly like him and I think he dislikes me."

"You barely know him and vice versa." John's black denims blended in with the darkness of the room. His shoes were dark, too. It was hard to tell where the floor began and he ended.

"Sometimes people don't hit it off. Is he from Jamaica?"

"I believe he has family there, but he was raised on the mainland. Why do you ask?"

He knows patois. The words were on the tip of my tongue but I didn't say it. So what if he picked up a few of the more interesting Jamaican insults? That didn't mean anything. "Perhaps he's accustomed to assuming a parental or guiding role with Adele. He might resent me."

"I doubt it. Grant isn't particularly interested in her. I think he's like me. I don't know anything about children. My own son was like a stranger to me. Bertti didn't really want children and she insisted he be sent off to boarding school." John looked at his drink. "I shouldn't blame it on her. I could have said no, but I didn't."

"There's not much to know about kids. They're people with a different focus than you or me. I discovered that when I taught college."

"What focus did your students have?"

"Partying and trying to pass my class." I grinned. "Adele's focus is figuring out who she is. She's at a cusp age."

"A what?"

"I think there are pivotal points in life, age points where we need to make significant choices. The early teen years are the first cusp. There are choices we make that can alter our lives significantly. Then there's graduation from high school and college. The late twenties are a crucial time for a woman."

"Why then?"

"Her biological clock is ticking. A woman needs to decide whether to have a child or wait. If she waits, it might not happen."

"You didn't have children."

I remembered the miscarriage I endured, weeks after Nick died. "No, I didn't." I sipped my wine, my hand trembling. "We were planning to start a family, but he died."

"Family is so important. I didn't realize it until I got older. I deeply regret my disagreement with Edward," John said. "I thought there was plenty of time to make it up with him." He sipped his port. "We didn't."

"Why were you estranged?"

"I disagreed on his choice of a wife."

I winced. "That's a deal breaker."

John's mouth quirked up. "You could say that. We had a bitter argument about it. I was afraid he was making the same mistake I made when I married an island woman. Edward never talked to me after they were married. In fact, he took Antoinette's name as his own, rather than she changing her name, which explains why Adele has a different surname than mine."

"That's unusual."

"Edward was an unusual young man. Very strong-willed and with a strong moral sense. I didn't know I had a grandchild until Bertti told me."

"I didn't think you and your wife stayed in touch."

He went to the sideboard. "She called me now and again. We were amiably separated."

Something didn't make sense. Well, a lot of things didn't make sense, but the chief one was this. "Why did the police investigate you when you had her declared dead? I'm not questioning that you and she were amiably separated. What I'm asking is what prompted the police to investigate you?"

He came back to sit. "You're good at putting puzzles together. What do you think?"

"The police don't initiate an investigation unless they have a good reason to do so. That means they thought there was a case. Which means someone tipped them off about something suspicious or they had evidence." Thunder crashed overhead and I instinctively ducked. Luckily my glass was empty, otherwise I would have spilled red wine on myself.

"That was close." John glanced at the windows. Lightning lit the room and his face was highlighted by it. Thunder crashed again and this time the lightning came immediately. The lights flickered.

He came back to his seat while thunder shook the house again. I stood. "I think I'd better unplug my computer." I finished the last few drops of my wine and put the glass on the end table between my chair and John's.

"Thank you," he said.

"For what?"

He put a hand on my arm. "I'm glad you're here."

My casual, *Happy to help*, died on my lips. The expression in his eyes was far different than his usual distant look. It was still there but something more personal was there, too.

"I like Adele. It would be nice to see her have a normal childhood or at least as normal as it can be with someone as rich as you."

"My wealth doesn't have to be an impediment." He removed his hand, his fingers sliding along my bare arm. "Once I'm sure she's safe I'll see to it she has the opportunity to participate in more normal childhood pursuits."

"Are you worried she'll be kidnapped and held for ransom? Is that why you have armed guards watching her constantly?"

His lips thinned and I saw a nerve twitch on his forehead. "That's part of it."

"Part of it? If you want me to become a member of your household, I need to know what's going on."

He frowned, evaluating what I said. "It's not my decision to make."

"Whose is it?"

"The police."

"What?"

As though to accent his words, thunder shook the house again and lightning flared.

The lights went out.

Chapter 7

Faint nightlights clicked on, triggered by the loss of power. It gave the room a hazy glow, punctuated by the next strike of lightning. "Is it the storm?" I asked softly.

John was already moving, a dark shadow at his desk. "No. We have backup generators."

I followed him, narrowly avoiding our chairs at the last second. "Does the power outage trigger the security alarm?"

"It should, unless the system is compromised." He moved around the desk.

"How many guards are in the house tonight?"

A nightlight behind John's desk highlighted his movements. I could see him remove a gun and a shoulder harness from the drawer. "Paul, Frank, and Mark. Paul is outside. Frank and Mark are inside."

"How long before the police arrive?"

"Five minutes, maybe ten. Possibly longer given the weather."

I gestured to the automatic he held. "Do you have another? Mine's in my room."

John straightened. "You're remarkably calm about this."

"It's not my first rodeo."

"I expect you to explain that remark later." He reached into the desk and pulled out a 9mm in a belt clip and handed it to me. It was heavier than my S&W but familiar.

I checked the safety then attached the belt clip onto my jeans, holding the gun at my side. "Where do you need me?" I whispered.

John went to the door. "Stay with Adele. I think she's in her room."

"If we need to evacuate, I'll take her to the woods and the patio below. From there we can hide if we have to."

"You're not a regular nanny, are you?"

"I've done some security work."

"Like I said, we'll talk later. Let's go." He led the way from the room, pausing in the doorway, his gun raised. I followed, keeping watch behind me every step or two, straining to hear anything unusual.

We hesitated by the opening into the kitchen. John peered inside quickly then pulled back. He was trained. He knew about hostile search tactics. One more little fact to add to my knowledge about John Aire. With a quick gesture, he moved past the opening. We reached the stairs. I saw movement in the living room and froze. John saw it, too. He crouched, his gun up.

Frank materialized out of the shadows. "Rochester," he whispered.

"What?" I asked, one foot on the stairs.

"That's the passcode for the night," John said. "Don't trust anyone unless they give you the passcode."

"You used my name for the passcode?"

John gave me a gentle shove. "Go."

"Where's she going?" Frank demanded.

I didn't wait to hear John's explanation. I dashed up the steps, thankful I was wearing my lightweight summer fabric shoes and not leather sandals. Those shoes weren't meant for running. And they were loud.

I dashed around the balcony and glimpsed Adele going through the door leading to the outside balcony. *What the hell?* Maybe she and John had an arrangement, one of those "if the power goes out, go downstairs" or something.

If they had an arrangement, he would have told me. I ran after her, reaching the balcony door. I expected to see her standing outside or going into the guard room at the other end.

The balcony was empty.

That's when I remembered the spiral staircase. I turned. It was partially hidden behind a decorative metal grate. I pushed the grate open and peered into darkness. The black iron of the stairs blended in with the night.

I held my gun in front of me and descended cautiously, keeping hard against the back of the stairs as much as I could to present a minimal target. When I got to the bottom, I stayed in the shadows of the house, John's bedroom against my back. French doors were on my left. I glanced inside when I moved past. His bed faced the doors. I saw it in the faint nightlight.

I was still under the shelter of the overhead soffits. The yard in front of me was soaked but the rain was lighter, now a fine mist. On my right was the patio. Beyond it was the motor court. The exterior lights must have been solar powered because they were still on, although dim. A small sedan was there, parked so it faced the drive.

I glanced to my right, where the sunroom was a dark mass interrupted by windows set every three feet. They were floor-to-ceiling windows, so to get to the other side, I'd need to cross in front of them. I heard footsteps above me. I leaned forward from the shelter of the house and glimpsed a dark figure overhead on the balcony.

"Rochester," someone said softly.

"Rochester," I replied, stepping onto the lawn.

Mark peered down at me. "Where's Adele?" he called.

I pointed to the car. "There, I think." I trotted across the wet lawn.

"Wait." He moved above me, heading for the guard's room.

I saw figures around the car. I stayed under the overhang of the house, keeping to the shadows. I got to the edge of the garage just as Mark opened the door leading to the game room. "Stay behind me," he whispered.

I wanted to argue but it made sense. I fell into position, keeping the bulk of his body ahead of me while we crept around the side of the garage. I peeked around him and saw Adele, her hand on the roof of a car while she prepared to slide inside. A man was behind her. It seemed like he was shoving or pushing her.

Mark ran forward, his gun raised. "Stop!" He headed for the driver's side of the car, probably to prevent anyone from driving away.

The garage door opened and two men ran from there, heading for the car with their guns raised. I sprinted toward Adele, who struggled with the man trying to push her into the car. I couldn't use my gun. Adele was too close. I dropped it on the grass and leapt at the man who gripped her arm.

Opponents always expect me to go in low because I'm so small. I have a good jump, though, easily three feet straight up. He faced me and my foot caught him in the thorax. He dropped back, his breathing cut short by the blow.

I went in, fists flying, landing a solid punch to his nose and feeling the cartilage crack. I stomped on his foot then spun, using my elbows to pummel him when he tried to fight. He staggered back, pulling Adele with him. She fell away, hitting the pavement and rolling.

I kicked again, this time landing a hard blow on his thigh, not enough to break the bone but give him a bad bruise. He fought back, punching at me. One blow landed on my already injured left cheekbone. The pain was blinding. I dodged backward, barely missing Adele. I spotted my gun and reached for it now that she was out of the line of fire.

"Stop!" someone bellowed.

I halted before getting to the gun, recognizing authority when I heard it. I turned, my arms up. My opponent came at me, his arm cocked to deliver a right cross. I finally got a good look at his face.

It was Grant Pool.

I dodged his punch, ducking to the left. I kicked his left knee and it buckled, dropping him to the pavement. I stepped back, raising my arms again. "I'm unarmed! I'm clear!"

"Damn, remind me not to take you on in a fight." Mark jogged to me, picking up my gun from the ground. He handed it to me. I holstered it while he turned to Pool. "What the hell is going on here?"

I went to Adele. "Are you okay?"

She scrambled to her feet, her jeans torn and her hoodie sweatshirt tangled around her upper body. "What are you doing? You had a gun. Were you going to hurt him?"

"He was hurting you." I reached for her but she drew back.

"He was helping me get away," Adele said tearfully.

The floodlights outside the garage came on, momentarily blinding me. When I could see again, John was in front of Pool. "Explain yourself," he snapped. "What's going on?"

A sedan careened into the drive, screeching to a halt behind John. Two men leapt out of the car. I think one was on duty the day before. Even if I didn't recognize his face, his bulky physique and professional way of moving told me they were part of the guards assigned to the house.

"It's a misunderstanding." Pool kept his left hand to his face, covering his nose. I don't think it was broken but when he moved his hand away, I saw blood. Thunder rumbled overhead. A fat raindrop hit my bruised cheek, making me jerk in surprise.

John noticed. "Inside. Now."

"Let's go." I put an arm around Adele's waist. We followed John and Pool into the shelter of the garage.

Pool made a beeline for the door leading to the house, but Frank emerged, blocking his way. John turned to me and Adele. "Go inside." I started to protest but he said, "I'll be in shortly and we'll discuss this." He met my eyes. "I promise."

"It's a misunderstanding," Pool repeated, his voice muffled when he pushed a handkerchief against his face.

"Is the house clear?" John asked Frank. He nodded. "Thank you. Charlotte, please take Adele inside."

Adele and I moved past Pool and John, Adele clinging to me. Pool kept his gaze fixed on me when I moved past him. If looks could kill, I would have been a quivering lump of meat. Adele and I went up the steps into the house. When we did, I noticed the door open on the fuse box panel next to the door. Frank reached over and closed it.

We came into the hallway going past John's office and the kitchen. Lights were on overhead. "Mr. Pool said he talked to John about it," Adele whispered. "He did. I thought you and John knew about it. He said it was okay. Jamie and I just wanted to meet."

I paused at the foot of the stairs to view her in the brighter lights of the house. She appeared sincere but I wondered. "Whose idea was it?" I asked.

Her mouth sagged open in astonishment. "What?" Frank moved into place behind her, listening.

"Whose idea was it? Yours or his?" I went up the stairs.

Adele automatically followed. "Mr. Pool. He and I were talking the other day. I told him about the Gems forum and how I wished I could meet other kids my age."

I looked beyond her to Frank, who nodded and went back downstairs. "Come on, let's get changed. You're wet and so am I." Plus my pants were grass-stained, my shirt was ripped and my shoes were a wet mess. At this rate, I wouldn't have any more clothes left to wear and would need to go to my house to re-stock my wardrobe.

I stopped at my bedroom door. "Come down when you're ready. I think your grandfather wants to talk to us."

Adele went toward her room but stopped and turned. "You're not a regular nanny, are you?"

"I'm kind of specialized. Get changed now." I went into my room, sucking in deep breaths to calm my still-booming heart. I was sick with adrenaline but it would pass, I knew.

I longed to know what bullshit Pool was spreading, but I trusted John would fill me in on it later. John's reaction to what could have been a simple power failure spoke volumes about his level of paranoia. Something was going on. I *would* get to the bottom of it.

I cleaned up and pulled on a pair of jeans and a denim shirt, clipping the gun and holster to the waistband. My bruised face didn't appear any more bruised than before, but my cheek was a dark red and my eye seemed puffier. I'd need to make sure I sat with an ice pack before bed.

I dug my feet into my bunny slippers and left my room. Adele was outside her room, staring at her phone. She had changed into clean jeans and a T-shirt, her expression so woebegone I suspected she was crying. I waited until she noticed me then waved her to join me.

"My grandfather will be really mad," she said in a small voice. "I didn't mean to do anything bad."

I almost believed her sincerity. "You were trying to sneak away at night," I pointed out. "That doesn't look good."

"But Mr. Pool said he cleared it."

I raised a hand. "Let me give you some advice. If you do something wrong, apologize and move on. Don't try to make excuses. Say you're sorry, you've learned your lesson, and it won't happen again." I peered into her eyes. "Okay?"

"Yeah. I just wanted to hang out with kids my age."

"I know." I nudged her toward the stairs. "I'll talk to your grandfather about that. But first we have to deal with tonight's problems."

"He'll never let me out of his sight again." Adele

inched down the steps, the picture of dejection.

She was right, but I wasn't about to tell her that. "Let's get it over with."

We reached the bottom of the steps. I spied Paul, standing in the doorway to the kitchen. He gestured us closer.

Adele and I met him at the doorway. John and Mark were inside the kitchen. Grant Pool was nowhere in sight. "Come in," John said. "Check the grounds one more time and reset the alarms," he said to Mark. "And make sure the police know this was a false alarm. I talked to them but it might be good if one of our people follow up." Mark nodded and left the room.

Our people? What did that mean?

"We need to talk." John gestured to the stools flanking the kitchen island. "Have a seat."

"Where's Grant Pool?" I was too antsy to sit, so I began to pace the length of the room while Adele slid onto one of the stools.

John didn't answer. He went to the cabinets alongside the fridge, opening doors. "Do you want something to eat?"

"Not really," I said. "What did Pool say?"

John appeared totally at ease, not like a man who recently hunted through his house, gun in hand. My nerves were still jangly but he seemed ready to kick back and read a newspaper. "He said it seemed harmless enough. She wanted to meet her boyfriend. He reasoned that if he went with her, it would be okay." He regarded Adele. "I didn't know you had a boyfriend."

"Is he crazy? She's a thirteen-year-old child. You don't help a kid sneak out of her house in the middle of the night."

"Calm down."

"We were just attacked."

"Actually, we weren't. Not really. Besides, we're fine. Sit." John opened an upper cabinet and pulled out mugs. Then he got powdered sugar and cocoa powder from another cabinet and what looked like baking soda and flour.

I continued to move around the kitchen, stopping once to watch him. "What are you doing?"

"I'm making us a treat. Sit down before I tie you down." He dug in a drawer and got out a large spoon.

"Sorry, I need to work off energy. What kind of treat?"

He went to the fridge and got a carton of eggs. "If you don't sit I'll make you sit."

I glared at him over the expanse of the kitchen island. "Try it."

He started around the corner of the granite. I clambered up on the stool next to Adele. "Okay, okay."

Adele put her hand on my arm. "Please." Her voice was tremulous. I saw the panic in her eyes.

Her fright cooled my adrenaline. She needed calmness now, not action. I looked at John and he smiled. Damn it. He already knew that. I propped my elbows on the counter and rested my chin on my clenched fists. "What kind of treat?"

"You'll see."

"What do you know about cooking?"

"You'll see." He cracked an egg into each mug and dumped in sugar and cocoa powder and some other ingredients I wasn't sure about. Then he dug through a couple of drawers, finally finding a whisk.

"Mrs. Fairfax will be pissed off if you mess up her

kitchen stuff," I warned.

"I'll handle Mrs. Fairfax." He whisked each mug's contents vigorously and put them in the microwave, inspecting the controls. I was about to give him pointers but Adele nudged me, shaking her head before I could speak.

"Milk?" he asked. "Maybe a little shot of something to liven it up?" He returned to the fridge and got a carton of chocolate milk, setting it on the island counter. He disappeared into the living room briefly and came back with a bottle of coffee liqueur, a bottle of white crème de menthe, and a cocktail shaker.

He dumped generous measures of the liqueurs into the shaker with ice and handed it to Adele. "Shake it up."

The microwave pinged. He used the oven mitts to extract three piping hot individual chocolate cakes. Next he poured chocolate milk into martini glasses and set everything in the middle of the island with three forks. He put a tiny bit of the liqueur mixture into Adele's glass and a heftier measure into the other two. "Dig in."

I sampled the cake. It was darn good and it was especially good when the alcohol combined with it. We ate in silence for a minute or two then Adele said, "Where did you learn to fight like that?"

"I'm a small person, in case you haven't noticed," I said. John made a noise that sounded like a snort. I ignored him. "I decided a long time ago it made sense for me to know self-defense. One thing led to another. Before you know it, I had a black belt and firearms training."

"You were mean," Adele said. "You looked like you might kill him."

"I know when to pull a punch. It's like you go to

another place where hope and love and anger are only words. All that's left is a goal, a mission, a need. You have to stop the other person no matter what."

"Have you ever killed anybody?"

I looked at John. He shook his head.

"No," I lied. "That's serious shit. I haven't."

"Tell me about this boyfriend," John said, sipping his cocktail.

"He's not a boyfriend." Adele twirled her fork in the remains of her cake. "He's a guy I met online. I wanted to talk to somebody my own age. You know, talk, and you know, stuff." She drew a deep breath. "I'm sorry. I shouldn't have done it. No matter what Mr. Pool said."

"It's not an unreasonable expectation," I said before John could answer. "It's natural for her to want to be with other kids."

He didn't say anything immediately but regarded Adele, his blue eyes narrowed in thought. "I'm sorry," he finally said. "Please cooperate with us for a while longer. I know this has been boring for you. I should have known you'd find someone you'd like to meet in person. Follow our directions for a while longer then I'll find a school here in town for you."

Adele's head jerked up and she smiled. "Really? A real school?"

"I'm sure we can find a school that would be suitable." He looked at me. "Perhaps Miss Rochester can help."

"Sure," I said absently. I was mulling his wording about *just a bit longer*. Was he on a schedule? A timeline?

"However, I think you must be punished for what you did, but I'm not sure how to do it," John said, drawing my attention back to the present. "I'm disappointed you wanted to sneak out, but I blame Mr. Pool more than you." He put his empty coffee mug into the sink. "Charlotte, do you have any ideas?"

I considered him and Adele. The alcohol calmed me and the adrenaline drain was making me sleepy. "She could go shopping with me tomorrow. That's enough of a punishment for anyone."

"Shopping?" John took my empty mug and Adele's and added them to the stack in the sink. "For what?"

"I need a dress for the party you want us to go to. I don't have anything that's fancy enough for a dinner party." I eyed the remains of my drink, wondering if I dared check the cocktail shaker to see if it was empty. "Unless you don't want us there," I said hopefully. "Maybe we should stay home."

"We'll talk about it later." John looked past Adele. Paul was in the doorway. "Why don't you go to your room now?" he suggested. "We can continue this conversation tomorrow."

Adele and I slid off our stools. "Not you," John said to me. "We need to talk."

Adele whispered, "I think you're in trouble."

"It won't be the first time." I gave her a little shove.

To my surprise she put her arms around me and hugged me fiercely. "Thank you. For protecting me."

"Silly kid." I hugged her in return. "Get some sleep. No playing online games tonight." She nodded but I said, "I mean it, Adele. No games. I don't care how many people are in trouble from trolls or how close you are to winning the contest. You stay offline tonight."

"Okay," she said reluctantly. She left, Paul behind her.

John came around the kitchen island. "Let's go to my office. We have a few things to discuss."

I followed him to his office. "Thanks for the loan." I pulled the gun and holster off my waistband and put it on his desk. "Glad I didn't have to use it." I sat in the chair I'd vacated earlier, surprised to see the wine glasses still sitting on the end table. It felt like our earlier conversation happened days ago.

John poured two glasses of port, handing one to me before sitting. "Why didn't your security background show up when we ran a check on you?"

"Perhaps you didn't dig deep enough."

"I doubt that."

I smiled. "It's useful to keep aspects of my life private."

"But—"

"I didn't lie. I work for Simmonds Security. It's a division of Lerner, Incorporated. I do tech work for them as well as security work. Specialized jobs, usually for elderly clients, often those who are being terrorized by their own children."

"Why didn't you tell us?"

"If I didn't feel I could handle this job, I wouldn't take it. That's one reason Burns recommended me. Most of his people have some security training. I probably have the most." I sipped the port. It tasted velvety and rich. Mingled with the aftertaste of cake and chocolate, it had a soothing but stimulating effect. "Now it's your turn. Why is Adele under lock and key? Why are your guards armed and why are you so well armed? Why weren't you surprised when the lights went off?"

"That's three questions to my one. Not fair." John smiled at me above his wine glass.

"I can quit, you know," I warned. "Watch me."

"I know. And I'd hate it if you did." His eyes were fixed on mine. I read something in the depths of his. I wasn't sure what I saw, but it made me shiver. "Adele is in danger."

"I figured that. Why?"

"Her grandmother."

"What?"

"Her grandmother. Sabine Verrens." John's voice was cold when he pronounced the woman's name.

I sipped my wine, dredging up memories from a long-ago life. "Sabine and Antoine Verrens. They ran the drug trade on Jamaica. Rumor had it she was as ruthless as him, if not more so. She's from an old island family."

"She's also crazy."

"And she's after Adele? Why?"

He smiled faintly. "I doubt you'd believe me if I said it was familial love."

"You'd be right. I wouldn't believe it."

"She's obeah."

"You said that before."

"She believes Adele can help her resurrect her daughter."

I let the words sink in. "Antoinette, your daughter-in-law?"

"Sabine didn't sanction the killing of her daughter. Her husband did it. From what I was told, she was beyond grief when she discovered what he did. Antoinette was their only child. Sabine killed the men who killed her daughter. She had them bound. She cut out their hearts and burned them on an alter to the old gods, trying to bring her daughter back."

I went to the decanter and topped up my glass of

port. I resumed sitting, my hand trembling. "Resurrect?"

"She believes if she has Adele, she can call her daughter back from the dead. Her daughter will inhabit Adele's body and Sabine can have her daughter again."

She's crazy. That's stupid. That's insane. "Powerful magic." I remembered talking to elders when I lived in Jamaica. Their belief in magic was complete. I could never understand how they lived in the modern world while still believing in witches, demons, and the walking dead.

"She'll do anything to get to Adele now that Adele is—" John stopped, his tanned cheeks flushing a dark red.

It suddenly made sense. "She's menstruating," I said, pieces falling into place. "She's a woman now."

"She's a child," he snapped. "No matter what anyone says."

"You know that and I know that." I was momentarily sorry for him. Men had no idea about the threshold a girl crossed into womanhood. It was a profound change in a woman's life. "To someone from the islands that's powerful juju."

"I know. I've done everything I can to keep Adele safe but I know Sabine is after her."

I barely heard him. A piece of the puzzle was missing. "Who told you this? How do you know?"

John looked away, staring at the photograph on the wall. "I have sources on the island. They keep me posted about what is going on there."

I put my hand on his where it rested on the arm of his chair. "John. Tell me."

He finally met my eyes. "Bertti."

"She's—" I almost said *dead.* "She's gone."

132

"She's alive. She and I have stayed in contact."

I managed to take another sip of port but it was a challenge. A series of questions raced through my brain. What came out was, "How?"

John was silent for a long moment. "She fell in love with a fisherman on the island. All she wanted was a normal life. To be a regular person. But she didn't want anyone to know."

"How could she do that? She's—" *Rich. Famous. Beautiful. She's Angelina Jolie combined with Jennifer Anniston. She's the Kardashians.* "She's notable," I finished lamely.

"Bertti was beautiful, true. But much of her beauty came from cosmetics and other artificial means. Once she allowed herself to be natural…" He shrugged. "She's not so notable."

"And you knew this? You knew she wanted—" I struggled to find the correct word. "She wanted out?"

"Of course I did. She and I got divorced very quietly years ago. We maintained a public façade for years but eventually she wanted more. So she vanished."

"And you went through a trial for her?" I sipped the port, my thoughts buzzing around my brain. He might have gone to prison. He might have been convicted of a crime.

"She would have come back if needed. But there was no body."

"And no evidence," I finished for him. "You went through that for her. Why?"

"Like you said. Because I could. She needed it and I could." He smiled at the photograph of the bay.

"But you might have gone to prison. Innocent people have gone to prison before."

"Not this time."

I put my empty glass on the table between us. I needed to process this one fact at a time. John's wife, or ex-wife, being alive was relegated to the back of my mind while I considered the events of the night. "What about Grant Pool?"

John's face changed. It was a subtle shift of his jaw and eyes, a tightening that showed his anger was under control. "He's either in Sabine's pay or he's stupid. I'm not sure which. I fired him, of course." He rested his head back against the chair to regard me. "He blames you."

"Me? I'm not the one who tried to sneak out of the house with a kid."

"I think he's embarrassed you got the better of him in a fight."

I rolled my eyes. "I've seen that before. Men get weird when they're beaten by a puny little woman. I've learned not to pull a punch and for some reason it surprises people." I looked at the doorway, visualizing Adele in her room. "I still think you need to explain why you're being so protective. She's a smart kid. She'll understand."

"That's the whole thing. I want to her to stay a kid."

"I get it. But I still think you should."

He put a hand over mine, his fingers tightening and releasing. "No more arguing, okay?"

I felt it then. Maybe it was the adrenaline. Maybe it was the fighting. That always seemed to activate the hormones in me. A shiver of anticipation made me tremble. "Who's arguing?" I said softly.

He leaned closer and so did I. Our faces were inches apart. "I don't want to be accused of harassment," he said.

I grinned. "I doubt I'm your type. I'm not too worried."

"And you know my type?"

"Sure. You were married to one of the most beautiful women in the world."

"The key word there is *was*. I was married. I've been divorced a long time."

"Still, you married her."

"I was young with different tastes then. I prefer a more mature woman now."

"Well, that leaves me out. I've never been accused of that."

He smiled. "Good to know."

"Excuse me." Mark stood in the doorway, his gaze bouncing away from us to the desk behind John as though proving he wasn't gawking. "I wanted to report in."

I moved away from John and stood. "You've given me something to think about. I won't discuss it with Adele but I think you should tell her. I'll leave it up to you, though." I went to the door. Mark moved to one side to let me pass.

"I would like you to consider a suitable punishment for her," John said behind me.

"Trust me. Shopping with me will be punishment enough. Good night." I smiled at John and slipped out of the room.

Something to think about? I went up the stairs. That was an understatement.

Chapter 8

Thursday dawned cooler and less humid than the previous days. My Tai Chi and swimming were pleasant, not the sweat-filled exertion they were earlier in the week.

John met me at the pool when I emerged. Today he wore faded jeans, an untucked pale-yellow shirt, and sandals. It was a surprisingly sexy outfit, probably because his hair was tousled and his cheeks were unshaven. That gave me the impression he rolled out of bed and grabbed the first clothing at hand. If so, he'd chosen well because the outfit highlighted his tanned arms, gray hair and smoky blue eyes.

He handed me a towel and a mug of coffee. "How are you this morning? Any aftereffects from last night's excitement?"

I dabbed the towel against my cheek. "I meant to ice this last night but I was so tired I forgot. I suppose I'm a rather violent shade of purple this morning." I sipped the coffee. It was fixed the way I like it, with cream and sugar. Mrs. Fairfax's doing, I suspected.

"Purple looks good on you. Have you considered Adele and how to handle her?"

"I think Adele is the least of our worries. A psychotic woman who's after her is more of a concern to me." I put my mug on the wicker end table and picked up my shirt.

"Now you understand why we have so many guards and why I was adamant that Adele stay close to the house."

I pulled on my T-shirt over my wet swimsuit and wrapped the towel around my lower half. "Let me talk to Adele and explain how serious this is. I won't go into details," I added hastily when I saw him draw breath to protest. "But I'll say you've been threatened and it has you worried for her safety."

He nodded reluctantly. "I wanted to keep her unaware of the problems if I could. She's had a hard enough life as it is. I didn't want her to worry."

"Worry is one thing. Being alert is another. I'll talk to her. I'm sure she's confused and would like an explanation." I started to walk to the house, picking up my coffee along the way.

John put a hand on my arm, pulling me to a stop. "Thank you, Charlotte." His blue eyes were intent on mine. "It's easier to have you here to share this with me. I appreciate it."

I was acutely aware of my nearly naked body next to his. I couldn't blame my rampant hormones this morning on the after-effects of an adrenaline filled fight. "I'm glad to help," I said, dabbing my face again so I could hide my reddening cheeks. "She's a good kid."

"And I need all the help I can get?" He moved his hand on my bare arm, causing goose bumps to pop up.

"I didn't say that," I protested. "It's tricky handling teenagers. This isn't your usual *I don't want you dating that boy* scenario." I inched away from him and ran a hand through my tangled curls. It was either that or pull him closer. Somehow I didn't think that was the right move to make, at least not in front of the windows facing the house.

"Are you really going shopping later today? Do you think that's wise after what happened?" John kept pace with me when I entered the sunroom.

"It's either go shopping or I show up at your party in blue jeans. I don't have a party dress. My idea of a big night out is to go to the local bar and have beer and pretzels. They make the most awesome pretzels."

"Pretzels? What can make a pretzel awesome?"

"You have to taste it to believe it. Hot out of the oven, lightly salted and served with their famous dipping sauce. That and a cold beer is like heaven on earth."

"I'll have to try it sometime. Where is it?"

"Brockle's Tavern, on Lowood Street." I grinned at the idea of John Aire walking into the neighborhood dive and ordering a beer.

"You don't think I'll do it?" He stopped at the door leading to his bedroom.

I glanced at the unmade bed before looking in his eyes, which made me even more flustered. "Oh, I'm sure you would. I'm not sure the pretzels are up to your standards, though."

He raised an eyebrow. "You might be surprised about my standards when it comes to pretzels." A phone rang in the house behind him. "That's for me. I asked your friend Mr. Allen to call me. I need a new assistant. He did such a stellar job of finding a governess, I'm sure he can find someone who will suit me. I'll see you at breakfast." He touched my arm again and went into the house.

I managed to make it to my room without stumbling, which I thought was doing damn good given how goofy I was. My hormones were sure wacky. I showered, dressed in a clean pair of jeans and went to Adele's room. "Am I in trouble?" she asked as soon as she saw me.

"Kind of." I entered her bedroom. As I expected, the Gems game was displayed on the wall-mounted monitor. "What did I tell you?" I pointed to the screen. "I told you to lay off the game, Adele."

"You said I couldn't play it last night. I just wanted to check in and see where the contest ended." She frowned at me. "I didn't do so good."

"I'm sure there will be other contests."

"Oh, yeah. They have them all the time. Anyway, I wanted to talk to Jamie and tell him what happened." She went to the keyboard and typed a few commands. The game cleared and an online message forum appeared. "Oh, look. He gave me a black pearl. I can use it to buy my way into the Tailor's Shop. I haven't opened that level yet."

I glanced at the wall chart near the monitor. "That's a pricy one. The pearl is valuable. Have you sent him any gifts?"

"Sure. I had dragon eggs I didn't need so I gave him some." She clicked a few more keys. A picture of her Gems inventory showed on the screen next to the forum message.

Princess: Here's the black pearl you need. I wish we could meet in face. Hard to find some who knows as much as you about Gems. When you going to library again? Maybe talk there.

"Wait a minute," I said, skimming the message. "He was at the library? He was the guy you were talking to?" There was something else in the message, something I couldn't put my finger on, something that sounded familiar.

Adele shook her head so vigorously I knew it was a lie. It would have been funny if I wasn't so pissed off. "No, that wasn't him. I mean, I went to meet him there but it wasn't him."

"Remember what I said last night? If you screw up, admit it, ask for forgiveness, and move on. Don't play me, Adele. I'm on your side. I went out on a limb for you."

"I know and I appreciate it." She smiled at me so winningly I wanted to slap her. "It's been so hard with John. I never know what he's thinking. It's so much better now you're here."

I stared at the screen, reading the message again. "Why don't you call him Grandpa?"

"What?" Adele went to her vanity table and eyed herself in the mirror, touching her hair and turning her back on me.

"John. Why don't you call him Grandfather or Grandpa? Why do you use his given name?"

"Grandpa is my other grandfather. I don't want to think about him as my family."

"I guess it makes sense." I pointed to the computer screen. "Did you know Jamie is Jamaican?"

"What?" Adele turned. "What do you mean?"

"The phrasing, the way he forms his sentences. That's patois."

"I thought he was using slang."

"That's what patois is. It's a form of Jamaican shorthand. Did you know he was Jamaican?" When Adele turned back to her vanity table, I strode across the room and grabbed her arm. "What are you up to?"

She jerked away from me so I overbalanced and stumbled back, catching hold of the bedpost to keep from falling. "I left there when I was a kid. I don't have anything to do with the island. What does it matter if he's from there?"

I longed to wipe the smug expression off her face, but I restrained myself. Somewhat. "Do you know why John has so many guards in place?"

Adele shrugged, her linen shirt sliding off one brown shoulder. The thin strap of her black bra was revealed along with most of her upper chest. "He's paranoid. He's rich and he's afraid somebody will kidnap me and make him pay money."

I lunged at her, pushing her hard against the wall. "Is that your game?" I kept my hand below her neck, pinning her in place. Her eyes were so wide I could easily see the white around the dark gold irises. "Are you and that Jamie guy trying to cook up a scheme to get money out of John?"

"No," she gasped. "No, I didn't—no, I don't know anything about—"

I released her, my finger marks dark red on her skin. "This isn't a game, Adele," I said, speaking directly into her face. "If someone kidnaps you, there's a good chance you'd be raped and killed. The kind of people who do kidnapping aren't like people you see on TV. They aren't nice. John is doing everything he can to make sure you're kept safe."

"From my grandparents?" she whispered, rubbing her throat.

I took a step back. "What do you know about them?"

"They're still alive."

"Nobody knows for sure." I moved away so she couldn't see me. I always have a hard time lying to someone's face. "But it's safe to assume they might be and they might want to get in touch with you. So you can see why I'm a little bit pissed off when I discover you've been in touch with a Jamaican guy who might be in the pay of your grandparents."

Adele was so stunned I knew it wasn't an act. "He's a high school kid. He told me he and his family lived in Kingston for a few years. They moved to Chicago last year. His parents sent him here to live with an aunt when his neighborhood got too rough. That's why he got in touch with me. He doesn't know anybody because he just moved here."

It was a nice sounding story. And it would be believable to a thirteen-year-old girl. "I suppose that's why you and he hit it off so well. Because he knew you were from Jamaica."

"I never told him that," she said. "I never even mentioned Jamaica. I suppose you'll tell John about it."

The doorbell rang. "I don't know what I'll tell your grandfather. If you promise me you'll stay off the game and won't be in contact with Jamie again, I'll do what I can to make sure your grandfather doesn't get too pissed off." I went to the bedroom door and peered over the balcony into the living room.

John and a woman were walking into the room, talking. He had changed into a charcoal-gray business suit with a dark tie and shirt. The woman was as tall as him with long legs in shiny nylon stockings, a gray pencil skirt and a fitted gray jacket emphasizing her small waist and statuesque bosom. Her dark blonde hair was pulled up and back into a neat chignon. It highlighted her long, elegant neck and high cheekbones. The woman was familiar but I couldn't place where I knew her from.

I gestured to Adele to join me. "Come to breakfast now. Your grandfather will want to talk to you."

"Do I have to?" She stood up reluctantly.

"Yes, you do. Don't worry. I won't let him ground you for life." I nudged her in the ribs. "Maybe ground you for a week, but not for life."

"Geez, thanks." She laughed shakily. I knew I was forgiven once again for being a grown-up. Talk about hormones! Maybe being a teenager and going through menopause had more in common than I knew.

We went down, John and the woman joining us at the foot of the stairs. "Adele, do you remember Catherine White?" John asked.

"Sure." Adele stuck out her hand and gave the woman's hand a firm shake. I smiled proudly. Adele and I practiced handshakes the day before. She was an apt pupil.

"This is Charlotte Rochester. She's joined our household as a teacher for Adele." John stood between me and the woman, his gaze going from me to her. "Charlotte, this is Catherine White, a business associate."

The woman smiled and extended her hand. "We're more than business associates, John. We're friends, too." Her gaze fixed on my black and purple face and her smile faltered.

I took her hand. Her nails were painted a dark pink color, her grip firm and businesslike. "How do you do. I thought I recognized you. I saw a story about you in the newspaper a few months ago, didn't I? You won an award?"

"Yes, it was quite an honor. Businesswoman of the Year." White smiled at John and moved closer to him, her hip near his. "John nominated me. I was so flattered."

I'll bet. Who wouldn't be flattered if the richest guy in town noticed you? I forced a smile. "Adele and I were going in for breakfast. Are you joining us, Miss White?"

"No, I don't have time, I have a meeting at eight o'clock. I stopped by to talk to John about Grant Poole. He's so distraught about what happened." White frowned at Adele, her brown eyes censorious. "You got him into trouble, young lady."

Well, who the hell are you to be scolding Adele? I straightened, pulling myself up to my almost-five-foot height. "Adele and I discussed what happened. She's aware of her culpability in the matter. Just as Mr. Aire and I are aware of Mr. Poole's culpability."

White crossed her arms and rested back on one foot, a pose I've seen women employ to make themselves look more combative. It was bravado, of course. Such a posture was ridiculous in a real combat situation. "I'm sure it was a misunderstanding. After all, Grant would never do anything to endanger Adele." She smiled perfunctorily at Adele.

"I'm sure Grant appreciates your intercession on his behalf." John moved so he was between me and White, closer to me than to her. "But as I told you, I can't condone that kind of behavior in my home. I expect anyone who works for me to be totally honest, especially where Adele's safety is concerned." He glanced at me. "Why don't you and Adele go to the dining room? I'll join you in a minute."

I considered ignoring him but Adele plucked at my sleeve. "We shouldn't keep Mrs. Fairfax waiting," she murmured.

I felt a burst of affection for her for trying to defuse

my anger. "Of course. How thoughtful of you. I'm sure you won't mind if we begin without you, Mr. Aire."

I could tell from the bemused look he gave me that he knew exactly what my opinion was of Business Girl Barbie. "Please do. I hate to keep you waiting." His blue eyes positively twinkled with humor.

When Adele and I left them I heard White say, "I'm surprised, John. You never used to eat breakfast at home."

"Breakfast was never quite so interesting before," he replied.

Adele and I went into the dining room where Mrs. Fairfax was putting the last of the chafing dishes into a rack. She regarded Adele, her head tilted to one side and a fierce frown on her chubby face. "I must say, miss. I'm disappointed in you."

Adele slid into her seat. "You and everybody else, I guess. I know I shouldn't have tried to leave the house at night."

"Well, that and taking Mr. Poole's word for things." She shook a finger at the girl. "If you're going to get into trouble with somebody, at least pick someone you can trust." Mrs. Fairfax turned to me. "I hope your morning mug of coffee was to your liking."

"Yes, it was exactly the way I like it. Thank you."

"Thank Mr. Aire. He's the one who fixed it for you." She smiled smugly at me and left the room.

Adele shook out her napkin. "Will you tell John about Jamie?"

"I suggest you tell your grandfather yourself." I went to the chafing dishes and inspected the contents. Pancakes, bacon, and eggs scrambled with peppers and onion. I filled up a plate and took a seat opposite her. "It would be much better if you explain things to him, not me."

"Explain what?" John came into the room. I looked across the table at Adele but she studiously ignored me. Before I could prompt her, he said, "I hope Charlotte explained to you the seriousness of the situation, Adele."

She nodded, her eyes on the table. "She did."

"Good. I'd rather not dwell on this, so let's try to put it behind us." He went to the sideboard and filled a plate with food. "What do you ladies have planned for today?"

I glanced to my left, at the living room where Catherine White stood a few moments before. "I think we'll need to go shopping." Adele met my gaze. She recognized, as I did, I needed to step up my game for this dinner party. "I'll be glad to have your help. I'm not well acquainted with haute couture. Or any kind of couture."

"Shopping is my superpower, remember?" Adele frowned. "Of course, it'll depend on your budget. But I'm sure we can find something at the mall."

I shook my head. "I doubt it. Whenever I've tried to find clothes in the past, I always have a hard time. You know. I'm small."

"I believe Charlie and Jason will be going with you. They'll handle any finances." John met my surprised look with one raised eyebrow. "I want you and Adele to feel comfortable tonight. Cat's dinner parties often are featured in the society pages."

"Cat?" I hastily swallowed the bite of pancake in my mouth. "It's her party?"

"Yes, she's hosting the business dinner at the country club. Several people from different companies will be there as well as business students from the local high school," he said to Adele. "You'll have a chance to chat with kids your age."

Just my luck. The chick is the businesswoman of the year and the hostess of a party at the country club. A woman whose parties are featured on the society pages. Why am I not surprised? "Well, won't that be interesting. Is she one of the investors you mentioned?"

"Her company is." John slathered jam on a piece of toast and took a bite.

"When can we go?" Adele asked. "Stores open at ten at the mall."

"We'll go this morning. I have the feeling this might take a while. What time do we need to be at the country club?" I asked John. "Do we meet you there?"

"Yes. The guards will drive you, of course. Cocktail hour is at five-thirty and dinner is at seven."

Maybe we could arrive fashionably late and get there at seven-thirty. I didn't mind socializing, but the idea of hanging around in a dress and making small talk gave me the willies. "Oh, boy. Something to look forward to."

Adele sprang to her feet. "I'll get my homework done before we go so we can spend as much time as we want." She sped from the room, the picture of energy.

"Ah, youth." I sighed.

"You don't enjoy shopping?" John asked.

"I don't have the shopping gene. I tend to find something that fits and I buy it in three colors and call it done. It's not easy being me, I guess."

"I think Adele is up to the challenge. Besides, shopping is a bonding kind of thing for women, isn't it?"

I rolled my eyes. "For some women. For me, it's more like bondage."

"Really?" He arched an eyebrow. "Interesting."

I went to the sideboard, more to hide my flaming red cheeks than to replenish my food. "So how important is this party?" I speared another pancake and sat. "Is it critical you have these investors in your business?"

"Critical? No, but Cat's company has market share I'd like to capitalize on."

I'm sure that's not the only thing he'd like to capitalize on. "She must be one heck of a businesswoman to get an award."

"She's driven. There aren't many women in executive roles in the entertainment industry. Cat has worked hard to get where she is." John regarded me across the expanse of table. "She reminds me somewhat of you, actually."

I dropped the piece of bacon I was nibbling. "What?"

"You're intelligent, independent women who are succeeding in fields normally dominated by men."

"I'm only a governess. That's a woman-dominated field if ever there was one."

John shot me a disbelieving look. "A governess who understands firearms, can plan escape tactics, and who keeps her head in a dangerous situation. You're special."

I beamed at him. "Why thank you. Does that mean I get a raise?"

He laughed out loud. "I'll discuss it with Mr. Allen. I'm meeting him later today."

"Say hello for me and tell him he owes me a favor. I told him he'd owe me big time if I took this job."

"Has this been so tough?" John asked softly.

Our eyes locked across the table. "No," I whispered. "Not bad at all."

Mrs. Fairfax came into the room. "There's a call for

you, Mr. Aire. I think you'll want to take it." She glanced at me. "It's the police."

I was happy to break away from John's hypnotic eyes. "Probably calling about the ruckus last night. I thought you sent one of your people to talk to them?"

John stood, dropping his napkin on the table. "I'm sure it's a formality. I'll see you tonight, Charlotte. Would five-thirty suit you to arrive?"

I scowled at him. "How about seven?"

He smiled. "Five-thirty it is." He left, passing Mrs. Fairfax on the way out.

The plump cook regarded me, her hands on her hips. "What was that about?"

"Adele and I have to go to a dinner party tonight. The one with gowns."

"Nothing so bad about that," she commented.

I pointed to my cheek. "In case you haven't noticed, I'm kinda fluorescent today."

She waved a hand. "Nothing that foundation won't take care of."

I shook my head. "I don't do makeup. Or gowns. Or high heels. Or nylons. Or any girly stuff."

"Hmm." Mrs. Fairfax tipped her head to one side, regarding me. "Then I guess you should stop at the makeup counter in the department store and ask for help, shouldn't you? As to high heels, well, you might be surprised. Sometimes they can be sexy." She gave a little shake of the hips and left, grinning.

"Sexy?" I asked the empty room.

I finished my meal and went to the sunroom, checking my email on my phone. No surprise, there were several from Richard, each shriller than the last. I thumbed a quick reply. *I'm still working so can't answer in detail. Will call you next week.* That would shut him up.

I had one excited email from Burns. *It's working! You're a magic woman. Aire wants me to find him a personal assistant. We're on the way!* He went on to describe various people I knew who he was considering for the job. I gave him my evaluation of them based on my interaction with John and ended on a cautionary note. *He doesn't take any bullshit so make sure the candidates are straightforward and honest.*

I sat back in the chair and stared at the morning. The sun shot light off the pool. I remembered John standing there, the mug of coffee in his hand. He was surrounded by the green grass. Combined with the blue of the water, I was transported back to Jamaica and those lazy days with Nick, swimming in the ocean and loving on the beach.

John. Was I misinterpreting things or was he sending me signals? I'd never had a romantic entanglement with an employer before so I wasn't sure if this was workplace nonsense going on. I had a couple of affairs after Nick died, but I never met anyone I respected and loved.

I went to the patio. The warmth of the day was beginning but the choking humidity was gone. The breeze was even cool here in the shade. Summer was beginning to wane. This property would be beautiful in wintertime with the trees and large expanse of lawn. I glanced up at Adele's room. She was a good kid and surprisingly normal given the shit she'd been through in her young life.

Sabine Verrens was insane. I remembered my time on the island and the way religion was woven into everything people did there. Nick's sister was into voodoo. His younger brother ran with kids who reportedly were in the pay of one of the sects. Nick's mother did what she could to keep the younger kids out of trouble, but a lot of the responsibility fell on Nick. I lost touch with his family after Nick's death. A friend of a friend told me Nick's brother was killed in a gang war not long after Nick died.

I shuddered, one of those all-over shakes. This job was raking up old memories, memories best relegated to the closets of my mind. I went back into the house to experiment with my meager supply of makeup.

Adele found me in the TV room a couple of hours later. "I've made a map of the mall," she said excitedly as we went downstairs. "If we don't score there, we'll go to—"

"I'll bet you and I shop at the same stores," I interrupted. "I often wear a junior size, so wherever you're shopping is fine with me."

She drew back. "Me? I have dresses."

"Anything dressy enough for this party?"

She frowned. "I see your point. Okay. I have it all mapped out."

"Tell it to our guides." I smiled at Charlie, who waited for us near the garage door. He rolled his eyes and led the way to the sedan.

The shopping mall was awash in humanity, or so it seemed to me. "Why are these people here?" I stuck close to Adele while people ebbed and flowed around us. "They should be at work or school, shouldn't they?"

"People like to shop."

"Some people do. Let's go to Target. Or one of those discount stores."

"No way. John told me to buy whatever you wanted."

"Oh, for heaven's sake. What I want is a good pair of jeans but I doubt it would satisfy him."

She dragged us into the first store, the two men following in her wake. I took one look around and said, "Nope."

"What? Why not?"

"There's nothing my size here. Trust me." I smiled at the saleslady who bustled to help us. "Nothing my size, right?" I asked her.

"We have an excellent seamstress who can modify—"

"I need it in four hours."

Her outraged expression was her answer. "Four days, maybe. Four hours?"

I turned around. "Let's go."

We met the same reception at the next two stores. "We'll go to the department store then I'm done," I told Adele. "I have a black pantsuit at home and I'll wear that." I stomped into the Petites department, glaring.

A saleslady with gray hair and affable smile met us. "You look like a woman who can't find a damn thing to wear," she said.

I held up my hands in a *why me* gesture. "Business dinner tonight. I've been told I need a dress."

"I'm sure we can find you something. Follow me." She wove her way through circle racks of clothing and I followed in her wake. I glanced back and saw Adele and Jason heading for the Juniors department while Charlie kept pace with me in the main aisle.

The saleslady paused, swept a gaze over me then picked two blouses from the rack on her right. She continued onward, gathering up clothing and draping it on one arm. By the time she was done there were eight or ten items waiting for me at the fitting room.

"This with this." She showed me a flimsy blouse with a blue and pink floral print and a sapphire blue skirt cut loose and flowing. "Top it with this jacket," and she flourished a pale pink silk jacket with wide lapels, cut so the side panels hung along my hips in long points.

I eyed the clothing skeptically. "I don't know. The neckline on the blouse is pretty low."

"Then this." She held a blue dress with white polka dots. It had a halter neckline, discretely plunging décolletage and a flowing skirt cut on the bias. "With the jacket. Give it a try." She put the clothing into one of the dressing rooms. "I'll go in search of shoes while you do. Size five?"

"Or six depending on the shoe."

I shucked off my jeans and pulled on the clothing. I tried the blouse and skirt. While it was comfortable it made me seem chunky. I considered the dress. I didn't have a halter bra so I'd have to go braless. I was small chested so I'd be okay while I wore the jacket. I slipped it on and was surprised at the overall effect. I was dressed up but still businesslike. I turned, pleased at the way the dress hung. It had a zigzag hemline so the skirt swirled when I moved.

I emerged from my dressing room just as the saleslady entered the larger fitting zone with boxes in her arms. "I was right," she said with satisfaction. "Those colors are perfect for you." She put the shoe boxes on a table and circled me, eyeing me critically. "We could go down a size in the jacket, I think. It should be more fitted. Otherwise, I think it's fine. Try these shoes." She emptied one of the boxes and held up a pair of blue high heels.

"No way," I said. "I can't walk in those."

"How about this?" She tried another box. "Try them. They're surprisingly comfortable."

I drew breath to protest when Adele burst in. "Ooh, those are pretty. Try them on. See what I found." She flourished a strapless red dress that looked like it contained about a yard of fabric.

"You're not wearing that," I said flatly. "You're showing too much skin."

"Everybody does it."

"Not someone your age." I shook my head. "Absolutely not." I stuck my feet into the shoes the saleslady put on the floor. It had a chunky heel but it wasn't too tall. I examined myself in the full-length mirror. "What do you think?"

"It's perfect," Adele said. "John wanted you to get something blue."

"Why?"

"I don't know. He said to make sure you got something blue. I saw the makeup counter. I think we need to get something to cover your black eye." Adele dangled the dress in front of me. "I'm trying this on." She pirouetted away.

"No you won't." I turned to the saleslady. "I'll take it. Can you toss in nylons and a purse? It has to be big enough to hold a small revolver and has to have a shoulder strap."

She didn't even blink. "Of course. Leave it to me. I know just the dress for the young lady. I'll go help her while you get changed." She hurried away, gesturing to another saleslady to join her.

I went back into the dressing room and surveyed myself in the mirror. The outfit was quite nice. "Bonding experience?" I muttered. "Yeah, right."

Chapter 9

I upended the cosmetic bag from the department store on my bathroom counter. There were surprisingly few items given their prices. I once again thanked my stars John paid for this day. "What do I do with this?" I asked Adele. "It looked so easy in the store."

"Here, I'll show you." She sorted the small tubes and containers littering the countertop.

"How do you know about all this?"

"I read magazines."

"Thank God for it," I muttered. "Otherwise I'd be lost."

"Didn't you learn about any of this when you were young?" She lined up the tubes in front of us along with the little wands and sponges the saleslady sold us.

I shook my head. "We weren't rich. Fashion wasn't high on Mom's list of priorities." I handed Adele the makeup sponge and tilted my face up toward her. "Go at it."

Five minutes later she stepped back. "What do you think?"

I surveyed her handiwork in my mirror. "My God, you're a miracle worker." I was myself but smoother. My bruising was hidden and my skin almost glowed. "It doesn't even feel glunky."

"Glunky? Is that a word?"

"You know." I touched my cheek. "Not makeup-y."

She grinned. "Do you need any help getting dressed?"

"I think I can manage." I gave her a little shove. "Now go get ready. We can't be late. Your grandfather would be annoyed with us if we were."

"I don't think so. I think he'd forgive us."

"You, maybe. But I'm the hired help trying to keep you in line."

She paused in my bedroom doorway. "I think you're more than that," she said before scampering off to her room.

I examined my purchases and discovered the nylons were thigh-high, held up by a band of elastic. I breathed a sigh of relief. I gave up pantyhose long ago. I was glad I didn't have to endure that misery.

I dressed quickly, smoothing the folds of the skirt. The jacket was a delicious silky feeling against my bare arms and back. The bodice of the dress was skimpy but the jacket covered it. Mostly.

I emerged to find Adele downstairs, peering up at me on the balcony. "Come on. You're the one who's worried about being late."

I moved cautiously down the stairs in the high heels. They were solid enough that I didn't teeter but they added a few inches to my height, so I had to be careful. I reached the last step. Mark was there, looking surprisingly elegant in a dark suit and bow tie. "You clean up good."

I fluttered my eyelashes at him. "We do what we can." I settled my chic little beaded handbag on my shoulder on its slender silver chain. "I'm ready to face whatever comes."

Mrs. Fairfax peered out from the kitchen. "I hope

you don't mind. I wanted to stay and see how you girls look. I must say, Miss Rochester, the outfit is perfect." She beamed at me and Adele. The girl wore a floral print dress on a dark brown background with a demure hemline and a somewhat low neckline, a compromise I agreed to. Her hair was upswept and braided with small ribbons holding it in place. "And you, too, Adele. You're beautiful."

The girl smiled at me. "I had fun shopping."

"Fun?" I shook my head. "You have an odd definition of fun."

"Shall we get this show on the road?" Mark asked. "We're running late and you know how Mr. Aire is about being late."

Adele and I exchanged a glance and she giggled. "By all means," I said.

Adele was quiet on the ride to the country club, staring through her window at the night scenes. "I never get to go out at night," she murmured. "This is so much fun."

"This won't be the last time," I assured her. "You heard what your grandfather said."

"I may have a normal life someday."

I took her hand. "You will. I'm sure of it."

"I wonder what it will be like," she whispered. "I've been running so long."

I squeezed her hand in sympathy. I hope John meant what he said about letting her go to a school in town. If he didn't, I'd track him down and guilt him into doing it.

Des Moines has three private golf clubs. I've never been to any of them except as an escort for one of the older ladies I occasionally stayed with in my capacity as live-in help. Our destination tonight was the newest entry in the Elite Club set, on the south side of town.

The long drive to the clubhouse gave us time to admire the sprawling edifice of windows, light, and steel atop a hill. It seemed to float above the immaculate green fairways like an alien spaceship. The building was designed by a renowned architect in conjunction with the golf course, which was designed by a PGA professional. The setting and the building combined to make me feel as though I'd entered a fairy tale world.

Mark pulled up to the entrance and a valet immediately took over. Adele and I fell into step together with Frank and Mark flanking us. We entered a massive foyer glittering with chandeliers.

John must have been waiting for us because he came striding across the marble floor as soon as we entered. I glimpsed a roomful of people through a doorway behind him with waiters moving among them. John wore a dark navy suit with a pleated white shirt and dark blue bow tie. I guess it was a version of a tuxedo, but I wasn't well versed in the intricacies of men's evening wear. Suffice it to say he looked like he could take a walk on a red carpet and fit in perfectly. There was something to the old saying that a well-dressed man was the erotic equivalent of a woman in lingerie. He looked good enough to—well, you know.

His gaze flickered over Adele and me. I swear I glimpsed a relieved expression on his face before he hid it behind a smile. I suppose he was worried we'd show up in something inappropriate. "Good evening. Thanks for doing this."

Mark and Frank moved so John, Adele, and I were effectively hidden from anyone around us. John pulled a small blue box from his jacket pocket. "I thought you might like this," he said to Adele. "I believe it belonged to your mother."

She opened the hinged box. Inside was a large red-brown oval gem on a fine golden chain. "What is it?"

"It's citrine," John said, glancing at me. "It's a stone of protection, or so it's said."

I took the box from her when she removed the necklace from the velvet backing. "Help me put it on," she said, handing me the necklace.

John stepped forward and took the necklace from me, draping it so the large gem hung midway on her chest. He fastened it and smiled at her when she turned. "I'm sure your mother would want you to wear it."

She touched it, her eyelashes dark against her warm brown cheeks. "Thank you," she whispered. She quickly brushed a kiss against his cheek before turning away.

"Why don't you go inside? We'll join you in a minute." John handed the jewelry box to Mark, who held out his arm. Adele slipped her arm through his and they headed for the large open doorway, Frank behind them.

"That's a nice gesture," I said. "Adele will treasure her necklace."

"I'm glad. I thought you might like something, too." He reached into his other pocket and extended a similar box to me.

"Oh, no, that's fine," I said. "The outfit is more than enough."

"Please." He opened the box. Inside was a stunning teardrop-shaped sapphire with a large diamond atop it. The stone was an amazing deep blue, not overly big but still beautiful in its simplicity. John took it from the box and held it up, dangling it on a slender silver chain. "It matches your eyes."

I stared at it, hypnotized by its simple beauty. "I can't accept a gift like that," I stammered. "It's totally inappropriate."

"I insist." He moved behind me, raising the necklace over my head and clasping it.

"But I can't…"

John put his hands on my shoulders. His body was warm behind me and his aftershave was a seductive scent, making me long to rest against him. "You can and you will," he said, his voice near my ear. "Didn't you tell me a girl needs some color in her life?"

I shivered. "Are you giving me orders?" I turned my head to stare in his eyes.

He smiled, small lines making creases around his blue eyes. "If that's what it takes to make you accept my gift, then yes. I'm giving you an order." He squeezed my shoulders gently, turning me so I faced him. "I appreciate what you've done."

"Like I said. It hasn't been a tough job. Adele is worth the effort."

He moved closer. "It's not only Adele I'm talking about. I appreciate what you've done for me, too."

"I don't understand." I had a hard time getting the words out.

"You've made me view her, and my life, in a new way." John touched the necklace where it rested on my chest. It was an intimate gesture, one that made me shiver.

"Thank you. It's beautiful."

"No, thank you, Charlotte." He moved forward toward the open doorway. "Shall we?"

For an instant I wasn't sure what he was asking. Then I remembered where we were. I drew in a long breath to still my hammering heart and slipped my hand through his arm. It's funny. I used to dislike my name, but the way he said it, so soft, with a faint slurred accent, reminded me of the island and my days there with Nick. I decided maybe my first name wasn't so bad after all.

John led me into what appeared to be a ballroom with tables at the far end. The location where we entered was designated for cocktails and mingling. Mark and Adele stood near the windows by the golf course. She was talking to a tall young man, smiling at him while Mark did the bodyguard thing and eyed the guests. I saw Cat White talking to four men, all intent on whatever she said. Her cocktail dress was a shimmering black number, form fitting and reminiscent of one of those evening gowns from the Fifties that looked painted or poured. She saw me and swept me with one cool, evaluating glance then did the same to Adele, as though fitting us both for strait jackets.

"What can I get you to drink?" John paused inside the entryway.

"Anything wine," I said. It appeared there were maybe twenty younger people, college age or younger. The rest was a mix of mostly older men with a few older women and younger women thrown in. Everyone was Old Money and Old School except for the teenagers, who seemed surprisingly at home in their suits and ties.

John disappeared into the crowd. I inched away from the doorway, searching for somewhere unobtrusive to stand. I ended up near a wall not far from the tables, which were laid with an impressive amount of silverware and crystal.

An older man in a dark suit meandered over to stand next to me. "I saw you come in with John. How do you do? I'm one of John's investors, Stan—" and his name was drowned out when the crowd around us shifted.

"How do you do?" I said politely. "I'm Charlotte Rochester. Miss White certainly puts on a nice show, doesn't she?" I waved a hand to take in the glittering crowd. "She's quite the hostess."

The man glanced quickly at me, as though questioning my sincerity, but I merely smiled. "Yes, she does. Of course, she's interested in this opportunity with John."

I appeared suitably curious. "I'm sure she is."

"Frankly, I was surprised to see him with you tonight. We thought, well, I mean, we wondered. Well, he and Catherine have spent a great deal of time together." The man's tanned cheeks turned a healthy shade of red.

I considered the many ways I could play this game. I decided on one that might work to John's advantage. "I'm an investor, also," I said in a low voice, moving closer to him. "This is a great opportunity. When John heard I was in town, he offered to let me join tonight's gathering."

"Really?" One bushy white eyebrow raised at this news.

"Yes. It's a natural extension of his business, of course. Today's teenagers are tomorrow's consumers." I smiled. "Who am I kidding? They're today's consumers. Adding an attraction for tweens and teens is a brilliant marketing move. It's a great chance for families to participate in an activity together, one cool for both kids and adults."

"I suppose so," the man said doubtfully.

"It was also genius to invite students from the

business program at the high school to join us. I'm sure he's gathering feedback about how best to market this. I can't wait to see how it turns out." I spied John moving through the crowd, two glasses of wine in his hands. "Excuse me."

"Of course." He moved to one side, turning to talk to the man next to him while I joined John.

He handed me a glass of wine. "I hope this won't be too boring for you," he murmured. "I'm afraid I won't be able to spend a great deal of time with you or Adele. I need to mingle."

I looked to my right, where Adele stood with four other teenagers. "I think she's found her niche. I admit I'm surprised. I wondered if she might feel shy around other kids, but she seems comfortable."

John watched his granddaughter talking excitedly with another girl and the tall boy I saw her with before. "I guess I didn't realize how much she must have missed being around other kids. When I was growing up, it didn't seem to matter too much to me."

He sounded wistful or maybe confused. He and I had more in common than I guessed. I didn't have many friends growing up because our family was poor and I was ashamed to bring kids to our house. "Adele is a social child. Look at those online games she plays. It's a way to interact with other people."

John frowned. "I meant to continue our talk about that. I'm not sure it's wise to let her play those games. I've read it's easy for kids to get addicted to them."

"I agree. That's why I told her to limit how much time she does spend. I haven't enforced it because I wanted to discuss it with you. We can set parental controls on her tablet and her laptop. Also, if you limit how much money is available to her, we can effectively curtail playing the one game she loves."

"Is it hard to do? Set those controls?"

"I think I know how to do it. I need access to her laptop and her tablet."

"We should consider that, then," he said, sounding relieved. "Let's discuss it with her and make sure she understands why we're doing it."

I frowned. "I'm not sure."

"John, I was hoping you could talk to some people." Catherine White appeared at John's side, slipping her arm through his and pulling him gently away. "You won't mind, will you?" she said to me, John's arm pressed against her breast. "This is a business dinner, after all."

Bitch. I considered my pistol in my handbag. Oh, to be allowed to use it. "Of course," I said with what I hoped was graciousness. "I'd hate to get between these people and their money."

John flashed me a grateful smile while he was led away. Mark appeared immediately, which told me he was keeping an eye on me. "How's it going?" he asked, his gaze evaluating the crowded room.

"It's oh so much fun," I muttered, drinking my wine. I smiled at an older woman swathed in a too-tight dress and the wrong shade of pink for her complexion and her age. Then I chastised myself for the uncharitable thought. Who was I to act as the fashion police? Good lord, if it wasn't for an astute saleslady, these people might be critiquing me. I touched the necklace dangling near my breasts.

"Nice rock," Mark commented.

My face got hot. "I shouldn't have accepted it. It's

too expensive. I've never had such a pretty piece of jewelry."

Mark frowned, his eyes still flickering through the crowd while he talked. "John doesn't think like that. It doesn't matter to him how much it cost. He saw it and he decided it would be good for you so he bought it."

"When did he buy it?" I asked.

"This morning. I think he was pretty impressed with you, the way you took a gun and went off to take care of Adele." Mark grinned quickly at me before continuing his perusal of the crowd. "We were impressed."

"Well, he shouldn't have done it. I can't accept such a gift from him."

"I've known John for a while, maybe three or four years. We've been handling his bodyguard duties since before the kid came. John doesn't think like most people think. He doesn't think in terms of price or what's appropriate. He wanted to get you something and he found what he liked. It didn't matter if it cost thousands of dollars."

My wine glass slipped. I barely caught it in time. "Thousands of dollars?" I touched the necklace nervously. "Oh, now I know I can't accept this."

"You're missing the point. It's not about the money. I'm not explaining this right. It's a gift from him to you. It doesn't matter how much it cost. It's something he wanted to do so he did it."

"I appreciate that. I was raised differently, though. An expensive gift like this isn't right."

Mark sighed. "Well, don't say anything about it to him tonight, okay? You'll spoil it for him. He loves doing stuff like that."

"Like what?"

"You know, giving gifts to people. Hell, he gives a boatload of money away to charities and museums and all kinds of stuff. It's something he enjoys doing. He doesn't advertise it because it's not about the money. It's something he can do so he does it."

Like going on trial to give his ex-wife a chance at a new life. Like taking in a granddaughter he'd never met and trying to protect her. There were more sides to John Aire than I imagined.

Mark touched my arm. "I think we're getting the high sign to go into dinner now."

I followed his gaze and saw people moving toward the linen-covered tables at the other end of the room. "I suppose there's assigned seating."

"I already scoped it out. You're here." Mark led me to a table near the window where eight place settings were arrayed.

"Where's Adele sitting?" I turned, looking for her among the moving people.

"She's with the teenagers." Mark nodded to the table next to mine where the younger people were taking seats. He moved away and joined Frank at another table. John appeared on my left.

"I hope you don't mind acting as hostess at my table," John murmured. "The people here are the ones who aren't sure about investing. I need to spend more time with them."

I saw the Unfortunate Pink Lady take a seat at the table. "No problem." I went to the spot opposite John where my place card was situated. I picked up the glossy booklet on my chair and smiled at the young man taking a seat on my right. "Hi, there," I said. "I'm Charlotte Rochester. Who are you?"

I glanced through the booklet while people around me made introductions. It was marketing material for John's theme parks, with artist renderings of the proposed additions. I tucked it under my seat with my purse when the salads were served.

Talk at the table turned to a funding issue coming up for a vote soon, the one about school renovations. It was somewhat controversial because it was an overall funding vote for all the elementary schools in town, not only ones in specific districts. The general population was being asked for a flat one-percent tax to upgrade the schools in the poorest neighborhoods. No tax breaks, no loopholes, no exemptions. A simple tax on every taxpayer.

"Why should I pay for it?" the man next to me said. "Those aren't my kids in that school."

"But those are the kids who may handle your nursing home," I pointed out. "They might be the janitor or the secretary or the doctor who dictates what your life is like in twenty or thirty years." I glanced at the people nearest me. "Like it or not, we're in this together. Believe me, I understand why you might resent it. I don't even have kids and I'm being asked to fund it. But the kids in those schools are our future. I think it behooves us to give them a good start."

"Hear, hear," a lady next to the young man murmured.

"It's a fair tax, too," I continued. "Everybody chips in."

"I can guarantee you one percent of my net worth will be far more than most people are paying," the young man grumbled.

I restrained the snappish response I longed to hurl.

Instead I said, "Consider this. It's cheaper to fund a school than it is to fund a prison. Do a cost analysis and tell me what you think."

"But it's still not fair for me to pay more than most people." He stabbed at his chicken as though it was responsible for him having to kick in the cash.

"What do you think, John?" I looked across the table at our host. "I guess you will pay more than anyone else at this table."

John's eyes met mine. "One percent to a cab driver has a far greater impact on his or her life than one percent does to me. I'd be willing to pay even more if it's needed. After all, the only reason to make money is to spend it. The way we choose to spend it tells us something about ourselves, doesn't it?" He shifted his attention to the young man, his gaze cool and evaluating.

The man wasn't easily intimidated. "I'm getting tired of funding a bunch of do-nothings and lawbreakers."

"We're funding education, not welfare. I doubt an eight-year-old child is a lawbreaker," I said dryly. "And I'm sure many of them would like to be do-nothings instead of being in school." Someone near me laughed softly. The man scowled but didn't reply.

When we were on the dessert course, Cat White arose from her seat at a nearby table and approached a podium set in front of the windows. The buzz of conversation faded while she waited expectantly. When it was finally quiet, she said, "Thank you for coming here tonight. I appreciate your attendance and your attention. I know I speak for everyone in the room when I say I was interested when John Aire approached me with his proposal." Her smile, directed at John, was at once seductive and secretive.

John picked up his glass of water. When he did, I glimpsed the hard set of his face and the forced smile he gave to the man sitting next to him who murmured something to John. He must have sensed me watching him. He met my gaze across the table with a slight raise of his eyebrows, as though to say, *I had nothing to do with that.*

I relaxed while Cat continued in the same vein, talking about what a fabulous opportunity it was to "join forces with one of the guiding businessmen in our community" and "discover for ourselves how John Aire has become such a success today." By implication meaning anyone who took advantage of the deal would become a similar success.

I sipped my wine, glancing around the room at the attentive faces, many of them watching John as well as Cat. The people here were successful but they weren't in the same league as John Aire. I checked Adele, who sat next to a tall young man at a table not far from ours. She, too, was looking around the room. I wondered if she was getting bored with the business talk. After all, she was seated at a table with students in the business program. She didn't have much in common with them.

Polite applause diverted my attention when John stood to join Cat at the podium. He thanked the various people involved, eliciting a preening smirk from Cat White. Then he made a simple business pitch about the proposed changes to his theme parks. "It's discussed in the brochures you have," he concluded, holding up one of the glossy booklets. "I won't try to sell it to you. I feel it's an exceptional business opportunity. But I'll let you be the judge of it. If you'd like to invest, you know how to contact me." He smiled and left the podium.

That seemed to be the signal for people to get up and head for the bar. I stood, moving slowly in my high heels. Mark appeared as soon as John disappeared into a crowd of well-wishers. "We'll be leaving soon," he said in a low voice. "John didn't feel it was necessary for him to stick around."

"Whatever you guys want to do is fine with me. My feet barely hurt. I'm good for another hour or so."

Mark flashed me a quick smile. "You've got endurance. I don't know how women manage those shoes."

"Very carefully." I took Mark's arm and we moved toward the exit. A few minutes later John joined us, a glass of wine in his hand.

"I think we'll have to pry Adele away from her new friends," he said with a wry glance at his granddaughter. She was with the tall kid with the dark hair near the windows. Frank the guard stood nearby, his dour look like a dark rain cloud on Adele's sunny expression.

"She's certainly having fun." I eyed the necklace she wore. "Did it really belong to her mother?"

John swung his attention to me. "Why do you ask?"

"Citrine was used in Jamaica to ward off evil spirits. Or to call them. If your daughter-in-law repudiated her family, I doubt she'd keep that gem."

John swirled his wine, focusing on the mundane action. He was in silhouette to me. His face appeared sharper, more angular from this vantage. "You're right. I have nothing from her parents except a few photos. Everything burned in the fire."

"She mentioned a fire."

"Edward and Antoinette were shot and the house

was set on fire." John's gaze went to his granddaughter. "She looks like Edward. Her eyes. They're his eyes. He was like her, too. So curious and adventurous."

I put my hand on his arm. "It's a terrible loss."

"We both lost someone at the hands of the Verrens family."

His words didn't make sense. "I'm not sure what you mean."

"Your brother-in-law was involved with a gang in Jamaica."

I heard Mark draw in a sharp breath next to me. I glanced at him. He watched John, an expression of— warning? confusion?—in his eyes.

"Yes, Nick's youngest brother, Bramwell, got pulled into a gang. He was such a sweet boy. Bram was his family name but we called him Willie. Nick did what he could but it wasn't enough." I was surprised to see sympathy in John's eyes. "Nick died before he could get Willie safe. But you knew that. You did your research about me."

"Yes, I did. I was in Jamaica when it happened."

"When what happened?"

"I saw your husband. I was there, on the island, when Antoine Verrens killed your husband."

The words made no sense. "Nick died of typhus."

John shook his head. "Antoine Verrens killed him because your husband was getting too close to the truth about the Verrens' drug operation."

"But the authorities said he got ill."

"They covered it up. Your husband was an American citizen. It would have caused an international scandal. Drug deals were being done every day. Governments turned a blind eye to it all."

"You're wrong," I said automatically, my mind racing.

"Did you see his body?" John looked directly at me, challenging me.

"John, this isn't the place to discuss this," Mark said. "Let's talk about it later."

I ignored him. "They couldn't return his body. He had typhus. It was contagious." Even as I spoke the words, I sensed John was right. Nick's death seemed so unreal at the time. Was it because it was a lie? "Why were you there?"

"I was desperately in love with a woman who was addicted to cocaine. Antoine Verrens kept her supplied. Because of Verrens, Bertti could function. Remember I told you about the fisherman she fell in love with?" I nodded numbly, unable to speak. "He helped her get clean, helped her kick the habit. You said she was one of the world's most beautiful women. She used to be. But the drugs took a toll. I doubt if you'd recognize her now."

"John, I hate to interrupt but I need to talk to you." Cat White moved next to John.

"I'm sorry, Catherine. We're leaving soon."

White pushed in front of him to confront me. "Ask her. Ask her about the boy Adele wanted to meet."

"I don't know what you're talking about." The last person I wanted to talk to was Catherine White. I needed to sort through what John said. Nick was murdered? I suppose it was possible. He was a police officer and he went back to Jamaica to try to extricate his little brother. "Wait a minute," I said. "The gang Willie joined. It was tied to a sect."

"What are you saying?" White demanded. "That has nothing to do with this. You knew Adele was going to meet that boy." She turned to John. "Grant said Adele told *her* about it." Cat stared at me while she spoke.

John set his wine glass on a nearby table. "Is that true, Charlotte?"

I barely heard him. Pieces of a puzzle were coming together. "Yes, I knew she was chatting with someone online. I didn't think it was critical to share with you."

"You withheld information?" John took a step toward me.

"I told you. I didn't think it was important at the time." I took a step toward him so we were only a foot or so apart.

"You were wrong."

"Then I guess you don't trust my judgement." I stared into his eyes, daring him to say it.

John's mouth hardened into a flat line. "I told you I won't tolerate anyone in my household who lies."

That's when it hit me. Lies. This was all about lies. "You used me." I clenched the strap of my handbag so tightly I was sure I'd break the fragile chain. "My background, my late husband, Jamaica. You needed me. Sabine Verrens knows who I am."

John stepped back. It was as damning as a full confession. I saw it in his eyes, in the way he glanced at Mark. But I also glimpsed something in the way Cat White moved, the way she stiffened and inched backward. I filed the knowledge away for later consideration. I was too busy with my righteous anger to care about it now.

"You needed me as bait. Sabine would see the wife of a man she killed next to her granddaughter. You know how her mind works. She assumes I'm out for revenge." One look at Mark's face confirmed what I was saying.

"She wasn't making a move. You had to force her to act. You wanted her to see me and get worried. You needed me to trigger a trap."

"I needed you in other ways, too." John raised his hand but let it drop.

I backed off. "Too? You admit it?"

"I didn't mean it that way."

I didn't wait to hear his stammered explanation. "You can't fire me. I quit."

Chapter 10

I whirled and strode away, heading for the foyer. I forgot I was wearing high heels. I slid on the marble flooring and almost did the splits. I wind-milled my arms and overbalanced. Mark grabbed me around the waist and kept me upright. "Where the hell are you going?"

"Call me a cab." I considered struggling but knew if I did I'd probably land on my butt.

"Where are you going?" he repeated, releasing his hold on my waist but keeping me upright by grabbing my elbow.

"To the house to pack." I continued my march to the entryway, which wasn't as dramatic as I wanted due to the fact I needed to slide and step my way.

"You can't get in the house. You don't know the passcode or the entry procedure. Stay here." He left me at the wide double doors leading to the outside world.

"I'm leaving," I fumed. "I'll break in if I have to."

"Wait." He went back the way we came, meeting Frank, who was emerging from the dining room. They conferred then Mark rejoined me. "Come on. I'll drive you home and come back to pick up John and Adele."

I glanced behind me. John stood in the doorway to the ballroom, watching. Cat White touched his arm. He turned his back on me, going with her into the building.

I pushed open the outer door and stomped onto the limestone steps. "Where's the fucking car?" I snarled.

"Just wait, Cinderella." Mark trotted down the wide steps to the valets at a kiosk at the parking lot. He conferred with one of them, who went racing into the darkness.

I followed more sedately, gripping the railing on the steps because I was trembling from anger or maybe a desire to hit somebody. Maybe both. Or maybe it was the damn shoes. I was tempted to kick them off and leave them behind, like Cinderella. But they cost a fortune. With my luck, Cat White would see them and commandeer them. The thought of it made my toes curl.

I was halfway down the steps when the doors crashed open behind me. Adele ran from the building. "Charlotte! Wait!" She careened after me, unmindful of her own heels.

Ah, youth. Ah, confidence. "I quit, Adele. I'm sorry, but I quit," I said before she could speak. "Your grandfather and I don't see eye to eye on what's best for you."

"Please don't quit." She darted ahead of me so we were the same height with her standing on the lower step. "What will I do? Who will protect me from him? If he has his way, I'll be under house arrest until I'm twenty."

I inched downward, forcing her to move. "I can't stay. He'll just fire me if I do." I reached the bottom of the stairs. I saw our sedan, going far too fast from the parking lot. Mark apparently had put the fear of God into the valet. "I'll stay in touch with you on the Gems forum, okay? You can always contact me there." I flung my arms around her for a tight hug. "I'll friend you and you can send me messages, tell me how it's going."

"I don't want to lose you," she whispered, clinging to me.

"You won't," I promised. "We'll stay in touch." I disentangled myself from her grip and walked unsteadily to the car, pulled up to the curb. The valet opened the rear passenger door for me. I ignored him and pulled open the front passenger door. I looked back and saw Adele, one hand on the railing and that woebegone expression on her face. John was framed in the doorway above her, glaring at me, his face harsh and unrelenting. I was tempted to give him the finger but Adele was there. I didn't want it to be her last sight of me.

"Asshole." I flung my beaded bag into the car and slid in after it.

"Quit throwing shit at me." Mark pushed the bag away from him.

"I didn't throw it at you." I fumbled on the seat belt and resolutely resisted looking back while we drove away. "Trust me, if I wanted to throw something at you, you'd know it."

"You shouldn't have quit." Mark eased the car into the sparse traffic of this mainly residential area.

"He would've fired me so what does it matter?" I glared through the window at the world sliding by. "Arrogant son of a bitch."

"That's the pot calling the kettle black."

"What?" I turned so fast Mark pulled the steering wheel, probably afraid I'd slap him. "Who are you calling arrogant?"

"What do you call it? You're making decisions about John's granddaughter directly contrary to what he said because you think you know best."

"If I told John about the kid, he'd go ballistic."

We stopped at a stop sign and Mark leveled a sarcastic look at me. "Geez. You think so?"

"If he'd told me what was going on, I might have told him," I conceded. "But he didn't. I thought he was being a jerk. By the time I was going to tell, Adele pulled her stunt with Grant Pool." My voice faded when a small detail clicked into place. "Cat White and Grant Pool. She said Pool told her about the online forum."

"So what?" Mark continued driving, merging onto the freeway circling the metro area.

"That means Pool knew about it, too."

"So what? You're over-reacting."

"Geez, you think so?" I mimicked. "I was hired because my husband was murdered by a woman my employer is trying to find. He put me and a teenage girl in jeopardy because he didn't tell us the truth. And to top it off, he calls me a liar when I didn't lie to him. I just didn't tell him something. He's the liar."

"You don't understand all that's going on."

"Yeah, well, spare me the details. It doesn't matter anymore. I'm fired, remember?" I simmered in silence for several long miles before asking, "You're not a bodyguard, are you?"

"Of course I am."

"Quit bullshitting me. Who are you? CIA? NSA?"

"I'd rather not say."

"Shit," I muttered. "How did you find me?"

Mark stared straight ahead. "Your name came up when we did a database search for anyone in the area with a connection to the island. When we found you, what your background was, we knew we could use you." He winced. "Sorry. That's not what I meant."

"That's exactly what you meant." I crossed my arms and stared at the dark fields and streets sliding past. "I don't trust Pool."

"Neither do we. And for a while, we weren't sure we could trust you."

"Yeah, well, some of you still don't trust me."

Mark was quiet for few minutes, frowning at the road ahead. "John's not accustomed to having anyone question his judgement."

"If he plans to raise a teenager he'd better used to it fast. That's what they do."

Mark snorted. "Yeah, no kidding."

I kneaded my beaded bag, feeling the reassuring lump of my gun. "You knew about my security background."

"No we didn't. I mean, yeah, we knew you did babysitting for old ladies and all. But Jason Simmonds never told me you had tactical and weapons training like what I saw." Mark's hands tightened on the steering wheel. "I may need to have a little chat with Jason about that."

"Don't take it out on him," I muttered. "It's good to keep details about my background somewhat secret. That way when I babysit, we get results."

He was silent for a minute, digesting that. "So you get in place with these old ladies and you see who oozes out of the woodwork?"

"Yep. Let's face it. People take one look at me and they figure they can intimidate me. Some heirs show their true colors when they think they can get away with it. I didn't know how much elder abuse there was in the world until I took a couple of those gigs."

Mark was silent until we left the metro behind. When we entered the dark countryside he said, "This is a mistake. We need you. You have a good connection with the kid."

"It wasn't hard to do. John could connect with her if he'd give it a try. But he's too damn worried about keeping her safe to make sure she's happy."

"That's not fair."

He was right but I wasn't about to admit it. "She plays this game, Guardians of the Gems. It's an online game. That's where she exchanged emails with a kid who calls himself Jamie. He told her his family used to live in Jamaica but they were living in the U.S. now."

"See, we didn't know about that. You've got a connection with her. You should've told us about it."

"You're right," I admitted. "But I didn't know until this morning. Then we got busy with the shopping crap. I'm sorry. It got lost in the shuffle."

His hands clenched and unclenched on the steering wheel. "The first thing John should do is cut off her Internet access."

"Big mistake. Limit it, yeah. But don't cut it off. If you guys are trying to draw out the old woman, you need to make it seem like nothing's changed, especially if they're tracking her online use." I thought about the home network. "You can set up a monitor and traceback on her computer. It'll track the computer sites she checks. You can use it to see if you can find who the kid is who's in touch with her."

"I'll talk to the IT techs about it. Good tip."

"Make sure she doesn't know about it. She's smart. She'll figure a way around it if she thinks you're trying to smother her."

He sighed. "Smother her?"

"She already thinks you're over-protective. If you mess with her Internet use, she might get creative. You guys have to tell her what you're worried about." Of course, I told her something about what was happening. I didn't tell her the crazy details, but she knew the general outline.

"Are you kidding? She's already tried to run away once."

"She was sneaking out to meet a friend." A small detail surfaced then vanished in my mind. Grant Pool. Something about Pool.

We entered the driveway. Mark parked the car and went to a keypad at the side of the garage. He tapped in numbers and the garage door opened. He rejoined me and pulled the car into its slot.

"I won't be long. You can leave the garage door open." I kicked off the damn high heels and was halfway across the garage before Mark got his door open.

Charlie opened the door to the house. "What are you doing home?"

"I was fired." I pushed past him into the hallway. "I came back to pack."

"Wait a minute, whoa." He reached for me but I was too fast. I skittered by him and went up the stairs, two at a time. I took a moment in my room to suck in a deep breath, trying to slow my racing pulse. I went into the bathroom and washed my face, wishing I could wash away my anger as easily. I tossed the cosmetics back in the bag and left it on the counter. John paid for it so he could keep it.

I removed the necklace and peeled off my clothing, hanging it up in the closet with the shoes underneath. I emptied the beaded handbag and put everything back into my regular purse. I pulled on a pair of jeans and a T-shirt, jamming the rest of my clothes into my suitcase. Everything would go into the laundry when I got home so I didn't bother with folding. I packed my tech bag and left the room, carrying the bulky St. John Bible book and the necklace with me.

Mark was waiting at the foot of the steps. "I still say this is a bad idea."

"Aren't you going back to the party?"

"I wanted to try one last time to talk you out of this."

"I have no choice. John doesn't trust me anymore, so there's no reason for me to stay." I regarded him and Charlie, who was in the living room, watching us. "Take care of the kid. This whole thing you're doing is crazy. If you fuck it up, I'll come after you all."

"Don't blame me," Charlie said. "Blame a lunatic witchy woman in Jamaica."

I shook my head. "You're going about this wrong. This isn't the way they do things on the island." I saw the skeptical expression on his face and Mark's. "You have to fight magic with magic. This isn't a simple snatch and grab. This woman has a deep-rooted belief in what she's doing. That will drive how she accomplishes this. John needs to think like her."

"We've been researching it all. John has a handle on it."

I dragged my roller bag along the hall, narrowly missing his feet. "You have no idea." I went into John's office, leaving the necklace in the middle of his desk.

Mark watched me from the doorway. "He wanted you to have it."

"He wanted me to have it before he decided I was a liar. I'm sure he regrets buying it for me by now." I looked at the two chairs where John and I sat in the evening, talking. "He has no idea what Sabine Verrens can do. None of you do." I left the room and continued to the garage.

"I know you have the best interests of Adele at heart, but we have this covered. I'll make sure we check the computer stuff, too. There's no way anyone in the Verrens family can get close to Adele."

I dragged my bags down the steps into the garage, pausing to get my car keys from the rack on the wall. "I hope you're right." I knew I was wasting my breath. John, Mark, Charlie—they were men, American men. They had no idea of the power of women and tradition. I saw it first-hand on the island. I knew what it could do.

Mark slung my bags into the miniscule boot of my car. "Take care, Charlotte," he said, bending over to speak to me where I sat in the driver's seat.

"I always do. Keep an eye on the kid. And John," I added grudgingly. "He's his own worst enemy."

"Yeah, well, you should know." He moved away before I could fire back with a retort.

I shot out of the garage and drove off, glancing once in the rearview mirror before the darkness swallowed the house.

I considered calling Burns when I got home but I was too exhausted by then. I dumped my clothing into the laundry room and flopped on the sofa with days of mail. My mind kept playing and replaying everything John said. I finally drowned my woes in a glass of wine and an over-the-counter sleeping pill.

I spent a hot and humid Friday getting caught up on a week away from my home. I called Burns, prepared to spin a story, but I could have saved myself the trouble. "Aire called me last night," Burns said. "He explained he no longer needed you. He paid for the entire contract, even though he didn't have to."

"I thought I was there on a week-by-week." I sipped my orange juice while I considered the contents of my fridge. I needed to make a grocery run.

"No, he hired you for a month. I'll pay your salary, of course, so that's a nice bonus for you. Did everything go okay?"

"Sure. No problems." I nudged the enormous picture book of the Bible, sitting on my coffee table. "No problems at all."

"Are you available for any jobs soon? Are you teaching this fall?"

"No, I'm taking the semester off. I need a break." And I needed to put my scattered thoughts into a semblance of order. Something was still nagging at me, a buried bit of information nudging me for attention. "Give me a month or two and I'll be ready to work again."

"That sounds good. Talk to you later."

I hung up. John hired me for a month. Why a month? I wandered to my She Shed and worked for a time on a sketch of a new sculpture. My mind kept returning to the conundrum of Sabine Verrens, John Aire, and Jamaica. I finally gave up on creativity and went into the house to sit in front of my computer.

I did a few searches on obeah and turned up the usual mix of fact, legend, and superstition. I dug out my address book and sent an email to a couple of old friends from my Jamaica days. Anne was now a professor of religion at a college on the East coast. I asked her what she knew of reincarnation rituals, using a vague story of a friend's child who got involved with a sect.

I was more specific in my query to Emily, a retired police officer who used to work with Nick. "I know someone who might be involved with the Verrens," I said in my email. "Are they still operating? I'm worried my friend may be in over his head."

I pushed away from the desk and went back to my She Shed, but the restlessness didn't let up. When I came back inside I found a message on my phone machine from the animal rescue organization. Was I available for another foster opportunity?

Sure. Why not? I drove to the shelter, not far from my house. I came home with two cats whose late owner was apparently a gothic romance fan because the cats were named Heathcliff and Catherine. Heathcliff was a bad-tempered black male with three legs. Catherine was a petite yellow tabby. Upon release from their cages they promptly hid under my bed and no amount of coaxing brought them out. I was accustomed to this kind of behavior and knew in a day or two they'd acclimate. With luck, I'd find them a new permanent home soon.

To my surprise, I already had an email reply from Emily. "I was thinking about you and then I got your message. Isn't that odd? I'm working in Homeland Security now, pushing papers in an office. One of the agents here in the Kansas City field office knew I used to work with the Jamaican Constabulary. He mentioned a new investigation was ongoing into the Verrens drug ring. That *stakki* old bitch was supposedly seen in Miami by one of our confidential informants. It wasn't verified and our people here are pretty sure it was bogus."

I grinned at the word *stakki*, which was patois for bat-shit crazy. Sabine Verrens was spotted in Miami? I wondered when.

"Sabine ran the gang after Antoine died. In fact, she ran it before he died. She's one tough lady. It made me think about Nick and you," Emily continued. "I can't believe it's been thirty years since he was killed. He was one of our best, you know. I always wondered what would have happened if he lived."

She included more news in the email about her life now, but I skimmed it. I went outside to dig in the garden, letting everything simmer in my brain. I kept coming back to Emily's phrasing. *Since he was killed.* Killed by typhus? Or did she know something else? Was John right? Was Nick murdered? How could I even find out after all this time? And why dig into it? Nick was gone. My life took a turn after his death, which set me on the path to security work and teaching.

I trimmed, cut, and raked, beginning the process of putting my yard to bed for the winter while I let ideas scatter around my mind. The days were growing shorter, a reminder that September was just around the corner. That reminded me of the oddity of John hiring me for one month. Why?

I quit working when darkness nudged me back into the house. I grabbed a box of files and flopped in front of the television. The two cats emerged from hiding to join me in the living room while I watched TV and munched on a bag of chips. The female was friendlier than the male. He hunched near the doorway to my office, keeping a wary eye on me. But Catherine soon joined me on the couch, sitting not far from me and even letting me pet her now and again.

I leafed through the legal papers regarding Nick's death, mostly different certificates: death, foreign burial, permission to bring part of his ashes with me into the country, and cemetery papers where his family buried their part of his ashes. Everything appeared legit. What was it John said? The government covered it up because Nick was an American citizen.

I returned the papers to the box and logged in to the Gems game on my tablet. I tapped around and found the user forum, where my persona, Clueless Newbie, friended Princess Ada, requesting help. It was minutes later I got a reply from Adele in the forum.

I wondered if you meant what you said. Thank you for finding me, I've missed you. John won't tell me why you quit. I don't understand what's going on. He and the guards are acting weird. I hardly see John anymore. He stays at his office or he's with that Cat woman. I don't like her. I think she's mean.

"Out of the mouths of babes."

Catherine inched closer to me, curious about this object which diverted my attention from her. *I'm sure your grandfather is busy,* I replied. Yeah, busy with Cat White. He was working on more than one kind of merger with her. *Make sure you do what he says and what the guards say. They're just trying to keep you safe.*

Her reply came back a few minutes later. *I know. I heard from a couple of kids from the party. I want to meet them at a coffee shop but John won't let me go. Oh, and I asked Mrs. Fairfax to get me chamomile tea. I think it helped. And the heating pad helped, too. Thanks.*

Poor kid. She was a fellow female going through the pangs of womanhood. How I hated having periods. One benefit of menopause.

Talk to Mark about meeting the kids, I replied. *He might be able to talk to your grandfather. And quit playing the game so much. I see you're to level 100. You're playing way too much!*

She didn't answer so maybe she took my advice,

although I doubted it. I clicked on the TV and immersed myself in a re-run of *Patriot Games*, one of my favorite Harrison Ford movies. I fell asleep on the couch with Catherine curled up near me and Heathcliff on a nearby chair.

When I woke on Saturday morning, I struggled to remember the bits of a dream that had parts of *Patriot Games* interspersed with Sabine Verrens and the Gems game. Something in the dream seemed urgent or important, but I couldn't put my finger on it. The feeling persisted during my quick run to the grocery store. I was putting my purchases away when a car pulled into the driveway. I peeked out the front window to see Mrs. Fairfax, John Aire's cook, popping out of a small blue sedan.

I opened the front door to greet her on the porch. "What a surprise. I didn't think you could take time away from your cooking."

"I was on my way to do some shopping and thought I'd drop by, if you have time for a little chat," the small woman said.

"Would you like to come inside? It feels like another hot day. Can I get you an iced tea? Lemonade?"

"No, thank you. I can only stay a minute." She followed me into the house. "You have a pretty home. I'm sure you're happy here."

"It suits me. Please, have a seat." Catherine, alerted to the sound of a strange voice, edged around the doorframe leading to the hallway.

"Oh, a kitty. I adore cats. My little Cathy, a tabby cat, died a few months ago." Mrs. Fairfax sat, peering at Catherine.

"Cathy?" I took the seat in the matching armchair.

"I always name my pets after characters in novels. Cathy was named for Cathy Linton, from *Wuthering Heights*."

"Isn't that a coincidence? The previous owner of these cats named them Catherine and Heathcliff. True to his name, this Heathcliff is moody." I stopped when Heathcliff sauntered into the room to rub against Mrs. Fairfax's black slacks. "Well, he seemed moody with me."

"He recognizes a kindred spirit." Mrs. Fairfax tugged on her pant leg and lifted the fabric to reveal a prosthetic leg. "I lost my leg in the Army, years ago. I had to retire from active duty."

"You're one of them. A bodyguard."

"Yes, dear. Of a sort." She rubbed Heathcliff's head, eliciting a throaty purr. "I stopped to see you because I'm worried about Adele. I never see her anymore. She spends her time in her room. I do wish you and Mr. Aire could put aside your differences."

"I doubt it will happen. He has a low opinion of me."

Mrs. Fairfax sighed. Heathcliff apparently took it to mean he was needed, because he jumped on her lap, turned around, and lay down, returning my shocked expression with a smug look of his own. "Mr. Aire has a difficult time apologizing," Mrs. Fairfax said, stroking the black cat. "I'm sure if you reached out to him, he'd meet you halfway."

"I'm not so sure of that." An idea began to glimmer in the back of my mind. "Do you buy the groceries for the house?"

"Of course."

"What about for Adele? Do you buy any of her personal products? She told me she's been having such heavy periods. Are you in charge of buying her sanitary things?"

Mrs. Fairfax nodded. "She tells me what she wants and I add it to the shopping list. As I told you, I get most of our produce and meat locally, but the other items I get at the local grocery store. The poor child, she's alone in the house with those men. I'm sure she was happy to talk to you about her problems." The little woman beamed at me with motherly approval.

"You go shopping?"

"Well, no. Sometimes I send a list to the store and they send it to us. Or I do the shopping, like I did today."

"So someone could know what's on the shopping list." Was I being paranoid? Was it crazy to think Sabine Verrens would be interested to know if Adele, the only young female in the house, needed sanitary products?

"I suppose so." She glanced at her watch, a difficult maneuver because Heathcliff butted her arm, insisting on more petting. "I suppose I should be going. I'm making a soufflé for lunch and I need to get eggs." She got up, putting the cat on the chair behind her.

"These cats need a permanent home," I said, going with her to the door. "If you're ready to adopt again, it might be a match made in heaven."

"Oh, I'm not sure about that." Heathcliff sprang from the chair, wobbling then trotting to her to butt her leg. "Well, maybe. I'll call you and we'll talk about it."

"Say hello to Adele for me."

"I will. And I'll say hello to Mr. Aire, too." She left before I could advise her against doing so. I finished putting away my groceries then went into my office where I found an answer to my other email. Anne, the college professor, sent me links to articles about magic ceremonies as well as information culled from her own research.

"But by some accounts, the victims of the ceremonies did appear to assume the personalities of the reincarnated," she wrote. "Of course, drugs are often used and that may account for it. This is a closed society and one that's dangerous to try to infiltrate. If you know anyone involved in this, I hope they know what they're doing."

"They have no idea," I said to Catherine, who had followed me to the den. Heathcliff stayed behind at the front door, probably wishing Mrs. Fairfax would return.

"Many of the leaders develop their own practices," Anne continued. "Some operate by phases of the moon, some by the tides, others on certain days of the week. If you want to know details you need to talk to someone in their group. They won't accept outsiders into any truly deep mysteries. You tell your friend to get their child out if possible."

I stared at the computer screen. John hired me for a month. Was he assuming Sabine had a specific time in mind for the ritual she was planning? I turned to my tablet, charging on the desk next to the computer, and logged in to the game. A small icon popped up, telling me I received gifts. I checked the gift box icon and saw Adele sent me a life preserver. I could only use it once I got to Level 50 when the Docks location was opened to me. Odd. I was at level 10. She also sent a coffee cup and a buggy whip, which I could use now. I sent her a quick *Thank you* in the forum and got an immediate reply:

Can't talk now. Too busy with friends. Hope you explore using the tools I sent.

I got up, restless and not sure why. Maybe creative

work was what I needed. I leafed through the St. John's book, coming to pictures of the Genesis panels Adele liked. Maybe I could make her something. I changed into my raggedy jeans and an old Hawaiian shirt over a pale green tank top. I slipped on my steel-toed work boots and opened the working side of my garage, propping open the book on my workbench to the page with the illustration.

There were seven panels representing the seven days of creation. I didn't plan to make solid panels. My idea was to have small items as my interpretation of the panels. This would be a small, tabletop sculpture. It was taking shape in my mind while I visualized how I'd solder the different components together. I flicked on the fan to stir the humid air and pulled on my terrycloth headband to keep hair and sweat from my face.

I went through my tubs of found-objects, bits of things gathered at garage sales or discard bins. Here was a piece of costume jewelry, a silver bird with faux ruby eyes, which would serve as the centerpiece. I had a narrow piece of metal with raggedy edges I could burnish for the "chaos" side of the panel. I'd add special paint to it to make it look right. I also found a bracelet, about an inch-wide, of faux gold to serve as the "order" side of the design. In between them, like a painting in a frame, would be the actual sculpture.

I found bits of gold art glass I could glue to the armature in the middle. I picked through a box of toys and found two small silver charms, a man and a woman. Perfect. I could solder those to the armature. I discovered blue metal, part of a defunct drum, and some green plastic which I could use to represent grass. I arranged the pieces on the workbench, frowning while I tried to imagine a way to tie it together.

Tie it together. Like from the movie, and how it tied together different plot pieces. The man in the movie who was "undercover" in the bookstore. The mousy little man who looked like Grant Pool. I rummaged through a shoebox of jewelry pieces, searching for the sun and the moon in the fourth panel, between "grass" and "creatures." I found a gold crescent moon and a smiling sun face. I arranged them in their spots and bent over the table, studying my work.

Grant Pool. He spoke patois. I straightened. The moon. Phases of the moon. A woman's cycle was known as the moon cycle. I went to the calendar on the opposite wall. A quick glance confirmed what I thought. Tonight was the new moon, the start of the new cycle.

Adele. She was just finishing her period, beginning a new moon cycle for herself.

Powerful juju.

I reached for the phone but realized I didn't know John's phone number. It was probably unlisted. Wait a minute. He called me when he hired me. I picked up my cell phone but stopped when a burgundy Jaguar stopped in my driveway.

John stepped out of the driver's side.

Chapter 11

"Speak of the devil," I muttered. "That's quite the role reversal," I commented when Mark emerged from the passenger side.

"I need your help." John wore his "at home" faded jeans and black T-shirt under a lightweight denim sports coat. Today he was rumpled, not pressed. His hair was tousled, like he hadn't bothered to comb it. His cheeks above his goatee weren't shaven. *He's tired. He's worried or exhausted?* I couldn't explain it but something was wrong about him.

"You fired me. I don't have to help you." I grabbed a rag and wiped my sweaty face. The fan moved torpid air, stirring the humidity. At least I didn't have my soldering torch going. That's when things got toasty hot.

"Adele is gone," John said flatly. His gaze bounced around my garage workshop, taking in the workbench, soldering tools, and oddments scattered around before coming back to me.

I turned to Mark. "Have you checked with Grant Pool?"

"Grant is gone, too." Mark joined John in the garage, peeking around the dense black curtain separating my workshop from the car side. "No one can find him."

"Well, shit," I said softly. "How long has she been gone?"

"I'm not sure." John paced to the far wall to glare at snow shovels and garden tools before coming back to glare at me. "She and I argued yesterday. She was upset I fired you."

"Yeah, well, so was I." I dropped the rag on my work stool and dug my hands into my pockets. "I got over it. I'm sure she got over it, too."

"That's not the point," he snapped. "I don't know if she ran away from home or if she was kidnapped."

"How am I supposed to help? I'm not psychic. I can't tell you why she's gone." His nasty temper was rubbing off on me.

Mark stepped between us. "Adele may need your help. Please. She's missing. That's what matters, isn't it?"

Damn it. He was right. If my suspicions were correct, she might be in trouble with Sabine or her minions. Of course, I was guessing. I had no idea what that *stakki* old bitch might be up to. "You didn't answer my question. How long has she been gone?"

"We think she left early. She told me last night she wanted to swim this morning. I saw her leave the house at daybreak. She never came back in." Mark glanced at John while he spoke.

"I was gone. I spent the night at the office." John looked away from me when he said it, his gaze on the St. John's book propped open on my workbench.

Office my foot, I thought. I'll bet he and Cat White were spending the night together. Well, not my business although I had to admit, I was disappointed in his taste in women.

I checked the time on my phone. "It's noon. She's been gone about five hours, right?"

"Yeah. We got an email from her." He handed me a piece of paper.

"How can you be sure it's from her?" I unfolded the paper, a computer printout with a date and timestamp on it from today.

John moved around Mark to stand directly in front of me. "I can't be. That's why I need your help."

Grandpapa: I'm with friends at a mashup I think you'd like. Everything's okay. Don't worry. I'll be home later. I gave Charlotte the presents like you asked.

"What's it mean, about the presents?" John tapped the paper impatiently. "What did she give you?"

"Come inside." I went through my other garage and into the house, not bothering to check if they were following. I didn't have to. John was treading my heels. We entered the mudroom then through the kitchen to the hallway and my den. Heathcliff took one look at the men following me and vanished, springing away into the spare bedroom where I'm sure Catherine was already hiding.

"Adele sent me something on the game she plays." I led the way to my desk. I logged in to the Gems game on my computer, the convoluted game map springing to life on my twenty-four-inch monitor. "She sent me a coffee cup, a life preserver, and a buggy whip," I explained, touching each object in my inventory chest.

"I have no idea what you're talking about." John rested his hands on the edge of my desk on my left so he could peer at the screen. I caught a scent of mingled soap and sweat.

I tapped the game on my touch-screen. One of the locations opened. "She plays this game and I joined it, too. Players can give each other gifts. I can't use the life preserver yet. I can't access the location where it can be used. I've only been playing this for a few days."

"Then why did she send it to you? She knows what level you're at, right?" Mark stared over my shoulder on the right. I was hemmed in on both sides by testosterone. For the first time in my life, I felt small.

I examined the email printout. The timestamp said it was sent an hour earlier, but that didn't mean anything. Some servers held email and sent it in batches, or an email could be delayed if a router connection went down. There were several reasons why the timestamp couldn't be believed. "Yeah, she can see the level I'm at when she sends a gift." I tapped a small avatar on the game board, drifting from spot to spot. "That's her. She's at an advanced level."

"What kind of game is it? Why does she play it?" John peered at the screen as though he could find the answers there.

"It's a standard hidden-object game. You have to find items at different locations. She has a map of the whole game in her room. Haven't you seen it?"

John shrugged. "I thought it was only scribbling or something."

I rolled my eyes. "She's got it figured out." I stared at the screen, ignoring his exasperated look. "The coffee cup," I said, thinking aloud. "I can use it at this location." I tapped open the location for the café. "If I use the coffee cup here, I'll get more energy and can play longer."

"I don't understand any of this." John straightened, crossing his arms and glaring at me. "Where is she? What does this game have to do with anything?"

"Where is the life preserver used?" Mark asked.

I tapped the Docks. It opened but the details were

grayed out because I wasn't at that level. "Why did she send me something I can't use?"

"What about the other one? The buggy whip." Mark stared at the screen, his face level with mine.

"It's earned when you complete level 8." I tapped open the location. "That's the street scene."

"None of this makes sense," John said. "Why did she bother sending you stuff? When did she send them?"

"I don't know when she sent them. I didn't log on to the game until an hour ago, just before you got here. She could have sent them any time and I wouldn't see them until I logged in. There's no timestamp on the gifts." I stared at the screen and the contents of my inventory box. Life preserver, buggy whip, and coffee cup. Why did she send me those specific items?

I re-read the email. "Wait a minute." *Grandpapa.* What was it Adele said? *Grandpa is my other grandfather.*

"Her email mentioned you," John said. "So she must have wanted me to contact you."

"Wait a minute," I repeated. John started to speak again but Mark raised his hand. John paced my small office, covering the distance in a few strides to come back and stand next to me.

"Damn it," I muttered softly. "Pool."

"What?" John looked like he might throttle me if I didn't talk fast enough.

I ignored him, focusing on the ideas rattling around in my brain. "I wonder if White is involved or if she was a patsy." I considered it. The woman was devious and vindictive, but would she put a child at risk? I remembered the calculating, cool expression she had when she saw Adele. Yeah, she would.

"What are you talking about?"

"Pool is from Jamaica." I sprang up from my chair, pushing past John to leave the room.

"No, he isn't. He grew up not far from here. Why do you think he's from Jamaica?" John trailed behind me, Mark following him.

I went back through the kitchen and into my bedroom at the back of the house, heading for the weapon safe in the drawer of my nightstand. "He spoke patois," I said while I pressed the fingerprint lock.

"Lots of people…" John's voice faded when I stared at him. He knew as well as I did that few non-Jamaicans spoke patois. "Maybe he heard it."

"Bullshit. When will you learn I know what I'm talking about?"

"When will you learn I don't like being bossed around?" John took a step toward me.

"When are either of you going to learn this is all about Adele?" Mark's icy voice made me jerk back in surprise.

Damn you, John Aire. How do you always bring out the anger in me? I sucked in a deep breath, pushing my anger to the background. "Pool used a particular expression I've only heard on the island. I completely blanked on it until I watched a movie." I shook my head. "It's a long story." I pulled out my knife, my handguns and ammo clips. "They needed to get rid of me. Pool knew I was tracking Adele's online access. I need to get on her laptop and her tablet. It will tell us more."

John eyed the weapons I held. "What do you think happened?"

I pivoted, eyeing my open closet door. We might get into a situation where I would need more options. I made a fast decision and dropped my guns and knife on the bed before unzipping my jeans. "I think someone posed as a teenager in the game and lured her out."

"What are you doing?" Mark asked when I shucked off my jeans.

"Changing clothes. Stay or go, I don't care." I didn't bother seeing their reaction. I dug out my black combat jeans from the dresser. The jeans were elastic-waisted and looser than my regular jeans. More importantly, there were interior pockets for weapons. I bent and slipped my knife into the hidden sheath near the side seam on my calf.

"What the—is that a Buck?" Mark sounded kind of strangled. I peered up at him while I adjusted the knife.

"Modified Buck Intrepid. I'm short. It's hard to find a fixed-blade knife with a good fit to my leg." I straightened and checked my Glock, verifying it was on safety and loaded. I slipped it into the holster I secured to my waist. "I think Grant Pool was waiting for her and took her somewhere. I think he and Cat White are working for Sabine Verrens."

I watched John absorb the information I was leveling at him, his eyes distant while he evaluated what I said. "I'm not sure about Cat," he said.

I checked and secured my second gun, a small Smith & Wesson, into the hidden interior front pocket. When the gun was angled properly, it appeared like a fold of fabric. "I'm not sure, either, but I think I'm right." I looked at Mark. "Do I need my other gun?"

His mouth opened, closed, then he said, "I think we're good."

"Okay, let's go to the house. I need to find where she sent those game gifts from. Did she send them earlier today from her computer or from someplace else?"

"What will that tell us?" John asked.

"It'll tell us if she's trying to send us a message because somebody is staring over her shoulder." I left the house through the garage, the two men behind me. They went to the Jag. I tapped in my security code to shut the garage door.

Mark opened the front passenger door for me. "You're taller." I pulled open the back door. "You take the front." I slid onto the black leather seat in the back. "Mrs. Fairfax stopped by this morning. She didn't mention Adele was gone."

Mark dropped into the passenger seat, barely getting the door closed before John backed up the car. "She didn't know. Adele hasn't been coming down for meals." He glanced at John. "We don't see much of her lately."

"Why did you hire me for one month?" I asked John, meeting his eyes in the rearview mirror. "Why did you specify a length of time?"

"I had reason to believe Sabine Verrens would act within the month," John said, returning his attention to the street and his driving.

"Double whammy," I said. "New moon and Adele just finished her period."

Mark shifted on his seat. "This is so freaking crazy. Why the hell does it matter if the kid is, you know. I don't get it."

"I told you before, you guys wouldn't understand. It's a woman thing. Not only is it a woman thing. It's an island thing. It's all tied to the earth and the earth mother. A central facet of it is a woman's fertility cycle. It's about fertility and life and birth." I regarded the perfectly normal twenty-first century town outside the car. "You need to think like Sabine thinks. She's attuned to those kinds of rhythms. She believes in the power of a woman's fertility. Sabine absolutely believes a combination of the moon phases and Adele's cycle will give her the power to bring back her daughter."

"I still say it's freaking crazy," Mark muttered.

"That's because you're a guy and you never worried about fertility," I shot back. "A woman is always aware of it. She's reminded of it every month." I wanted to laugh at the disbelieving look Mark and John exchanged. Men. They didn't get it.

I knew I was right, but I was missing something central, something critical to understanding what was happening. "Tell me about Sabine Verrens and her husband," I said to John. "Tell me about your daughter-in-law."

He glanced at me in the mirror. "What about her?"

"She was an only child, right? How old was her mother when Antoinette was born? How was she raised? Did she go away to school?" I let ideas and guesses take shape in my head.

"I don't know much about her," John said. "I think Sabine and her husband were married awhile before Antoinette was born."

"They were married twelve years," Mark said. "We did some research."

"We?" I asked. "As in the FBI or CIA or Homeland Security?"

"Uh-huh," Mark replied. "Sabine's husband, Antoine, was older than her, more than twenty years older. They got married when she was young, only eighteen. It was one of those dynastic marriages."

"Dynastic?"

"Two crime families merged their operations."

"Good heavens," I murmured. "Who knew that kind of thing went on in the world?"

"Anybody who's in law enforcement," Mark said. "From what we can piece together, he slept around. Like, a lot. Eventually she refused to have sex with him because she was sure he would give her a disease."

"So why did they stay married?"

"These are gangs. Think of the Godfather or the Mafia. Her family would never have approved a divorce. It suited her to be married to him. Power and prestige and all that. We think he had the fear of God put in him when he did get sick. Syphilis, which nowadays is curable. But I guess he remembered the stories from the old days when it was a hell of a lot worse than it is now."

"How do you know so much about the intimate details of their love lives?"

"Servants, doctors, pharmacists. If you know the right people to pay, you can get information."

"Isn't stuff like that supposed to be kept private?"

"This is the underworld we're talking about. There isn't honor among thieves, no matter what you might think. Antoine got infected, got cured, and he decided to be faithful to his wife from that day forward. They were married ten years before he got sick. Then he got the cure and two years later, she got pregnant. He was in his fifties by then."

"That might explain why they had only one child. Did he have other children by any of the women he slept with?"

"No and that's weird because he slept around so much."

I nodded, facts coalescing. "So their daughter was

the miracle child," I said softly. "I'll bet he became the doting father and nothing was too good for his little girl."

Mark glanced back at me. "Yeah, something like that. Antoinette was given anything she wanted. She was sent to the best schools, had parties at their mansion, a pony and riding lessons. She was treated like royalty."

I considered that. It would have been after my time on the island. I met Nick and left Jamaica before Antoinette was born. We returned to the island once a year to visit family. Nick probably had knowledge of the Verrens because of his connections with the constabulary, but I didn't know anything about them other than rumor.

"Antoinette met my son when they were both teenagers." John stared straight ahead, his hands tight on the steering wheel. We were driving west and the sun shone on his taut, harsh face. "I wanted them to wait to get married. But Antoinette got pregnant."

"Was it a big wedding? Did the Verrens put on a big show?" I asked, anxious to break the tense silence settling over the car.

"It was enormous. Very Catholic, very proper." John left the Interstate, driving into the suburbs leading to his home. "I heard rumors about her family. Her father was elderly. I think he had dementia, but the mother, Sabine, wouldn't let anything stand between her daughter and a society wedding. I tried to warn Edward, but he was in love. And she was pregnant." John sighed. "Sometimes history repeats itself."

I belatedly remembered it was his story, too. Falling in love with a beautiful woman from the island, getting pregnant, and getting married. "It didn't exactly repeat itself. Your son loved his wife."

John was silent for a long moment. "He did. I should've paid more attention to him. They tried to be independent of her family but Sabine insisted on being involved with Adele. Antoinette tried to get away from them. Edward said she had no idea how deeply involved in the drug trade her parents were."

"That's hard to believe," Mark said. "She must have known."

"She may not have," I said. "Jamaica has a strict social structure. If the Verrens kept their daughter segregated from other classes, she may not have been told about her family's business until she mingled with the other classes. You need to remember this was before social media and the Internet and global news outlets. Their child was tightly supervised and watched. It's possible she didn't know until she got away from them how terrible they were."

"Edward said the same thing," John said, his voice soft with memory. "He defended her. He said she was innocent. I think that's one reason they testified. Antoinette wanted to prove she wasn't tainted by her family."

"Prove to who?" I asked. "Her parents?"

John gazed at me in the mirror. "Or to me."

"But if she was kept separated from the family business, what good was her testimony? What kind of evidence could they give?"

"I think it wasn't evidence so much as it was locations and people," Mark said. "I read through their depositions. They talked about places they heard about and people Sabine and the old man associated with. I think the parents believed their daughter was still oblivious to their real profession, so they talked about things in front of her."

"And your son?" I asked John.

"I think Edward and Antoinette decided they had to act and they acted together. I wish they had talked to me first."

"But you and your son argued and weren't speaking." What a tangled web of circumstance. "Adele said their testimony didn't do any good. She said the Verrens weren't sent to prison." I looked at John but it was Mark who answered my implied question.

"They weren't, but it put a serious dent in their operations. The old man, Antoine, died shortly after the trial. Sabine faded from sight. We're pretty sure she kept a tight hand on the family business through intermediaries."

"Then Edward and the family were placed into the witness protection program. I never had contact with them except through anonymous email and short phone calls. I never saw them again."

"What about your wife? Bertti? Did she have contact with him?"

There was another tense silence. I realized the two men in the front seats had a connection in the past permeating their current life. "I've never told her this," John said. "But it may be because of her Edward and Antoinette were killed."

I blew out a long breath. I could envision what was coming. "Poor woman. Did she contact them? Try to see them?"

John glanced at Mark. I glimpsed the bleak expression on his face. "She wanted to meet her granddaughter. Bertti thought her disappearance was complete. She didn't think anyone was searching for her.

She convinced Edward to meet her, with Adele. It wasn't much of a meeting, only a brief chat at a coffee shop in Albuquerque for a few minutes. But two weeks later, Edward and Antoinette were dead."

"You can't blame Bertti," Mark said quietly. "We screwed up, too. We shouldn't have let Edward go, no matter what he told us. We should have known it wasn't just a simple trip out of town with Adele."

Now it made sense. Mark was part of the security detail who protected John's family, or else his organization was. Either way, he felt responsible. "And Adele was kept in custody until you could come up with a plan to finally capture Sabine once and for all," I finished. "By using her as bait."

Mark shifted in his seat. "We thought we had the bases covered."

John's house loomed ahead of us. "Think again," I said.

We entered the house through the garage, John leading the way. "What do you need?" he asked. "Her computer?"

"Her room. She has the map of the game there. It might tell us something." I walked past him to the staircase.

Mrs. Fairfax peeked from the kitchen. "Miss Rochester! It's good to see you again." Her gaze went from me to John and Mark. "Is there a problem?"

"Adele might be missing," I said. "Could you please make me a sandwich? I missed lunch and I think we're going to be busy."

"Of course. I'll put together something. Do you want me to call in the other guards?" she asked Mark.

"Yeah, let's get a couple more guys here. Bring in

Frank and Paul."

I headed for the stairs, John behind me. "Why didn't you tell me she was communicating with someone?" he asked.

"I got sidetracked. And I knew you'd go ballistic if I told you and you'd ground Adele for life or something." I reached the top step.

John pulled me to a stop. "You didn't tell me. It's my decision how to handle Adele."

"You don't *handle* a person. Not if you love them. But I was never sure if you loved her." I faced him, daring him to contradict me.

He was silent for a long second. "That's none of your business, is it? You don't work for me anymore."

I stepped closer to him, so I was chin-to-chest. "I care about Adele. So it's my business." I whirled away, striding to Adele's room.

"Why do you think Cat is involved in this?" John said behind me.

"She's friends with Grant Pool so that makes her suspicious to me. Maybe I'm jealous, too." I pushed open the double door to Adele's room and paused inside.

"Jealous about what?"

"The fact she's tall and young and beautiful." I glanced around the room. "Let's face it, she's one hell of a woman."

"So are you."

"Yeah, right. Where's her tablet? Did she take it with her?" My gaze skidded over the vanity table, her bedside table, and the desk. "There." I grabbed the tablet from the corner of her desk and turned to her computer. "She has it paired with this computer, so if she doesn't have a password, we're good." I switched on the monitor and the game appeared on the screen. "Whew. She stayed logged in."

I opened a new computer window and opened the network usage monitor. "Were you online this morning?" I asked John, checking the graph of usage.

"I got home around nine o'clock. I went online then." John stood in front of Adele's large monitor, staring at the screen. "I didn't know anyone could access usage data."

"If you know where to look, it's there." I pointed to a spike in the graph. "Adele was online early in the morning so she might have sent the gifts then." I went back to her game screen and found the "gift" interface. Players could send gifts every four hours. Adele had two hours to go until she could send another one. "That means she sent it two hours ago, when she wasn't home," I explained to John and Mark, who watched while I maneuvered my way around the game.

I opened the location on Adele's game I couldn't access. The docks. "Can you print that? Enlarge it?" John stepped closer to the monitor.

I took a screenshot and printed it, magnifying the image so it printed on a couple of pages, which emerged from her printer on a nearby stand. "This is the location where I'm supposed to use the life preserver," I said, putting the pages on Adele's desk.

"What's that?" John peered at the computer monitor. "There."

I froze the screen and stepped closer. "It's a shack. I suppose prizes are hidden inside. You have to enter the shack."

"Not the structure. The wires above it." His finger traced a line in the air over the image of the building.

"Those aren't wires. Those are ropes," Mark said.

"It looks like *West Side Story*," John said.

"What?"

"The mashup thing you showed me. When they were dancing in *West Side Story*. On a road with electric wires above them." He picked up the email I dropped on the desk. "The eastside warehouse district. The mashup." John thrust the email at me.

"The warehouses, by the river," I said. "But which one? Where?"

"What about the other gifts?" Mark stared at Adele's map of the game and the interconnecting lines that made it seem like some kind of crazy road atlas.

I opened another computer window and brought up an online map of our city. I zoomed in on the warehouse district. It was south of town, at the junction of two major highways, the river, and a nexus of railroad lines. Boats on the river could unload directly to a semi-truck or rail car. It was an efficient way to ship grain and livestock in this farm-centric part of the world.

Mrs. Fairfax entered the room with a tray holding a plate of sandwiches, several bottles of beer, a pitcher of iced tea, and a bag of potato chips. "I called the boys as you suggested," she told John. "They'll be here shortly. I wasn't sure what was needed so I made up a variety." She stepped back and regarded Adele's handiwork above the computer. "Now why does she have a map of Kingston Village on her wall?"

I took half a sandwich from the plate. "Kingston Village? Where?"

"What's Kingston Village?" Mark took the other half of the ham sandwich I was biting into.

I went to Adele's map, comparing it to the map of

the town on her computer screen. "It does look like Kingston," I said.

"Kingston Village is the name for part of the original settlement. Immigrants and working-class people lived there. They worked in the meat packing plants and the factories. I suppose it's our version of Shanty Town." Mrs. Fairfax stared at the map on the wall, her head tilted to one side. "If the café picture was moved closer to the stables, it would be the spitting image of the old Spanish Village part of town. That's where most of the Hispanic people lived and worked. My father worked in Kingston Village but we lived north of there, in Laurel Highland. I remember that part of town because I used to go there at lunchtime to see my father." She shook her head, frowning at the map. "No, it's not Kingston. I thought it might be because of the railroad and the river."

"I don't think that's a river. I think it's supposed to be a street," I said. "And that's not a railroad. I mean, it can't be. This is a kind of pre-industrial village, I think."

"It's a drawbridge," John said. "Those lines are ropes holding the drawbridge."

Mark sat at the desk, peering at the monitor while he ate. "Where could you use those other things she gave you?"

"In the café and the stables."

"What's that?" He zoomed in on the city map.

"It looks like a restaurant," John said. "That part of the warehouse district has cafes and stores. They're trying to gentrify it. A real estate developer put in lofts and condos. Most of the shipping moved further downstream when the town got so densely populated around the district."

"It used to be a mechanic's shop," Mrs. Fairfax said.

"And next door to it was a café."

"The buggy whip," Mark said. "It might have been a stable at one time."

"How would Adele know that? She couldn't know the history of Kingston Village."

"Oh, of course she did." Mrs. Fairfax went to the doorway. "I think I hear the boys coming in. I'll make sure they come up here and join you."

"Wait a minute," John said. "Why do you think Adele knows the history of Kingston Village?"

"Because she did a paper on it for school." Mrs. Fairfax gestured to the computer. "Or what passes for a school nowadays. She had to write about the history of her home. I saw her moping around one day in the library, going through some books. We got to talking and she said she might write about the American Indians, but everybody writes about them. I suggested Kingston Village. After all, it's where your father got his start," she said to John. "Working on the railroad there. You mentioned it to me."

"Kingston," I said. "It's the capital of Jamaica."

"I'll go get Frank and Paul." Mrs. Fairfax left the room, unaware of the stunned disbelief in her wake.

John tapped the city map on the wall monitor and it enlarged, showing a maze of short streets and alleys on the shore of the Des Moines River. "She's here."

Chapter 12

"Why did they let her send an email?" I asked.

"To reassure us," Mark said. "To make us think everything was okay."

"Keep in mind, Sabine has no idea what kind of relationship Adele has with me," John said. "To her, this might seem perfectly normal."

Frank and Paul came into the room. The four men moved to one side to talk. I took another sandwich half and sat at the computer, staring at the city map. I wasn't convinced the email was as simple as they made it sound. Or maybe I was giving Sabine Verrens more credit than she deserved.

I printed a close-up version of the city map then went to another online map site with a different view of the area. I'd visited the riverside once, long ago, when I was a student and went on a pub crawl with fellow classmates. I doubt if the bars we visited were still there, especially if that part of the world was becoming "gentrified."

John broke away from the other men to join me. "Do you want to eat?" I nudged the sandwich plate his way.

"I had breakfast." He stood next to me, arms crossed while he examined Adele's handiwork on the wall. "At the office."

"Hmm."

"What's that mean?" He shifted his attention to me.

"Nothing. None of my business how you spend your evenings. Or your mornings."

"Reticence is not your strongest trait, Charlotte. If you have a peeve, tell me."

I swallowed the bite of roast beef sandwich in my mouth, which gave me a chance to frame my reply. "Adele said you were spending time with Cat White. Do you think that's wise?"

"Adele is wrong. And I think you're wrong about Cat." He took a sandwich half from the tray.

"Did she suggest Adele be invited to her dinner party the other night?" I chose a bottle of beer and took a swallow.

"Yes, she did, but it proves nothing."

"Who chose the teenagers who were invited?"

Mark rejoined us, flanked by Paul and Frank. "It was White's party so I suppose she chose who attended. Right?" He looked at John.

"One of those kids is the kid who was in touch with Adele." Little bits of intuition fell into place. I remembered how Adele seemed when she talked to the one guy, a thin young man with curly dark hair. The kid who looked like the guy in the library. "What are the odds Cat White would invite somebody Adele is in contact with?"

"You don't have proof about that," John said.

"What more do you need? Just because you're sleeping with White it doesn't mean she's not in the pay of Sabine Verrens. In fact, it would make sense. How better to find out about Adele than to sleep with her grandfather?"

John tossed the sandwich he held onto the tray. "I'm not sleeping with Cat White."

"The only thing that's important now is Adele," Mark said. "I agree with Charlotte. I think White may be involved in this but that can't be our focus now. How do you want to handle this, John?"

"Should we contact the police?" I took another swallow of beer to wash away the bitter taste in my mouth. I saw the expression on John's face when he denied sleeping with White. He was lying. I was sure of it. I only hoped his inability to tell the truth wouldn't endanger anyone.

"We have no evidence," John said. "By the time we convince them something's wrong, Sabine could be out of the country."

"Is that her ultimate plan?"

"I don't know. I think so." John's hands, dangling at his sides, clenched and unclenched. "Bertti knows someone in the cult who tipped her off. They weren't sure what would happen once Sabine performed this ceremony."

"I read up on rituals. They're often performed at seasons of the year or other cyclical things." I turned to the computer. "What time is moon rise and moon set?" I found the Old Farmer's Almanac website and checked the times. "Moon rise was at six-thirty this morning. Moon set and sunset are about the same time tonight. They're a few minutes apart. Maybe that's when she'll finish the ceremony, whatever it is."

"It means we have five hours to come up with a plan and get into place. We need to decide on possible locations." Mark and the other guards moved away, Mark talking and pointing to the map displayed on the wall monitor.

"Why does Adele play this game?" John asked me.

"I don't understand."

"It's kind of fun," I said. "More fun than the match-three kind or the Warcraft ones. Those can get tedious real fast. You always burn through lives too soon."

His head swiveled and he regarded me with what I think was amazement. Or maybe befuddlement. I wasn't sure. "What? You play games like that?"

"Sure. Online games. Apps." I dug my phone out of my back pocket and flourished it. "When you're waiting in line at the bank or at the airport." I dropped the phone on the desk next to the mouse pad.

"Why?"

"Have you ever tried them?" I asked.

"Of course not. I have other things to do with my free time."

"Like make money and schmooze with rich people." I was stung by his condescending tone. "You should hit your knees and thank God Adele is playing games like this and not sexting or trolling porn sites."

"What?"

"Porn sites. It's a problem with kids, especially tweens, like Adele. They get hooked on these sites." I shook my head. "I read up on it. There's a real epidemic."

"Don't parents set limits or blocks or something to keep the kids off?"

"Kids have phones and tablets and computers. They have access to data everywhere. I'm sure there are parental blocks that can be set, but kids are smart. They can find a way around it. The best thing a parent can do is talk about it with the kids. Even talking might not be enough." I drank the last of my beer, belching softly. "Sorry. I know somebody whose kid got caught up with a porn addiction. It was terrible. The kid went into therapy and everything. He was only fourteen when it happened. He had trouble getting his head screwed on straight after that."

"What a world for kids today." John pointed at the screen. "Show me how it works. Play the game, would you?"

"Why?"

"I want to understand her."

Well, it was a start. I opened the café scene. "I have to find the objects listed at the bottom." I tapped items while I spoke.

"Hold on. You're going too fast."

"There's a timer, see?" I pointed to the top of the scene. "I have to get everything before the clock runs out." I did slow down, pointing to objects before I tapped them. "That's one part of the game," I said when I finished the locale. "There's also contests and other events." I opened my inventory box. "When I successfully finish a level, I get prizes. I can trade those in for bigger prizes."

"She spent money on this?" John asked. "On what?"

"Buying things to help her win contests or get through a locale. I have a friend who gambles online. She plays slot games. She spends thirty dollars a month, no more, no less, just like she was at a casino to gamble."

John shook his head. "I don't understand it."

"What do you do to relax? To unwind?" I opened another locale and began playing. "Don't you ever go to a bar, kick back with friends, watch football? Read a good book or maybe play chess or backgammon or something like that?" I peered closer at the locale. "Damn. Where's the unicorn?"

John pointed at the lower left of the screen. "Behind the donkey. And why is there a unicorn and a donkey sitting on top of a wagon? It makes no sense. And look at that. There's a candle on the dresser. That pincushion might catch fire."

"Thanks. I need that pincushion."

"That dog doesn't look well. We should call the Humane Society."

I looked over my shoulder at him. He was struggling not to smile. When he saw me his expression became one of innocent surprise. "What? I'm just trying to make sense of this."

"It doesn't have to make sense. It's a game."

"Kind of like Sabine doesn't have to make sense because she's a woman."

"Hey. Don't try to belittle something you don't understand." I finished the round and put the tablet on the desk. "What's our next move?"

"Our next move is to find Adele. Yours is to go home."

"Bullshit. I'm going with you." I pushed away from the desk. John put a hand on my shoulder, keeping me in my seat. "Hey. You might need me to infiltrate or something."

"There's no way any of us can infiltrate," Mark said from across the room. "Grant Pool knows us. If he's involved, he'll be on the lookout. I sent Frank back to home base to round up some other guys. They'll go in and do recon for us. For now, we wait."

John's hand tightened on my shoulder. "Let the professionals handle this."

I peered up at him. "That doesn't sound like you."

"What do you mean?"

"You think you are a professional." I wiggled away from him and stood. "I don't think we have time. If Verrens is staging a ceremony, there'll be preparation. She might be drugging Adele or taking her blood or doing some other kind of thing that could harm Adele as much as any ritual. We need to go now."

"There's no way we can sneak up on them," Mark said.

"Fine. We don't sneak. We walk in on them. Better yet, we let them capture us. Pool hates me. He'll be happy to capture me. Sabine knows John, so ditto for him. John and I go in. We could be bugged and report back what we see."

"You're not making any sense. You can't do an operation like that. It's too dangerous. You've never—" Mark stopped talking when he saw my disbelief. "Okay, John can't do that kind of op. He hasn't been trained for it."

"He's a fast learner. He'll figure it out." I paced to the doorway and back. "I have a bad feeling about this. I don't think we have time to waste." My phone, sitting on the desk, blared my personalized ringtone, Elton John's *The Bitch is Back.* I glanced at the display. "I don't know that number."

"I'll bet your ringtone gets attention in the middle of a store." John picked up my phone. "Wait a minute. That's Adele's number."

"What?" I took the phone from him, sinking back into the chair.

"Put it on speaker," Mark said.

I fumbled with the controls and managed to get the speaker on. "Adele, where are you? Are you okay?"

"Ah, Miss Rochester, is it?" The voice was female,

husky with a faint lilt. "Good. I was hoping you would answer."

"Sabine," John whispered. "It's her."

"John Aire. Are you there, too? Even better." The woman laughed softly. "I need to talk to you as well. Two birds and one stone. Good. I need you both to help me."

"Why should we help you?" I countered.

"Because if you don't, you'll never see Adele again, John. I can call you John, can't I? After all, we're related. Somewhat." She chuckled then her voice hardened. "You both must join us. Leave your guards behind. Do not call the police. We'll be watching and if they follow, they'll be removed. You won't like what we do to you and your woman."

I opened my mouth to speak but John put his hand on my shoulder again. "What guarantee do we have that Adele is not harmed?"

"I'll give you the one guarantee that you know matters. I won't hurt her because I need her."

"Why do you want us?" John asked.

"That is not for you to know now. Maybe it's to give Adele comfort. Maybe something else. You must join us. There must be no police, no law. Things are getting ready there but I am missing a person. One of my participants has not arrived. I must have a replacement. Your woman will do fine."

"Now wait a damn minute," I said. "I am not—" John's hand tightened painfully on my previously injured left shoulder. "Ow."

"Where and when?" John asked.

"I'll send you a text. Be ready. *Likkle more.*" The line went silent.

"Yeah, right," I grumbled. "See you later. What the hell is she up to?"

"She's apparently getting things in place for whatever it is she's doing." Mark took my phone. "I'll see if I can get a trackback on this."

"You'll get a cell phone tower location," I said. "All they have to do is move around and it'll be no good."

"How do you know about trackbacks and cell towers?" Mark handed me the phone.

"I've had to do stuff for people before." I decided vagueness was best since I wasn't sure which government agency he worked for. "I suppose you'll want us to wear a wire."

"Yeah."

John's gaze shot from me to Mark. "Don't tell me," he said. "You've done this before."

"Like I said, this isn't my—"

"First rodeo," John finished for me. "I want you to tell me exactly what kind of security work you've done."

"Sure. Sometime." I turned to Mark. "They'll check us for a wire. Maybe have us strip. How do we do this?"

Mark touched the side of my head. "Good thing you have thick hair. I have something that'll work. It might be trickier for John."

"Why does she want us there?" John asked. "I don't get it."

"And what did she mean about a participant of hers going missing?" I tapped the desk impatiently. "A friend mentioned to me that Sabine Verrens was spotted in Miami a few weeks back. What if somebody with her was detained?"

"A friend?" Mark asked. "Like who?"

I waved a hand. "I know a guy who knows a guy.

Maybe we need to check any people coming from the island and see what turns up."

"We've been tracking that, but I'll double check. And we need blueprints for the buildings in the area. We can't be sure which one they're in." Mark pulled a cell phone from his pocket and moved to the other side of the room, gesturing to Frank and Paul to join him. They soon left, leaving Mark focused on his phone call.

"It'll be someplace where blood won't matter," I said. "Someplace easy to clean up."

"Good Lord, how can you talk like that? It might be Adele's blood." John stared at the game map. "I didn't think anyone could get at her if we were in place. I shouldn't have been gone. I should have stuck close to Adele."

I stood next to him, eyeing Adele's handiwork. "I should have investigated the kid she was chatting with online but I got too busy and it slipped past me. You should have told me earlier Sabine was planning something."

"I wasn't sure I could trust you."

"And I wasn't sure I could trust you. There you are. It doesn't do any good to dwell on it. It happened." I rocked back and forth on my heels, anxious to move. "They'll keep her alive until tonight. I'm sure of it, especially after talking to Sabine."

"What do you mean?"

"They're still getting things in place. That's what it sounded like."

"Come on," Mark said from across the room. "Let's get set up."

I took my phone and trailed behind him and John. We went along the balcony past the guest room I'd used and the library. Mark went into the guard's lounge and crossed the room to the wall unit holding the TV. He opened one cabinet door. I saw rifles and what looked like a box of grenades.

"What were you preparing for, the anti-Christ?" I peered around him at the armament. I counted two rifles, three handguns, a rack holding three knives and boxes of ammo.

"We weren't sure what to be prepared for." Mark took a box from a shelf to the table in the middle of the room. I lingered at the bookcase, eyeing the weapons cache.

"Put that knife down and get over here," Mark said.

I hastily replaced the USMC KA-Bar utility knife and joined him and John. "I just wanted to look at it. I haven't handled one of those in years."

John rolled his eyes. "What kind of training did you have?"

"Probably like what Mrs. Fairfax had." I smiled at his startled expression. "You know how us women love to gossip."

Mark handed me a flesh-colored circular plastic disc. "This is an in-ear communicator," he said. "Range is about fifty yards. It doesn't require line of sight. Anything you say will come across the wire and we can communicate with you. We won't be able to hear what others in the area say, though, so you'll need to repeat information."

"That's tricky." I fitted the gadget to my left ear, looping the thread-thin band around the upper part of my ear, pushing the flat disc into place. "I can't repeat everything they say without making them suspicious."

"Just repeat pertinent details. We'll try to get close

enough to deploy other devices. There's a good chance we can get into the basement or roof and be nearby."

"What about him?" I jerked a thumb over my shoulder at John.

"We'll try the standard mobile phone communicator," Mark said. "They'll find it. That will hopefully divert attention from you."

"Makes sense," I agreed.

"What are you talking about?" John looked at each of us in turn.

"They'll set you up with a Bluetooth in-ear communicator," I explained. "It won't be obvious but it won't be invisible. It's tied to your phone, which will send a signal to Mark and the others. Verrens' guards will find it and disable it. Maybe they won't find the one I'm wearing." I touched my left ear, hidden under my curly hair. "What about weapons?" I asked Mark. "They'll confiscate ours. At least, they'll confiscate the ones they can find."

"Yeah, I know. That's a worry."

"If we can figure where they are or where they're going, maybe we can get something in place." I wandered to the bookcase.

"Maybe they're already there," Mark said.

"No, you heard what she said. She said things are almost ready there. She didn't say ready *here*. It means they're going to a location. They aren't there yet." I stared at the rifles in the case, my brain churning. "Adele mentioned the mashup in her email. *West Side Story*. What if they mentioned where they were going and she overheard?"

John stood beside me. "Kingston Village. She knew the history of it. She probably also studied how it looks like today."

I met his stunned gaze with one of my own. "Come on." I dashed from the room, heading for Adele's bedroom and her map.

"The cup, the life preserver, and the whip," I said. "They're connected."

"How?" He was directly behind me, keeping pace.

"She knows this game inside and out." I waited until we reached Adele's room and I could point to the map. "You need the cup to get into the café where you can get the whip." I traced the line on Adele's game map between the items while I spoke. "You need the whip to make the key for the stable where you can get the life preserver for the docks." I tapped the image on Adele's wall. "The docks. The building will be on the river."

"Are you sure?" Mark peered over me at the wall.

"As sure as I can be." I studied the city map still on the computer screen. "There's a three block long stretch of buildings on the river. What's in those buildings?"

"Hold on." John wheeled and ran out of the room.

"Where's he going?" Mark asked.

"I have no idea." I sank into Adele's chair and swiveled it to peer up at him. "What are our odds for this op?"

"I don't know. It bothers me. We can't control the location. Who knows what kind of traps they might set? Will she kill the kid? Drain her blood? Drug her and take her back?" Mark shook his head. "There's too many variables we don't control."

"I don't think she'll kill Adele." I stared up at the game map. "The whole purpose of this is to bring her daughter, Antoinette, back to life."

"And that's freaking crazy," Mark muttered.

"I keep telling you guys. You don't get it. This is black magic. Sabine totally believes she can do this. She believes she has the support of her gods. She believes they'll do anything to keep her safe. What I'm not totally clear about is why." I got up and paced, going from the bedroom doorway back to the map. "What's motivating her? If she gets her daughter back, what does she hope to gain? Why is she doing this?"

"She's crazy. She doesn't have to have a reason."

He was right but he was wrong, too. Sabine took a huge risk to come here, kidnap her granddaughter, and do whatever it was she planned to do. What did she hope to gain from it?

Mrs. Fairfax came into the room. "Will you be needing anything else from me?" She set a plate of cookies on the tray she brought earlier.

"I don't think so," I said.

"Then I'll stay out of the way until I'm needed."

"That's wise. We're not quite sure what's going on yet."

"You let me know if you need backup. And unless I hear otherwise, I'll plan on dinner tonight with you, Mr. Aire, and Adele. Let's see, Adele is partial to my chicken and noodle casserole." She nodded emphatically. "That's the thing. A nice meal to welcome her home."

"I don't know what time we'll get back." I wasn't sure how to address such optimism.

"Not to worry. I'll handle it." She left the room, passing John when he entered with a large expansion folder under one arm.

"What's that?" I asked when he cleared off space on the desk.

"I got this from an investment group who wanted me

to buy into the development they're doing in the district." John undid the bungee band holding the portfolio closed and glossy brochures and documents fell out.

"This is residential stuff," I said, putting several of the booklets aside. "Where's the commercial stuff?"

"Here." John unfolded a big piece of paper.

I took the tray of food and moved it to the bed while John spread out a stylized map on the desk. It was like a regular road map but with callouts of photos of buildings, street scenes, and landscape. "What's that?"

"It's the architect's rendering of what the district will be like." John compared Adele's map, the town map and the one on the desk.

"There," Mark said, tapping the glossy marketing map. "The whole area along the river isn't slated to open until next year."

John pulled a glossy page from one of the brochures with pockets. "If this is still correct, it's not even under construction yet. They're clearing out the old buildings now."

"Perfect place to hold somebody hostage." I pointed to a spot on the map. "What's that?"

"One of those blocks along the river is for retail. There'll be clothing stores, a furniture store, and small shops," John said, skimming through the brochure. "The middle block will be condos. The third block is restaurants and nightclubs and a hotel. The hotel and one of the nightclubs is open now."

"That's it," I said. "The groundwork has been done for them. It will be somewhere in there, where there's new construction taking place."

Mark was already on his phone. "We have blueprints for those buildings. I'll see if we can get in and maybe set up weapons drops or comm units."

"Your guys need to sneak in. That's hard to do if it's all empty around there." I stared at the brochure. "Email me the blueprints. We need to check egress and access points."

He nodded and continued talking into the phone, moving away from us. I turned back to the computer. That's when I noticed John staring at me. "What?"

"You really do understand all this tactical stuff, don't you?"

"I was trained to think about it." I took a cookie. "It's like you're trained to think about profit and loss. I think about exits and windows and how best to ambush somebody. It's a way of thinking, that's all."

"It's foreign to me."

"Dinner parties are foreign to me. I managed. You'll manage, too." I munched the cookie. "There must be something else we can do. I wish we could get more intel on what's in the area. Why couldn't there be a festival or a celebrity sighting or something giving us eyes on?"

"What do you mean?"

"You can pick up a lot of detail about a location if you can get cameras in place. I remember once when I was helping a woman whose grandson was suspected of embezzling from her. We needed to know if he had connections to a group of people in town. They had offices in one of the buildings on the Plaza. You know it, the shopping area downtown? I went in as a tourist with another guy. We wandered around and snapped pictures during the big Christmas celebration. We found a side entrance he was using. Got pictures to prove it." I glared at the computer monitor. "Pity we don't have a Christmas festival going on."

"No, but we have something else." John went to Mark, who was still on his phone.

"What do we have?" I asked, following him.

"We have you. And me." He gestured to Mark. "We need to talk."

"Hold on." Mark pulled the phone away from his ear. "What?"

"Send the media a tip that Charlotte and I are having a clandestine rendezvous at the hotel."

"We can't do that," Mark said. "Verrens would know we're setting up a diversion."

"Sabine doesn't know we know where she is," John interrupted. "She thinks we're in the dark about Adele and where she's being held."

"And she doesn't know where we were when she called me. For all she knows, John and I were in a hotel room somewhere. If we play it right, we could be accidentally discovered leaving our love nest." I shot John a cautionary look. "This is acting. Just to be clear."

"Absolutely. It will give us a chance to check the area. We can use any news footage we get to verify details. Let's use the media to our advantage."

"I'll call Burns. He has people working there. He can get us in." I picked up my phone to call but thought better of it. What if Sabine tried to get in touch? I went to the landline phone on Adele's vanity table and dialed Burns' number.

Twenty minutes later John and I were in the back of the big sedan, Paul driving us. "Burns said to come to the side entrance, on Nineteenth Street," I told Paul. "Someone will meet us there. If I knew I'd be playing a femme fatale role today, I would have dressed more appropriately." I tugged on my shirt.

"We don't have to be caught in a compromising position," John said. "Being together will be enough." His face was harsh in the bright light of afternoon. "What is she doing to Adele? What's happening? It feels like this is taking so long."

I put my hand over his on the seat next to me. "She'll be safe," I said with as much confidence as I could muster. "Sabine Verrens has a specific plan in mind. She needs to keep Adele safe to make it work."

John wrapped his fingers around mine. "Thank you. For everything."

"Like I said. She's a good kid. She doesn't deserve to have this happen to her."

"What about me? Do I deserve it?"

I couldn't avoid the accusatory expression in his eyes. I didn't flinch away this time. "I'm not sure if you love Adele or not. I'm not sure if you care about her because of obligation or because of affection. But do you deserve this?" I shook my head. "No one deserves to be manipulated."

"The way I manipulated you?" His hand tightened on mine.

"Yes."

"Then why are you helping me?"

"I'm not helping you. I'm helping Adele."

John released my hand, shifting his gaze to his window. "Good to know."

Yeah, I thought glumly. Good to know.

Chapter 13

"Burns said to use the service elevator to the fourteenth floor." I followed John into the side door of the hotel, held open for us by a young man in a business suit. Paul followed behind us, his right hand pressed to his ear while he communicated with Mark through his Bluetooth comm unit.

"This way." The man hurried along a dark hall, claustrophobically narrow. "This will take us to the private kitchen staging area for the penthouse floor and the secure elevator." He stopped in front of a large wooden panel, which opened to reveal a gleaming elevator interior, far nicer than any service elevator I'd ever seen. "After you." He gestured us inside.

I went in and the men followed me. The man tapped numbers on a gleaming metal keypad. The doors closed and the elevator rose, so silent I could hear the hum of the motor. "This is pretty fancy for a service elevator."

"Only the best. The penthouses rent for a thousand dollars a night. We try to make sure the amenities are up to standard."

"Holy crap," I muttered. "Does it come with dancing girls and champagne?"

"Champagne, yes." He smiled briefly. "Girls, no."

Yeah, right. I'll bet if somebody requested a girl, something could be managed. I glanced at John, who stared fixedly at the doors. He'd avoided looking at me since our talk in the car. It might be tough to act the part of romantic lovers if this continued.

Well, it didn't matter. We just had to be seen together. "How's it going?" I asked Paul. "Are they in place?"

"Getting there," he said. "We need to stall for about five minutes."

"It won't be a problem," the young man said. "You can use Penthouse B. It has excellent views. You can wait there for your signal." He watched John when he spoke, obviously recognizing the influence standing next to him.

"Thanks," I said when John didn't answer. "This is a big help."

"Burns didn't explain much." The guy shot a questioning look at John, then Paul, before settling on me. "Only that you needed to use one of the penthouses for an hour or two."

"We'll pay for it," John said. "That's not a problem."

"Oh, no, no, I didn't mean that. It's just, well, it's an unusual request. Of course, we often get unusual requests. We're one of the premier hotels in the area, the finest hotel between Omaha and Chicago. We can offer any kind of service to our guests and..."

I tuned out his marketing babble, checking my phone display in case a call came in and I missed it. Nothing. It was more than an hour since Sabine called us. What were they doing? What if we were wrong? What if they weren't in this area?

What was Adele going through? I visualized her face, so young and hopeful, so naïve. Dear God, what if they were doing something to her to rob her of her childhood, her hope? My hands trembled when I jammed the phone into my pocket. If Sabine Verrens injured Adele in any way, shape or form, I would rip out the old woman's heart with my own two hands.

The elevator dinged. The hotel man led the way, moving past me to a short hallway. We went a few steps and emerged into a beautifully decorated foyer with three doors opposite an elaborately carved wooden panel.

"That's the lobby elevator," the young man said. "It uses a key code." He handed a slip of paper to Paul. "This is Penthouse B. I hope it will meet your requirements." He swiped a key card against a lock on the middle door and opened it for us.

"Holy crap." I walked into a suite as big as my entire house. It was done in a modern style but it wasn't angular and cold. Ahead of me was an expanse of living room with a wall of windows. To the right and left were doorways, presumably to bedrooms. Behind me on my left was a bar area, an island of wood and glass the size of my living room back home.

"Please help yourself to anything in the bar." The hotel guy gestured. "Or anything." He handed John the key card and went with Paul back to the door, their voices low.

"I've never seen anything like this," I went to the window. The city was in the distance like pieces of a Monopoly game in front of me.

John glanced around. "It's about time this town had a good hotel." He went to the door on the right and disappeared inside. I considered following him but instead I went closer to the windows.

"Yikes." I leaned cautiously on the pane, which was cantilevered over the street. I peered downward.

Everything appeared quiet, with no bustle or activity.

"You want anything?" Paul asked behind me.

I tore my gaze away from the view. "No, thanks." I went to the doorway on the left.

"Don't go far. We'll be on tap in a few minutes."

"I don't think that'll be a problem." I opened the door and entered a luxurious bedroom. A massive king-sized bed was against the wall on my left. The windows were angled so I could see a different view of the skyline. It was silent in the room, my footsteps muffled by dense carpeting and no hum of air conditioning, no sound from outside. I crossed the room to the attached bathroom. I decided John was paying for it so I may as well use it. Besides, it wouldn't do to need a bathroom break in the middle of a rescue attempt.

I laughed when I saw the controls next to the toilet. Apparently, I could adjust the temperature of the seat, the height of the seat and the type of air freshener I desired. I pressed a few buttons at random before doing my business.

I regarded myself in the mirror while I washed my hands. My black eye and bruising were faded considerably but since I didn't wear makeup, it was still noticeable. I ran cold water through my hair, making it fluff up. I pulled it forward to at least disguise some of my imperfections. Good Lord, who were we kidding? Why would anyone believe John Aire was involved in a steamy relationship with me?

I shook my head and tossed the plush towel on the marble countertop. It didn't matter what I thought. If we gave the media their field day, we might be able to get the information we needed. That's what mattered.

I left the bathroom and ran straight into John, who

was standing outside the door, waiting for me. "Are you ready for this?" He gestured to the window.

I peered at the street. A crowd was gathering on the sidewalk outside the building. The parking along both sides of the street was full. "Who's there?"

"Most of the local TV stations and newspapers, plus most of Mark's security people. They're mingled in the crowd. We need to walk to the next block. The crowd will follow us and the security people can break away and hopefully get in place. If we're lucky, they'll get into the buildings. If they aren't, we might still get details about the layout."

"It's a long shot," I said.

"It's the only shot we have." John moved to stand next to me. "You blame me for this, don't you?"

"That's irrelevant. The only thing that's important is to get Adele back, safe and sound."

"But what about afterwards? You don't think she should stay with me, do you?"

"Where would she go? You're all she has in the world. She's had enough disruptions in her life. She doesn't need a foster home or something like that." I edged away from him, putting distance between us.

"It might be better for her," he muttered.

"Believe me, it isn't. When my parents died, I was thrown in the foster care system. I was only in it for three years, but it was three years of hell. If you don't want her around you, find her a good school where she can be safe and nurtured." I headed for the door. "It's the least you can do for her parents."

I left the bedroom and went into the living room part of the suite. Paul was positioned near the door, not quite blocking it but creating a formidable barrier, nonetheless. I went to the bar area and rooted around, finding soft drinks and assorted booze in a fridge under the polished wooden countertop.

"What time is it?" I asked Paul. I poured a ginger ale into an elaborately cut crystal glass and took a swallow.

He glanced at his watch. "After three."

"What's she waiting for?" I muttered. "What's the delay?" I paced to the window and back, drink in hand.

Paul looked at the bedroom door. "Cut him some slack," he said in a low voice. "It's been a rough few days. He and Adele argued the night you left and they've barely talked to each other. Last night she lit into him and they had a big blow-up. I think he feels bad Adele is taking things so hard."

"It sounds like he's not around enough to really know how she's feeling." I returned to the bar and put down my glass. It was that or throw it at something. With my luck, I'd be charged a hundred bucks for breaking the glassware.

"He's been working overtime, staying at the office."

"Yeah, right." I went to the window, which had a view to the river. If it wasn't for the other wing of the building, I could see downtown from here. As it was, I caught a glimpse of the subdivision and the area beyond, where John's house sat.

"He's not with Cat White, if that's what you're thinking. I've driven him to the office and stayed there while he's there. She's not with him."

"It doesn't matter if she is, does it? He's not paying attention to Adele. That's what matters."

"Not everybody is good with kids the way you are." Paul crossed his arms, looking like a grumpy bear. "You're not helping."

"It's not my job, remember? I don't have to help him."

He shook his head. "Come on, grow up. Don't take it out on John because you can't get what you want."

I stalked over to him. "And what is that?"

"Him."

I stopped in my tracks. "What?"

He shrugged, massive shoulders lifting his sports coat. "You want to be with him but you think you don't fit in. It's bullshit, but there you are."

"Since when did you become a romance counselor?" I confronted Paul, my hands knotted on my hips.

"Since I saw you two together."

"It's time," John said behind me.

I whirled. "Now?" My face was, I'm sure, red. Did he overhear what Paul said? I dismissed my worry. Who cares if he heard? It was bullshit anyway.

"Mark called." John touched the Bluetooth receiver in his ear. "They're in place."

"Okay." I tried to move past Paul, but he shifted so I couldn't get by. "Now what?"

Paul stared over my head to John, who went to the bar. He poured a glass of water from the crystal tumbler, took a few swallows then put the glass down. It was like watching a robot. His movements were random, jerky, like he didn't have control.

I realized he was nervous, maybe as nervous as I was. The knowledge made me relax. I shifted my shoulders, tensed muscles unknotting. "Let's do it," I said.

Paul's lips quivered. "You really don't know you're small, do you?"

I jabbed him in the arm. "Sure I am. Small and

mighty. Come on." I inched past him and opened the door. "What's the game plan?"

"We get to the lobby and are swamped by reporters," John replied from behind me. "We end up getting diverted down the street. Mark has guys in place in the crowd. They'll fan out and see what they can find. If we're lucky, they can get into those empty construction sites."

"And get cameras and weapons in place," Paul added.

I started to speak but John cut me off. "I know. It's a long shot."

We went to the wood paneled elevator door. It opened as soon as Paul touched the call button. "When we get to the lower foyer, go right," he told John after typing in the code on the wall panel.

The elevator began a smooth glide downward. The only buttons on the panel were "P" and "L". What a life. No reason to be bothered with anyone between your world and the outside world. Your limo would meet you outside and you could be swept away from the hoi polloi. No need to be reminded anyone else existed. "The rich are different than you and I," I said under my breath.

"They have more money," John said. When I turned to him he said, "I read books, too. The rich really aren't different from anyone else."

"Says the man who's a billionaire. It's been a long time since you were anyone else."

Paul, standing behind us, cleared his throat. I saw his reproachful expression. "Give me a break," I muttered.

"I have," John said. "Don't you think it's time you gave me one?"

I transferred my glare to him. "What's that mean?"

"We need to make it seem at least plausible." John pulled me to him.

I pulled back enough so I could look up into his face. "What kind of plausible?"

"We need to give them something to talk about." He put his arms around me. "Like this." His lips came down on mine.

I tried to get away but his arms were around me tightly. He was hard and flat panes of flesh, pressing into me. His kiss was firm and explorative. I tried to resist but it was years since I fell into a wave of lust as powerful as this. His arms lifted me, holding me to him so I dangled like a doll in his grip. I put my arms around his neck and clung to him, a hot feeling of wanting making me breathless and bewildered.

I didn't care. I was safe, secure, and completely his. And he was mine. He wasn't holding back. This wasn't about control or power or anything like that. He was offering himself to me, vulnerable and open. I sensed it in his kiss, in the way his hands caressed me. This had nothing to do with dominance. It was surrender on his part.

We pulled apart, breathless. "You feel it, don't you?" he whispered. "You know it's real, Charlotte. Don't deny it." He kept his hands on the sides of my head, pinning me in place so I had to stare into his eyes.

"Don't deny what?" I wanted him to kiss me again. I wanted him to hold me and take me and push me against the wall. I wanted to wrap my legs around him and pull him to me.

The elevator door opened and lights exploded. I reeled back when two men lunged at me, cameras in their hands.

"Let us through," John shouted, pushing through the crowd of people taking our picture.

Paul pulled us back. He led the way, plowing a path for us against the herd of photographers, reporters, and news cameras. "Coming through," he yelled, jamming an elbow at a person with a cell phone aimed at me.

I wrapped my hands around John's arm. He dragged me with him when the crowd surrounded us. It was like being caught by a moving, flowing sea that pushed us with every step. We made our way across the foyer to the lobby, the people ebbing and flowing with us.

"Miss Rochester, how long have you and—"

"Mr. Aire, can you tell us—"

"John, why are you and—"

"When did you and Mr. Aire—"

"Charlotte, do you know that—"

"Does this have anything to do with—"

"What about Catherine White? We thought—"

Questions peppered me from all sides. John held on to my left hand, steering me forward. I kept my other hand up, shielding my face from the cameras and the people. We entered the main lobby. Even more people were there, some of them standing on chairs. Hotel personnel were running around, making ineffectual attempts to control the crowd. It was a scene from a Hollywood premier with paparazzi everywhere around us.

Paul and John pushed ahead of me, Paul on my right and John on my left. It was hard to keep pace with them when they broke through the press of bodies surrounding us. I stumbled once on the thick area rug. John tugged me back onto my feet.

"Where's the car?" John shouted.

"It's supposed to be here." Paul sounded appropriately worried and angry. I would have been convinced if I didn't know it was an act. "I'll go find it." Paul headed for the front doors, disappearing into the tide of people who blocked the entrance.

John kept his arm around my shoulders, steering me to a side door and away from the enormous revolving door at the entrance. I'm sure he was thinking what I was thinking. If we tried that door we'd be trapped inside.

Someone grabbed my arm and yanked hard. I spun, pulled away from John when we got outside. For an instant I was alone, twisted by people who shouted questions at me. Then John pushed people off me and swept me up against his chest. I wrapped my arms around his neck and pressed my face against his collarbone, his goatee scratchy against my face. People still shouted around us while I clung to him, questions coming at us from every direction. John pushed his way outside, ignoring everyone.

"I think we did it," I whispered, looking up into his face.

"What?"

"We gave 'em something to talk about."

One corner of his mouth quirked up. "Our car— where is it?" he shouted.

I hazarded a glance. Sunlight streamed into the area, momentarily blinding me. People milled around us, many thrusting cameras in my face or trying to angle for a shot at John's face. I checked over John's shoulder. "There," I said into his ear without the Bluetooth. "To the right."

John broke through the crowd and almost ran down

the block. People surged around us. I glimpsed Frank and Charlie and two of the other guards among them. They dashed ahead of us to the next block where television cameras were set up, capturing video of us running away. The people following us raced ahead. The crowd was suddenly in front of us. It was the perfect distraction for Frank and the others. I saw Charlie darting into an alleyway before someone jumped in front of John, forcing him to stop, making me lose sight of our security detail.

"Miss Rochester, is it true you're governess to Mr. Aire's granddaughter? What does she think of your romance with her grandfather?" A microphone was thrust into my face, knocking against my bruised forehead.

I was mostly recovered from last Monday's run-in with a photographer, but it surprised me enough to make me yelp. "Ow!" I yelled. "Stop it! That hurts!"

John stopped in his tracks. The crowd flowed past us then came back. He kept me firmly against his side with his left arm around my shoulder. I held my face pressed against his chest, glaring balefully at the people who pressed forward avidly. "Charlotte Rochester and I are friends. I do not appreciate having our relationship dissected for the local news."

"But you are news, Mr. Aire. You're one of the most reclusive citizens in this area and people are interested in what you are—"

I shook free of John, staring up into the face of the startled young blonde reporter who was speaking so earnestly. "Listen. You people need to get a life and report on real news. There are true injustices in this country, in this city, in this state. People are harassed because of their religion or the color of their skin. Our idiot elected representatives are overtaxing us so they can line their own pockets. Our environment is in the toilet. Animals are being slaughtered so people can be big game hunters. You should be reporting about—"

John pulled me back and clamped his arm around my shoulder. "You can see why I care so deeply for Charlotte. She's passionate about so many things." His hand tightened painfully. "And I do agree with her. I'm sure you can find many other things to report about."

"Can't you answer a few questions, Mr. Aire? You've been so reticent to speak to the press since your trial." The pretty reporter smiled sweetly at him. I'd seen her on the local nightly news, where she worked her way up from morning news to evening news in a remarkably short time.

I slipped my arm around John's waist under his sports coat, pinching him in the midsection. He let up the pressure on my shoulder. "I'm sure John would be glad to answer a few questions, but we won't discuss our relationship at all." I swept my gaze around the onlookers, giving me the opportunity to check the whereabouts of our guards. None were in sight, but I was so short I couldn't see well through the crowd.

The reporters seemed at a loss for words, as though my permission struck them dumb. Then several people shouted questions at once. John pointed to a man in the back and the man stepped forward to speak.

"We thought you and Catherine White, of Ingram Industries, were involved. Is that relationship now over?"

"Catherine and I remain business associates and good friends. We have never been romantically involved." John's hand opened and closed on my shoulder.

I spied Frank in the distance, emerging from a building half a block away. The crowd moved and I lost sight of him. When people shifted again I saw him ducking into another building. John was saying something about his company and his expansion plans. I listened with half an ear, shifting position now and again to try to catch a glimpse of the guys.

"...granddaughter feel about her governess being friends with her grandfather?"

The question was directed at me. I glimpsed a camera, balanced on a young man's shoulder. Sabine Verrens might be watching this. Maybe I could send a message. "Adele and I have become close in the short time I've worked for John," I said, lifting my chin and staring straight into the lens. "As you know, I'm sure, Adele had a precarious childhood. I will do everything I can to make sure she enjoys her time with her grandfather. She is a special kind of girl. I want to make sure she has the beautiful future she deserves." I smiled for the camera while John's arm tightened around me.

"Speaking of that, do you have any immediate plans for the future?" the young reporter asked. Her gaze was on John when she spoke.

"Yes, we do," John said. "We plan to leave here and go someplace where we won't be bothered so we can continue to enjoy our weekend." He moved forward and the crowd went with us like amoeba surrounding us. "I understand you want to have news stories, but I think you can appreciate that I would like to have a private life."

"But you're a public figure," Blonde Girl protested, keeping pace with John on his right side. "People are curious about you."

"Bullshit," I muttered.

"What's that, Miss Rochester?" someone asked.

"Like I said before. You people need to report news, not gossip." I spied Mark standing next to the car on the opposite side of the street. "There's our wheels," I said to John.

"Good. I think you're getting tired. You're becoming short-tempered."

"Becoming short-tempered?" I asked with an answering smile. "I've always been short-tempered. I'm becoming impolite because I'm tired."

"I stand corrected." He put his hand on the back of my neck and gave me a little shake. "Something you're so good at. Correcting me."

Mark and Paul came through the crowd, breaking a path for us. I kept my eyes on them and ignored the people around us. I wondered belatedly what my friends would say when they saw this on the television or in a newspaper. The initial reaction would be disbelief then an assumption, rightly so, it was a mistake. Everybody I knew would know John Aire and I were not a Power Couple.

I happily dropped into the back seat of the sedan. John slid in beside me. "I think our diversion was successful," he said to Mark, who took the passenger seat in the front. "Did they get in place?"

"We checked four buildings in the next two blocks. We couldn't do a thorough sweep but they seem deserted." Mark turned on the seat to speak while Paul pulled away from the curb.

"What about weapons? Did you get any in place?" I asked.

"We did what we could, but there's no guarantee they'll be there when or if you get in. We found a couple of rooms that look like they were scouted. That's where we stowed what we could. I'll brief you once we know the time and place." Mark's gaze went from me to John. "There's a good chance you'll be unarmed."

John sat next to me. "It won't bother me as much as it'll bother her."

I nudged him hard in the ribs. "Are you saying I'm combative?"

"I'm saying I wouldn't want to take you on in a fight." He rubbed his side. "That hurt."

"I pulled my punch. Believe me, if I want to hurt you, you'd know it." I subsided back on the seat, thinking furiously. We'd be at a big disadvantage if we were unarmed. Well, it couldn't be helped. All I could do was get in place, scope it out, and do what I could when I was presented with an opportunity. No worries.

My phone rang, sounding abnormally loud in the quiet sedan. I checked the display. "It's her."

"Wait a second." Mark snatched the phone from my hand and inserted a small square plastic gizmo into the headphone jack. He handed it back to me. "Answer it."

I tapped the necessary icons. "What do you want?"

"I see you have been busy," Verrens said, her voice frosty. "Such a bad example you set for your grandchild, Mr. Aire. I had no idea you and this woman were so foolish to be having your afternoon in public like that."

"Let's talk bad examples," I said. "How about a crazy woman kidnapping her own granddaughter?"

"You have no idea what you say."

"Oh, I have ideas," I said, my words slurring into each other. "I used to live on the island. I know what you're doing. I know why it will fail."

There was a long pause. "I cannot fail. My gods protect me and help me."

"You are evil and your gods will not protect you," I said immediately. "You are using an innocent child to accomplish something horrible. You will be punished, your punishment to match your crime."

Mark gestured frantically. "Hold on," he whispered. "Don't get her pissed off."

"I keep telling you," I hissed. "You don't understand this. Back off."

"Adele understands why I need her help."

"Cut the crap and tell us where you want us and when." I was so angry the hand holding the phone was shaking.

John put his hand on my leg, his palm warm against my skin where it rested on my ripped jeans. I glared at him but he just shook his head gently.

I sucked in a deep breath. "We want to talk to Adele."

"Not possible. She is resting, preparing for our ceremony." When I tried to interrupt, Verrens continued, her voice overriding mine. "I need you to be not far from where you are now. But you need to avoid the crowds which are so interested in you. Let's say ninety minutes. It will give us time to prepare. There is a building two blocks east of where you are now."

"You don't know where we are."

"Oh, yes, I do. I have people there and they watch you. Leave your car and wait for us at five thirty outside the buildings at the corner of Marsh and Morton Streets. We will find you."

The line went silent.

Chapter 14

"I have a bad feeling about this." I walked next to John past the buildings slated for construction.

"I'm glad to hear it," he replied. "I was afraid you were getting confident."

"Oh, I'm confident. I just don't like it." I kept my arm linked through his. He was taking shorter steps so we moved somewhat in sync with each other. I appreciated that. It gave me more time to check our surroundings.

"Mark said it's that building." John glanced to his left. "They've kept eyes on this entire block all afternoon. They saw a van pull up in back and people unloading."

I knew that, of course. I was in the briefing with him. But I think it made him feel better to repeat it. "Yeah. We caught a break on that. They didn't have time to do a thorough sweep of the building. It means the guns Mark put in place might still be there."

"Are you afraid?" John's voice was so soft I barely heard him.

"No. Worried, yes. Concerned and alert. But I'm not afraid. I can't be afraid. If I get afraid I make mistakes. I know that about myself. Fear works for some people, but it slows me down." I glanced around while we strolled on the uneven sidewalk. To my left was a boarded-up brick building, three stories tall. Yellow caution tape covered the front door, which was also crisscrossed with boards. On my right was the road, narrow here because of the construction zone. Straight ahead was the block with the hotel where we'd been mobbed.

"You know that about yourself." John's gaze was bobbing around, searching for anything unusual.

"Of course. It's something I've figured out." I paused at the street separating one block of construction from the next. "Like I said, I was trained to do stuff like this. There's never a sure outcome. If you think through as many scenarios as possible ahead of time, it makes it easier to react when push comes to shove."

"I suppose it makes sense."

"Of course it does." I squeezed his arm. "Don't forget the code phrase. Once I say that all hell will break loose."

A corner of his mouth twitched up in a smile. "I've seen you when all hell breaks loose."

"Oh, no you haven't. I held back."

"Then I have something to look forward to."

I was glad for his attempt at humor. He was wound tighter than a spring. I was afraid of what would happen when he let go. "We'll get her back safe and sound. Trust me." I winced when I heard what I said. "You know."

"Yeah. I do." John glanced at his watch. "It's fivethirty."

"And you are prompt." A woman approached us from the left, staying close to the old brick building and in its shadows while two young men hurried past her. Both were armed and both were big and muscular.

She stepped into the sunlight. I stopped in surprise. I don't know what I was expecting, but it wasn't someone like this. Sabine Verrens was beautiful. She was at least my age, if not older, but she appeared thirty or younger. Her skin was a coppery brown color, rich and warm. We were opposites, her and me. I had white, chin-length hair. She had long black dreadlocks. I was barely five feet tall. She was about six feet tall. I was small chested and somewhat overweight. She was lean and leggy, those features amply displayed in a flowing, flowered dress clinging to her like a second skin.

She stopped a few feet from me, looking at me with golden eyes. "You are the Rochester woman."

Her cool voice held only a faint hint of an accent, a lilt at the end of her sentence. "I am. Where is Adele?"

She turned her attention to John, dismissing me as little consequence. Good. That might help us later. "I vaguely remember meeting you at Antoinette's wedding." Her golden eyes assessed John, head to toe. "Your son looked like you."

John's arms lowered and my hand slid away from him. "Is Adele unharmed?" His fists clenched.

"Of course she is. She has agreed to help me. I've explained the ritual to her. She is unafraid and anxious to do what she can to assist me." Sabine tossed her head, her dark hair sliding on her silky dress.

"I don't believe you." I repeated what I could for the benefit of Mark and the others who were listening. "Adele would never agree to help you."

She glanced at me. "What you believe is irrelevant."

"Why do you need us? Why me and Charlotte?" John demanded.

Sabine turned, her skirt flaring and revealing her dark legs and high heels. "Bring them." She stalked ahead of us, hips swaying.

One man put a hand on my left arm and pulled me

forward. I considered slipping away from his grasp. Instead I acted like the helpless female he expected me to be. John followed me and the other man followed behind John. I stumbled and staggered while keeping a steady barrage of "Hey, that hurts," "Where are going?" and "Leave me alone,," All of which were ignored.

We came to the back of the building, this part in inky shadows. Sabine disappeared to the left and we followed. I took my time, giving my eyes a chance to adjust to the change in light. We passed through an open doorway to a hallway. It was long and dimly lit by lanterns on the floor positioned every few yards. Eight men lined the sides of the hall. They were young, black, and stood at semi-attention, their eyes fixed straight ahead like soldiers on display.

"Where are we? This was an old office building, wasn't it? Why did you bring us here?" I kept my voice whiny, which was what they expected from the stupid female.

"Be quiet," Sabine snapped. "I am tiring of your noise."

The man who was guarding me shoved me, pushing against my left shoulder. I sidestepped him. He stumbled ahead of me, hand on the gun in his waistband. Sabine whirled. "I told you, we will not harm you." She stopped when she saw it wasn't me who was stumbling. "What are you doing?"

"I'm trying to get away from your bully boy. He doesn't need to push me around." I drew in a calming breath, forcing myself to act the part of the helpless female. "He was shoving me. It's not my fault."

"Where's Adele?" John asked.

Sabine regarded me for a long moment before

shifting her attention to John. "We will join her now. I do not understand why you are with her." She eyed me disdainfully. "You can have a better woman than her. Such as Miss White." She smiled, her red painted lips parting to show white teeth.

"What about Cat White?" I didn't have to work to sound peeved.

"You are jealous," she said. "But no need for that. All she wants is business, not him. You have no reason to be jealous."

"What do you mean? What did Cat White do?" It was getting tough to rephrase everything she said for the benefit of my secret audience.

Sabine smiled. "In exchange for import waivers, she did as I requested and allowed Adele to meet someone." She smiled at John. "Your attraction was not as strong as you thought."

"Import waivers? So Cat's a patsy, too," I said. "Like Grant Pool was."

"Grant?" Sabine pushed one hand under her hair and lifted it in a languid, sensual motion. "Grant will join us soon."

Damn. If Grant Pool showed up, he would know I wasn't a bumbling woman who didn't know up from down. We needed to get this done before he appeared.

"Where's Adele?" John repeated, his voice harsh.

Sabine finally recognized how close he was to snapping. "Come. I show you." She gestured to the two guards who flanked her. "Take their weapons and their phones."

The guards who escorted us moved forward. I hastily raised my cell phone. "I'll give you my phone. Don't drop it. iPhones are notorious for their fragile screens." I handed it to him and backed up, my hands raised high. The guard patted me, confiscating the obvious handgun clipped to my waist. "That tickles." I shifted away so his hands slid past my side where my gun rested in the interior pocket. He finished with a cursory check of my legs, running his hands along the inside of my thighs. When he stepped away, I breathed a silent sigh of relief.

The other guard was more thorough with John, who they considered to be the obvious threat. He took the gun from John's inner jacket and the cell phone from his back pocket, like we expected. The other guard ran his hands over John's legs twice, making sure he didn't miss anything.

When they finished, the two guards stepped behind us. "This way," Sabine said, striding ahead. Two of the men from the hallway joined us, blocking our exit at the rear. I scanned the hall when we passed. Mark briefed us on the weapons they stashed here. If I wasn't mistaken, we passed by one of the rooms where he said they left a revolver.

We passed several closed doors then Sabine opened one on the left. This was a room that might have a gun if it wasn't found yet. I followed Sabine with John and the guards behind me. We were in what was probably an old conference room. A high intensity lantern outlined the long and rectangular space. A whiteboard was on the wall to the right. It was now covered with odd symbols written in red marker. They were vaguely familiar but I couldn't remember where I'd seen them.

Two men were in the empty room, standing behind Adele. She sat in an office chair facing the door, her hands bound in front of her with rope or cloth. A gray metal office desk was behind her. I spied a large bowl, several glasses, and a bottle of liquor or wine on the desk. Adele's body blocked my view of anything else.

She lolled in the black chair, held upright by a wide strip of bright red cloth looped under her breasts and tied behind her. Her faded blue jeans were dirty, with dark green stains on the knees. She wore one of her loose-fitting striped tops, her pastel bra strap showing on a brown shoulder where the material slipped off.

John walked toward her. One of the guards with us stepped in front of him. "Is she okay?" I peered around the guard. "She looks drugged. You said she wasn't hurt." I darted past the guard to Adele's side. The man behind her reached for me, but Sabine gestured and he stepped back.

"Leave her be." Sabine sauntered into the room to stand on Adele's left, between the girl and the whiteboard. "She is unharmed."

I touched the pulse point on Adele's neck. It was strong. I tipped her head back to peer into her eyes. "She's been drugged." I straightened, taking a moment to glance around the room. I spied a cold air duct near the floor under the whiteboard. That or the desk would be the only place to store a weapon.

"She's been calmed." Sabine shrugged, her dress shifting to show her cleavage. "I am curious. Why did you come? You're just the woman who was hired to stay in the house with Adele. A teacher. You have no reason to be here."

"A teacher and a protector." I put a hand on Adele's shoulder, squeezing gently. She stirred, her eyes fluttering.

"A protector?" Sabine crossed her arms under her

impressive breasts. "She has no need of that."

I gestured around us. "Really?"

"You don't understand. This is a chance for the child to give back to the parent. This is a chance for the child to fully embrace her life as a woman." Sabine looked at John. "I wasn't sure if you would come. I knew you felt guilty because of what you did."

"What I did?"

"You turned against your own son. You abandoned him. That's why I knew you wouldn't abandon his child."

The only reaction I saw from John was his narrowed eyes and the way his shoulders tensed, shifting his denim jacket.

I edged forward, putting myself between Adele and the guard next to the desk. "I don't understand why you're doing this. You loved her, didn't you? You loved your daughter."

"Of course I did. She was my life." Sabine said it off-handedly, with little feeling.

It was another clue, another piece of the puzzle. "You were jealous, too. Your husband loved her more than he loved you, didn't he?"

"You have crazy talk. My husband loved me."

"But he loved her in a way he could never love you," I said softly. "She was pure and untouched. You were not."

"You know nothing." Sabine's voice was harsh and low. "If I didn't need you, I'd handle you." She drew in a deep breath.

"Why do you need me?" I stepped forward, inching behind Adele, getting between her and the desk. "Why do you need John? What do your gods require?"

"The signs were hard to interpret. It took great power for me to find what was needed." Sabine blinked several times as though struggling to keep back her tears.

The four guards in the room glanced at each other. I couldn't quite interpret their expression. It seemed they were satisfied or proud, like pupils listening to an erudite professor. If they were her followers, I suppose it made a twisted kind of sense. "What kind of signs did you receive?" I struggled to keep my sarcasm out of my voice.

John went to Adele, kneeling on one knee in front of her. "We're here. We'll take you home soon." He covered her bound hands with his.

"I fasted and I prayed and the gods finally told me." Sabine stood near John, staring at him where he crouched. "I must have a woman who is at the end of her womanhood and a woman at the beginning."

"Makes sense, I suppose." *As much sense as anything you say, you crazy old bitch.* "But in that case, why not you? You're at the end of your womanhood. You're older than me."

"Who are you calling old?" Sabine stroked her hands down her full breasts, flat stomach and wide hips. "I'm still a woman, not a white-haired, washed-up hag like you. The gods love me and keep me young." She tossed her head and her dreadlocks danced.

"The gods are helping you?" I managed a credible chuckle. "Are you sure it's not a few little surgeries that helped you?" I ran a finger on the side of my face in the same spot where I saw a faint scar on hers. "Adele does not belong to you. She is not your daughter. She will not become your daughter."

"You know nothing," she spat. "Nothing."

"I know this. Your gods will not help you because you are tainted and your heart is evil." I saw my words hit home when she flinched. I continued, knowing I'd found her weak spot. "You want to do this because you failed your daughter. You want to make it up to her. But you can't. You let her down with your evil, wicked life. When she tried to get away from you, you became so angry you let that maniac you married kill her. You could not face her anger and her disappointment."

Sabine stiffened, her body so rigid she trembled. Then she inhaled deeply, her whole body moving with the rhythm of her breath. She moved around me to the desk, giving me a wide berth as if my words might taint her. "You do not know what you say. I'm not old and washed up, like you. I am still young and beautiful."

I came around the other side of the desk. I was only a foot or two away from the whiteboard and the air vent under it. I checked the guards. They stared at Sabine with predatory, hungry expressions. Two of them eyed me with such burning anger in their eyes I knew I'd have to watch my back if this came to a fight. They were out for blood. "They're young enough to be your sons," I said.

She smiled, the tip of her tongue moistening her bright red lips. "Yes, they are. Young meat is the best."

John went around Adele to face Sabine over the desk. "What do you want with me?"

"I need you to call Edward. Your spirit will call your son's. Your son will call my Antoinette. They were bound together in life and in death. If he is here, I can summon her."

Okay, I thought. *You truly are bat shit crazy.* The small receiver in my ear crackled. I heard two beeps, low-toned but distinct. Mark and the others were moving into place. The plan was for them to come in from the roof and from the ground simultaneously. Just a few more minutes. "What are you going to do? How will you call the spirits?"

"It's simple." She reached into the bowl and held up a knife with a wooden handle. "I will take John's blood which I will give to Adele. I will use your blood to summon the gods." She gestured vaguely to the whiteboard and the symbols there. "They will bring Antoinette's spirit to us."

Blood? I knew, in the back of my mind, that might happen but I had kept a vague hope this might not get messy. "That's the sign for God in man, isn't it?" I went to the whiteboard, pointing to the stylized eye in the middle of an open palm. "Is that what you're trying to do?" I glanced below it and saw the grate was loose. One good pull and it would be free. Was there a gun behind it?

Adele's eyes opened. She focused on Sabine. "I will never help you." Her voice was faint but audible. "I am not related to you."

Sabine strode to Adele, her face a mask of fury. "You are mine." She dug her hand into Adele's hair, drawing back Adele's head so the girl had to stare into her face. "Mine."

Adele spat. Sabine recoiled and raised her other hand. John lunged forward, barreling into her. Two of the guards clutched him and flung him aside. He hit the wall near the whiteboard. I ran to him but before I could reach him, a guard jerked me back. I stumbled and fell against the desk.

"It doesn't matter how I get your blood." Sabine took a gun from the desk and aimed it at me, her arms shoulder height.

I ignored the gun and focused on the sores I glimpsed on her palms. "You're ill," I said. "What is it? What is wrong?"

My words did exactly what I wanted. They made her hesitate. "What?"

"Your hands. The sores on your palms." I cringed away from the guard who still held me. "If you've lain with her I don't want you touching me."

The guard drew back, his hand still clamped on my upper arm. "What you say?"

"She's ill. If you've lain with her, you're ill, too." I moved as far away from him as I could, making sure he saw the distaste on my face. I forced myself to ignore John, who was inching the air grate to one side. "Don't touch me," I said shrilly.

Sabine's aim wavered, the gun wobbling. "She lies."

"Look at her hands." I pulled away from the guard. "It's the disease. She has it. She's ill."

"You're lying," Sabine said. "I'm fine."

"Poor boy," I murmured, turning to the guard so I blocked his view of John. "*Yuh salt.* Very bad unlucky to lay with her. She has the clap, boy. She sick."

"Your husband was sick with it." John stood. "What happened? Was the disease latent in him? Did he get you sick? Or maybe you were the one who gave it to him. Maybe he was innocent and you were the filth."

Sabine swung on him, the gun aimed at his head. "I can kill you now. It won't matter to my gods. I need your blood. Once I draw forth Antoinette's spirit, I will have her forgiveness. Then I can be healed."

"You're crazy," I whispered. "You're in the end stages. You can't be healed. Your brain is diseased. It happens with syphilis."

The guard who held me backed up, panic in his eyes. "Sabine, what you say? I don't understand."

"I needed your strength, your love." Sabine backed up, her arms trembling while she aimed at John. "I need forgiveness. I need blood to bring my girl to me so she can forgive me. I can be healed and live forever."

"She's crazy," I said. "She's insane."

The door to the conference room opened. Grant Pool stepped in. "Does he know?" I asked, hoping to throw him off guard. "Does he know you have syphilis?"

Grant hesitated, his gaze on Sabine then he locked the door behind him. "Tie her up," he said, gesturing at me while he strode into the room. "She's dangerous."

The guards moved toward me. Grant confronted Sabine. "What's going on? You said you wouldn't begin without me. You told me I could have her." He eyed Adele, his eyes intent on her. "You said you needed me to make her a woman."

John took a step forward. "What?"

"Well, shit. I guess we can't wait." I looked at John. "Let's get this party started."

All hell broke loose.

I turned on the guard behind me and got him with a blow to the upper chest. He reeled back, slamming into the desk. I followed up with a good kick. Since I was still wearing my steel-toed work boots, he went down hard. Grant Pool came after me, fists swinging. I dodged him and dove for the floor, rolling toward the door. I managed to pull my gun when I came up. I got off a shot at one of the other guards. He dropped, landing near Adele.

John was struggling with a guard so I couldn't get a

good shot. Then Pool came after me again, the knife in his hand and a crazed look in his eyes. I'd seen his expression before, on soldiers when they thought they had nothing to lose.

"Pool!" John shouted.

It was enough of a diversion for me to get Pool in my gun sights. I pulled the trigger. At the last second one of the guards rammed into me. The bullet went wild. I didn't see where it went because I was slammed into the wall and my gun went flying. I dropped to the floor and when I moved, it hurt to breathe.

I didn't have time to worry about it. Pool was coming after me again. I glimpsed John, struggling with another guard who had a gun in his hand. I crouched and pulled my knife from the sheath, bringing it up just as Pool reached me. He slashed and I deflected him, dodging under and bringing my knife up to score a cut against his arm. He wasn't trained. I could tell from the way he moved. But he was mad and he was desperate. That was worse.

"I'll kill you!" Sabine screamed.

I turned. She was aiming the gun at John, who still struggled with the guard, his back to her. Pounding at the door told me Mark and the others were there, tantalizingly close. I pivoted. Pool was almost on me, his arm raised high. Idiot. That's a good way to get killed. The thought surfaced and vanished in the time it took for me to ram my knife into his sternum.

I didn't wait to see the effect. I dropped my knife. "Sabine!" I launched myself at the woman at the same moment she fired.

The door flew open. Mark, Frank, and others spilled into the room. Sabine and I crashed into the wall in a tangle of arms and legs. I grabbed her right arm and slammed it as hard as I could against the edge of the desk. She shrieked and dropped the gun when she fell back in a faint. A broken arm could do that, I guess.

I rolled off her and dragged myself upright, using the desk for leverage. John lay on the floor, a guard on top of him. "Are you okay?" I called.

John pushed the man's body off him. "What about you?"

"Adele? Are you okay?" I stumbled over Sabine's body and went to Adele, who was huddled in the chair, her head drooped forward. "Adele!"

She raised her face. I saw her tears, her body shaking. I put my arms around her. "You're safe now. You're safe."

Someone's arms went around both of us. "I can't lose you," John whispered. He looked in my eyes. "I can't lose either of you."

I'm not sure what happened after that because I did something totally out of character for me. I passed out.

There is an annoying amount of paperwork involved in a kidnapping and gunfight. I, thankfully, didn't have to handle it. I was in the hospital, recovering from a bruised rib and a knife wound in my arm I didn't know I had. By the time I got out, everything was done. Grant Pool was in a hospital jail, Sabine and her minions were deported, and I made a statement to the local police with Mark in attendance. That confirmed my suspicion he was involved with government law enforcement.

After that, I went home to get on with my life. "Sabine is being shipped back to Jamaica," Mark told me when he stopped by my house a week after I was released from the hospital. "To a mental institution. It's a terrible irony. Her husband gets cured of the disease, they have a baby then she takes a lover and gets syphilis."

"What a fate. Who was the man?" We were lounging on my front porch, enjoying a cool September afternoon.

"A kid, really. Sabine's husband was so much older than her, I guess it's not surprising she took up with somebody younger. And you were right. All the husband cared about was the daughter. Sabine came in second."

"We know how she feels about that." I remembered Nick's brother, so young and impressionable. He could have been manipulated like that. "What happened to the lover?"

"He's dead now. Her husband had him shot as soon as he discovered she was stepping out on him." Mark eyed the large rectangular parcel propped against the porch railing. "What's that?"

"Something I need to return to the sender." I sipped my iced tea. "I'm going to leave it here and have the shipper come and get it." He scooted forward to get a closer look. "Go ahead. Open it."

He set down his beer and pulled the framed print from the custom-made box. "Wow. What is it?"

"The Song of Solomon, from the St. John's Bible. It's a custom print, a two-page spread."

"It's heavy." Mark hefted the big print, the glass glinting in the sunlight.

"Yep. Three feet by two feet. It's a full-size reproduction."

"That's racy stuff." Mark studied the precise calligraphy. "The artwork is amazing."

"Yeah. And expensive."

He put the print back in the box and picked up his beer again. "From John?"

"I suppose. Few people can afford a thousand-dollar custom print." I took a sip of my iced tea. "How are he and Adele doing?"

"Good, I think. They miss you."

"I've heard from Adele. You know, in the game forum. Sounds like she's doing okay. I think she's handled it good."

"Yeah. She's a tough kid. She might be going to school." Mark took a long swallow of beer. "John is checking private schools in town."

"That's a mistake," I said. "Why can't she go to public school?"

Mark shot me an exasperated look. "She's still the granddaughter of one of the richest men around. She needs to be in a private school."

"Bullshit."

Mark stood. "You're talking to the wrong person. Seems to me you should be talking to him about it."

"He doesn't want my opinion about raising children." I stared into my iced tea. "Was he right, Mark? About Nick being murdered?"

Mark stuck his hands in his jeans pockets. "Does it matter to you?"

I had thought about nothing else for the past few days and could answer him honestly. "I guess not. He's gone, no matter how it happened."

"I know he's sorry that he used you to protect Adele. Maybe you need to meet him halfway."

"What's that mean?"

Mark nodded at the parcel. "He's held out his hand. Why don't you take it?"

"You know as well as I do that John Aire and I get along about as good as fire and water."

Mark went to my front steps. "That's only because you keep putting out the fire. I'll see you around."

I opened my mouth to contradict him but he was already gone, stepping into the black sedan at my curb. I resumed glaring at the big parcel. When the skies darkened with rain clouds, I decided to drag it into the house. I may not accept it, but I didn't want to see it ruined.

Burns called me that night. "Let's go for a beer. We haven't gone out since you left the hospital. I know you want to say no, but don't."

"You know me too well," I admitted. "Sure. Why not?"

"I'll be there in fifteen minutes." He hung up before I could protest.

I put on a clean pair of jeans and a pastel plaid blouse, taking a sweater against the evening's chill. Burns pulled into my drive and opened the passenger door for me. "Your chariot, my dear," he said when I dropped into the seat.

We talked about work on the way to Brockle's, which wasn't too crowded for a Thursday night. Pro football was on the TV monitors. I settled down to cheer for the Bears while munching a pretzel.

Someone tapped me on the shoulder. I looked up and saw John, a beer in hand. He wore faded jeans and a sweatshirt with a Rolling Stones tongue logo on it. I had to do a double-take before I was sure it was him.

"What are you doing here?"

"I heard they have the best pretzels in town." He smiled at Burns. "She was right."

"She usually is," Burns said. "Excuse me. I think the jukebox girl needs advice."

I twisted in my chair. Adele waved to me then resumed studying the digital display on the music machine. "She's too young to be here," I said to John, who took Burns' vacated seat. "I didn't ask you to join me."

"She's not drinking so it's okay." John's hand inched toward one of the pretzels in the middle of the table. "Besides, I know somebody in law enforcement. They said it was okay." He looked over my left shoulder.

I slapped his hand. "Oh, no you don't." I turned and saw Mark Temple and Mrs. Fairfax sitting at a table, a pitcher of beer between them. She waved when she saw me. Mark raised a glass of beer in salute.

"Mark said you got my peace offering."

I thought of the gorgeous print resting on the floor in my living room. "I can't accept a gift like that."

"Why not?"

"It's too expensive."

"It's only money. I want to apologize. I should have trusted you. I wish I'd told you the truth about why I hired you and about your late husband."

I shot him a sidelong look. "I suppose I should have told you about the guy but it seemed innocent to me."

"I guess we were both wrong. You didn't trust me to understand and not overreact. I didn't trust you for the same reasons." He peeked at me from under his dark eyelashes to see how I was taking it.

He had a point. "Maybe," I conceded. "But I still can't accept the print."

"I suppose you can't accept this, either." John reached in his coat pocket and tossed the sapphire necklace on the table.

"Holy crap, John, be careful. That thing is worth a lot of money." I scooped up the diamond and sapphire necklace.

"I don't want it. It's yours."

"It is not."

"Is, too."

I tried to stuff the necklace in his pocket. He grabbed my hand, pulling me toward him. "It's yours. So is the print." He leaned closer. "So is my heart."

I kicked back from him so fast my chair tipped. "Whoa."

John caught the necklace when it fell from my hand. "Does it worry you? Are you afraid?" He had a look I never saw before. Or maybe I did, when we were in the abandoned building, fighting for Adele. The hunter, eyeing his prey.

I forced my gaze away from his. "Of course not."

"Really? You told me fear slows you." John stood so fast I didn't even see him get up. He tossed the necklace on the table and put his hands on the arms of my chair, leaning above me, his lips inches from mine. "I guess you're right. You are slow."

"I'm not afraid of you." I pressed back so hard my chair would have toppled if he hadn't been holding it in place.

"No, you're afraid of what you feel. The necklace is yours. The print is yours. I'm yours." He smiled, his cool blue eyes suddenly warm and sensual. "If you want me."

"But I can't—we just—it's too—You barely know me."

"Then let's correct that."

I tore my eyes away from his intense gaze. "This

isn't a romance novel, John. I mean, you can't come in here and sweep me off my feet."

He stood and my chair tilted. John put his hands under my arms and swung me bodily away from the table when music began to play. "Shut up and dance with me." He moved us both onto the dance floor.

I did.

A word about the author…

J L Wilson writes mysteries, reincarnation tales, and dystopian sagas. Stay caught up with her at her website (http://www.jayellwilson.com) or on Facebook (https://www.facebook.com/jayeAtplay).

Thank you for purchasing
this publication of The Wild Rose Press, Inc.

For questions or more information
contact us at
info@thewildrosepress.com.

The Wild Rose Press, Inc.
www.thewildrosepress.com